ID DIE FOR YOU

Copyright © 2024

All rights reserved.

ISBN:
ISBN-13: 9798324530204

*Deep down… you're a psychopath too and that's okay.
Least you're on a path.*

To all my readers who need to escape to another place, and to everyone who loves the unexpected. Enjoy the ride.

How far would you go for the person you love, and who do you trust along the way.

Warning
IMPORTANT NOTE

This book is linked with Dark Romance that contains very triggering situations such as graphic language, graphic violence and gore, murder, graphic murder, PTSD, miscarriage, human trafficking, mentions of rape, abuse, explicit sexual situations for readers 18+. Note that everything in this book is fictional including character names, businesses, locations and are a product of the authors imagination.

Recap

<u>I'd Kill For You</u>

6 months later

"You two got a visual?"

"We sure do, must admit you look like the best looking couple there is at this event." Gibb and Katie were in the van parked a few streets away which held a whole variety of computer systems, technology and connection to a satellite, so they were able to hack into anything close by.

"Good, did you get into the radio frequency to catch anything there?"

"Just come live now Hal, we are ready to go."

"Perfect. Wren you boys in position?"

"Indeed, all snipers in position and have visuals of the building and inside. May I just add sir that Hallie you look amazing tonight, will have to send a text to the missus showing that you can make an effort." Hallie chuckled and Seb pulled his arm around her, bending down closer to whisper in her ear, "You look amazing no matter what you are wearing. Or not wearing. Definitely think that dress would look better on my floor."

Hallie was wearing a long red tight dress which showed her body off perfectly, it hugged her in all the right places. The dress had glitter in it so when certain lights caught it, she would shimmer. Her hair was down with loose curls giving her the neat wavy hair look. With her makeup minimal and piercing red lipstick to match her outfit making her face pop.

"Okay, if you guys are going to do sexy talk or anything like that may I remind you this is an open line for us all so we will all hear it."

"What's the matter Gibbs, it's like listening to free porn." *Wren laughed making this comment whilst watching Seb and Hallie's reaction down the scope of his sniper.*

"Well, it might be for you lot but that is like hearing about my sister's sex life. It is weird okay." *Katie was laughing at Gibb, his confidence was so much better since he worked for Seb and Katie helped bring his personality out more.*

"Eyes on the target, he is sat right side of the bar, sixth person in. How are we going to get him away from his little group. I can cause a distraction so you can swoop in and grab him." *Wren was sometimes trigger happy, he enjoyed seeing the ones who were not good people suffer.*

"How about we call that Plan B, yeah." *Seb sat with Hallie on a nearby table to keep eye on the target without giving away their position.*

"Give me 5 minutes." *Hallie looked to Seb, he knew straight away he was not going to like this plan.*

"Absolutely not."

"5 minutes, I can get him out and heading up to his room and you can meet us there, sure Wren would be happy to assist you."

"With fucking pleasure, on my way. Boris take my position." Wren was already heading down to the van to grab a suit and ticket from Katie so he could get entry for the event.

"Hallie, he is probably one of the most dangerous men out there, I won't risk you."

"He isn't the most dangerous man out there. You are and I am yours, so I am safe. Everyone has eyes on me, Katie, Gibbs, you got camera footage of the elevators?"

"Sure do."

"5 minutes, if that doesn't work then I will leave and come back and will do Plan B."

Seb looked around the room not happy with this plan, but it was the best they had. "5 minutes. I am timing this darl."

"Wouldn't expect any different."

"Can I just ask what this plan is as I am confused?" Gibb questioned as he was tuning in the radio system the police use to communicate.

"Watch and learn Gibb. See how much Hallie has to act for this."

Hallie began to walk over to the VIP entrance however noticed it was ticket access only, she showed her ticket to the security man who allowed her entry. There was a seat either side of the target which was obviously there so no one could be too close to him. Hallie ignored this and went straight to one of the seats and asked the bar man for a Porn star Martini and a shot of tequila. This caught the attention of the target to which he looked Hallie up and down and approved of what he saw. By this time Wren was now in the building and sat with Seb ready to pounce if they needed too.

"Put that on my tab Tom would you".

"Oh really, you don't have to I am happy to pay."

"Nonsense, a woman like you should be spoiled. Who are you if you don't mind me asking?"

"My name is Anna Swift, and yours?" Hallie held out her hand to shake his awaiting his response.

"Charlie Henderson. What an intriguing name, are you from around here?" Charlie was a very well-built man, blonde hair with flakes of darkness through the roots. His eyes were a piercing blue and had a clean shaved face. Wearing a black suit and tie anyone would think he was taking part in a men in black look alike competition as he had the black sunglasses on his head.

"No, was invited by a friend who has gone to have sex with one of the Lord's over there." This was a lie, but Hallie needed to get his attention somehow and what do men think most about, Sex.

"So, are you all alone now then?"

"Looks that way." Hallie took her shot then began sipping her Martini. "What about you, from around here?"

"I travel a lot. I own the penthouse here though so least I don't have far to go when I am done being sociable." Charlie began to chuckle; this unsettled Hallie's stomach however she needed to get him alone so he could be extracted.

"Penthouse, blimey must have some money, this building is huge the views must be amazing!"

"I can show you now if you like, pretty bored here anyway, just old people, no one as interesting as you. Come on bring the drink if you like." Hallie got up and followed Charlie to the lift.

Seb stopped the timer and was showing four minutes thirty-seven seconds. Wren looked over his shoulder to see the time. "That was impressive."

"If he touches her, I will kill him."

"You are going to kill him anyway mate." Wren looked over to Seb as they made their way to the penthouse following Hallie and Charlie.

"Okay, then I will break his fingers one by one before I kill him if he touches her. Better."

"Much better." Wren went along with the joke, but he knew Seb was being serious.

Gibb and Katie had footage of all the cameras in the building and watched as Hallie and Charlie went up in the lift. "Well, he hasn't touched her yet sir, that is a good sign. Oh wait, nope he has her waist." Gibb thought he was helping. However, it made Seb angrier causing him to clench his fists as the lift was going up.

"Yeah Gibb, not helping on that one. Where are they now?"

"They have just entered the penthouse and, the door is now closed we don't have eyes anymore."

"Okay, Boris, do you have eyes through the window?"

"Yes sir, all okay so far, he has just laid down on the bed whilst Hallie is looking round the suite."

"Perfect, she is stalling. We are outside wait for our call okay."

"Yes sir."

"Perfect, you ready Seb."

"Never been more ready."

Three sharp knocks at the door make Charlie confused, "Oh, I told the bar to send up champagne, I paid for it as a thank you for the drinks and getting me out that event." This caused Charlie to lay back down on the bed and relax.

"Well, aren't you something else, how has no one claimed you yet." As Charlie had said this Hallie had already opened the door to Seb and Wren.

"Someone already has." With that a Seb pulled out a gun and shot him in the shoulder. A clear wound making sure no arteries or bone were hit, just a flesh wound making Charlie fall to the floor. Wren and Seb pulled him back up and tied him to the chair by the window so Boris would have the perfect shot if he needed it.

"You lying little bitch." That comment didn't sit well with Seb either, causing a hit to the face.

"I mean, you must be desperate, how long did it take me to get him out of there."

"Just over four minutes darl, pretty impressive."

"Why thank you."

"Do you know who the fuck I am!" Charlie was now shouting and pulling his arms trying to free himself.

"We do, do you know who the fuck we are?" Charlie looked at all three of them standing in front of him to which it finally clicked. He knew who they were and why they were here.

"Finally found me huh, you know they will find you before you are able to do anything to me."

"Nope, see that suitcase, you will be in it soon and knocked out so we can take you to another location where you will stay until we get all the answers. Unless you are willing to communicate now?"

"Go fuck yourselves".

All three of them looked at each other and smiled. Hallie reached into Seb's pocket and then kissed his neck before walking behind Charlie. "Have it your way then." *From this she stabbed the long needle into his neck, injecting a drug straight into his system causing his vision to start going blurry.*

......

As Charlie woke, he found himself tied up in Seb's basement, the same chains previously used on Fowler.

"Hello, anyone? Get me the fuck out of here. You are all dead you hear. Dead!"

"Best you start talking Charlie boy, already killed three of your men for being fucking idiots. You will die and I will take great pleasure in making sure it is slow and painful." Seb was sat on a metal chair in the corner of the room, he knew Charlie would crack eventually and would enjoy every minute of him being chained like an animal.

"Fine, what do you want from me huh?"

"The truth, names, the person behind it all. Start talking Charlie, got plenty of time on my hands and plenty of body parts I can break, rip off and tear until you die."

"My boss is Harold Kingston."

"Liar." Seb stood up in shock from this name, he didn't believe it at all.

"I swear I swear. He took me on five years ago, he gave me everything. I ran the show with his instructions so it would never trace back to him."

"Who else knows about him?"

"My brother, Jake. He is his personal human shield. We work together. Please man, let me go."

"You know, your name has been on my radar for some time. Now I have you, you are not getting away that easy." Seb walked away turning the lights off and headed up the stairs locking the door behind him. He went into the lounge where everyone was already eating except Hallie who waited for Seb like she does every night. Seb kissed Hallie before sitting down and grabbing his food.

"We have a name."

"Already? What did you do to him?"

"Hadn't even touched him yet. But we need to run checks behind this because if it is who he says it is, this just took a turn for the worse."

"Who?"

"Harold Kingston. Charlie's brother knows about it all so we need to find him, get the same name from him and get him to admit all of the fucked up shit they have done and then can go in that way."

"Fuck off." Wren was gob smacked by this response as were the rest of them.

"Hallie? You good?"

"Yeah, sorry just need a drink, I'll be right back." Seb knew something wasn't right so placing his food on the coffee table he followed Hallie to the kitchen.

"Darl, you know him. Don't you."

"Yes."

"How?"

"He was my foster parent, the last one, the one that encouraged me to go into the army, make a name for myself. That was the family that I thought truly cared but really wanted me gone at 16." Hallie began sipping her water when Seb came up behind her and turned her around.

"He now is one of our targets, are you okay with that?"

"Yes, I am fine. Just shocked me at first. I'm fine let's go back in." Hallie began to walk away before Seb pulled her back and looked her straight in the eyes.

"You're a bad liar, but I am here when you are ready. Okay."

"Thank you."

Multiple footsteps which sounded like running came straight for the kitchen which interrupted Hallie and Seb's moment. Both looking up to see everyone in a panic.

"What?"

"We need to go now! They have just put a new target out."

"But Charlie is here, how is that possible."

"The big boss must be taking control in his absence."

"Where is it?"

"Winchester Constabulary, we need to go there now."

part 2

1

Hallie was in a state of shock, she hadn't returned to the station since she packed her things and moved into the manor with Seb. Everything that happened with Fowler, all the lies he told, she never thought she would have to face going back there. But Hallie knew she needed to put her feelings aside and warn them, get them out as no one had any idea what they had planted or what they were planning on doing with the station. Also, the confusion as to why that was the target, there must have been a reason behind it but that was also something that needed time to think on. Right now, Hallie was trying to get a hold of her old boss, Sergeant, to pre-warn him. Still unsure what she was going to say, she just knew that she had to warn them.

"Fuck, why don't people answer there fucking phones. That is what they are made for!" Seb let out a little chuckle, he was driving at high speed to the station being followed closely by Wren, Katie and Gibb. Gibb and Katie were working on their laptops to try and find out what target has been put on the station.

Arriving at the station, Hallie runs in with Gibb clutching his laptop firmly under his arm. Wren and Seb took the perimeter of the building then would come in through the back, Katie followed still typing as they were checking the building.

"Detective, how great to see- "

"Not a Detective any more Elle so no need for that. But thank you, I am so sorry I don't mean to be rude but where is Sergeant?"

"In the board room having a meeting, is everything okay?"
"No, you got a spare key card?"
"I'm not supposed too- "
"Don't need it, already in the system." Gibb interrupted knowing he was able to open any door in the building. Katie also gained access to this system allowing herself, Seb and Wren to take the back entrance.

Hallie and Gibb ran up the stairs and along the long corridor till the last room on the floor labelled *'Board room'* appeared. Without knocking Hallie went straight in, slightly breathless but still able to run if needed. Gibb on the other hand was panting in the doorway attempting to get any oxygen back in his lungs.
"Urm, excuse me but we are in a meeting." A man Hallie had never seen before was in a suit sat upright. He had a vague look about him and something deep down told Hallie not to trust him, gut instinct.
"Hallie?" Sergeant stood up and went to walk over to Hallie.
"I'm sorry sir but we need to get this place evacuated or everyone into safety as soon as possible."
"I'm sorry, but who are you?" The same man now stood up and looked both Hallie and Gibb up and down. Hallie ignored him and continued to look at Sergeant, out of anyone in the building this was one person she knew would take her word.
"Okay, I need some more information than that Hal before I put in an evacuation."
Silence, now Hallie didn't know what to say, should she lie or tell her old boss that she now worked somewhere that killed people who don't deserve a second chance. Hallie looked around the room, she did not want to give all the information with all of these people here especially the stuck up mumma's boy in the suit.
Sergeant nodded, "Okay come with me." His office was just two rooms down from the board room he locked the door behind Hallie and Gibb and sat on his desk. "It really is good to see you, but you are going to have to tell me what is going on."
"I can't disclose everything sir, but I have a target who is a…" Hallie paused, she didn't want to say too much, "well a very bad person, still trying to capture them at present however we have been informed that someone has been sent to this station to plant a potential bombing or explosion." Hallie knew this sounded stupid and wanted to tell

Sergeant everything, but she still couldn't trust anyone since Fowler.

"Okay, what is the threat."

"Still working on that sir give me two minutes and I will have it." Gibb was still typing away and pressed his earpiece to communicate with Katie.

"I am still confused as to what you both do for a job now."

"It's complicated." Both Hallie and Gibb said at the same time. Sergeant nodded without asking any other questions.

"Hallie, we need to get out of here. Now!

"Why?"

With that everything went black, red lights were flashing as an emergency evacuation procedure was now in place.

"Gibb, did you do that?"

"No, we need to get out now!"

On the other side of the station, Seb and Wren had checked around the perimeter of the building and ended up in the underground car park of the station. There were concrete pillars everywhere you turned with a variety of cars on the second floor of this car park. Everything looked pretty normal until they caught eye of a man exiting the lift back onto the car park. Seb and Wren kept a close eye of this particular man as he looked somewhat familiar. As the man approached his banged up Citroen Saxo he got in the driver's seat and opened his laptop and began typing away. The door was caved in on the driver's side of the blue Saxo and the passenger door was red which indicated that this car is a piece of scrap, the perfect dump and leave vehicle. Seb knocked on the passenger window which startled the man slamming his laptop screen closed. The stranger looked up at Seb trying to figure out what he wanted, whilst Wren opened the driver's door and dragged him out holding him up by his shirt.

"You wanna tell us what your little plan is?"

"Get Fucked!"

"Wrong answer." With that Wren punched him square in the stomach causing him to squirm in pain. Wren hoisted him back up and made him stand straight. "Let's try again. What have you done here and where are the others?"

"You're too late" the stranger began to laugh when all of a sudden everything went black, and the same red light began to flash down in the car park. Seb tried radioing Hallie but there was no luck.

"What have you done?" Seb now got up into the man's face which caused him to move his head back as much as he could to create space.

"Nothing can stop it. It's already done." He breathed, Seb didn't move away from him.

"What is done?"

With that a large bang was heard from upstairs and the car park shook slightly with dust falling from the ceiling.

"Boom." The man mimicked the sound of the explosion and let out a chuckle. He didn't care what had happened and it was inevitable that this person was not going to talk. With this, Wren took the opportunity to slit his throat and allow blood to pour from his neck. His body jerked as he tried to use his hands to stop the bleeding, but the wound was too deep, his heart was just pumping the blood faster around his body causing him to bleed out. Colour drained from the man's body to which he still remained with a smirk on his face, knowing what he had done and got away with regardless, he knew was going to die. Seb and Wren headed back out of the building to try and find Hallie and Gibb as whatever just happened was not a good start.

"Bomb threat in the building, someone else has cut all the power to the station."

"I'll set the alarm and call it in." Sergeant had pressed a button under his desk and called the relevant people to which a message went out on the speakers around the station.

'This is not a drill. Please evacuate immediately. This is not a drill'.

The message was on repeat. Hallie was already ordering people out the building when she was at her old office. Refusing to let any feelings come out, she continued until she was back on the main floor.

"Hallie, Hal. Come on darling answer me."

Nothing. No response from Hallie or Gibb. Seb tried Katie to see if she could get a rough location of where they could be. "I have something, last active status on Gibb was on second floor, seventh room along." Katie seemed pleased that she was able to find them.

Seb headed into the building with Wren slipping past the officers trying to stop people gaining access. He was shouting for Hallie and looking around for her. Not knowing where to find her or where to even begin looking, he shouted Hallie's name as loud as he could. Surprisingly he heard banging on a door nearby, rubble was blocking the entrance to this causing the door not to open. Seb and Wren hooked as much rubble out of the way to find Hallie and Gibb on the other end of the door. Relieved and thankful that both were okay, Seb grabbed Hallie and hugged her tightly. Wren looked around and briefly reminded them that they had to go soon, Seb helped Hallie over the blocks and had his arm around her leaving the building. Sergeant caught eye of this.

"Hallie, are you okay?" Sergeant left his colleague on the pavement and walked over to Hallie.

Wren looked at Seb and nodded, "I'll get the car." Gibb followed Wren as he left with only a couple of grazes to his face.

"Yeah, I'm fine sir, just couple scratches, nothing major."

"How did you know about this?"

"It is a very long story sir."

"Well, I think it is a story that needs explaining don't you, and who are you?" Sergeant looked to Seb with confusion.

"My name is Seb sir, I work with Hallie." Hallie looked up knowing full well that Seb was in charge and the boss of everything. Hallie knew Sergeant would have questions as soon as Seb said his name.

"Seb, as in the Seb we were looking for before or is that just a coincidence?" Looking back down to Hallie concerned for her.

"No sir, you were looking for me, but I just sent all the information you needed to convict the right person." Seb tried to twist it back so he could stay out of the limelight.

"So, you work with Hallie? Okay well we all need to have a chat then don't we." Sergeant looked over to them both making sure they were following him into a quieter area. Ensuring that no one was around listening Sergeant stood looking vacant, waiting for an answer.

"Go on, cause if I have to make up some excuse as to why you are here and how you knew this happened. You deserve more than a thank you as that could've been so much more catastrophic. But if what you are about to tell me is something people shouldn't know about then I need to figure out a believable lie to tell the people above me. Understand."

Hallie looked over to Seb wondering whether she should say anything, Seb then took this as an opportunity to speak for them both.

"We work for a private company, like an undercover force. We are given targets to extract and remove from situations. An alert came through that this station was one that was due to be hit by one of the people we are after. Well, we believe it is down to this person, hence the evacuation. Do you know if there were many people injured or caught in the explosion?"

"We have confirmed 6 with injuries, no deaths which is good, all seem minor injuries thanks to your quick thinking. This private company, would I know it?"

"No sir, we are unable to disclose any information on the company." Hallie now speaking on their behalf, she knew that Sergeant would do some digging but right now she wanted to get out of there and get all the information she had back and find this target.

"Okay, I understand. Hallie, I want you to keep me updated with anything you are able to tell me about this person. We will run our own investigation as an anonymous source and as to why you were here for anyone that asks, you had seen unusual activity and came straight in as you know protocol. Understand?"

"Yes sir, thank you, will keep you in the loop."

"Thank you, and you." Sergeant now talking to Seb which made him wonder to what he was going to say. "Look after her, she's a good one that got away from us here. I saw you run in after her so if I find out you have done anything to harm her, I will kill you myself." Sergeant was like a protective dad to Hallie which made her smile.

"I can assure you sir, she is one that I'd kill for."

"Good, what I like to hear. Okay you both better go, I will clear up the mess here."

"Thank you." As they headed towards Seb's car Wren was already waiting leaning on his car bonnet.

"Took your time."

"Got held up by someone's old boss."

Hallie interrupted, "Who is not asking questions and letting us leave and crack on."

"Oh well that is handy, so didn't ask anything?" Wren was relieved as he opened the door for Hallie.

"He did but understood why I couldn't tell him who we worked for."

"So, he didn't catch on that your boss was the one with his arms around you."

Both just looked at each other and realised Seb was still holding Hallie. Hallie laughed and got in the car. Seb closed the door for her and walked around to the driver's side. Before getting back in the car he spoke to Wren. Gibb and Katie were already in the other car ready to go.

"So, they really aren't going to ask any questions?" his voice quietened not wanting to many people to hear.

"Doesn't look that way. Her old boss made up the excuse that Hallie saw suspicious behaviour and ran in as she knew the protocol."

"Handy, he should come be with us."

Seb chuckled, "Ex-military so he has it drilled into him like we did."

"Makes sense. So now what?" Wren still leaning on his car, Hallie was trying to lip read what was being said.

"Back at the house we will go through footage of the underground parking and see what we can find. You need to go home and see your wife really, then back to it tomorrow."

"No problem. The kids want to go out tonight so I said would take them all out but if you need me, I can move it."

"Go home Wren, enjoy it. If you ever need to you know your family is always welcome back at the house."

"Thanks, might have to take you up on that offer when it gets busy which judging on how today has gone looks like it will happen sooner rather than later."

Seb got back in his car and turned to Hallie to see that she was already looking at him. "Well?"

"Told him what just happened, what is going on and told him to go spend some time with his family tonight and come back in the morning." Seb pulled his seatbelt across his chest and placed the car into drive.

"Good, thank you again. Can't wait to get in the bath and just relax."

"Well, this will probably be our last quiet one for a while, be hands on from tomorrow, when this gets out that not many people were injured, they will try strike again."

The drive back was beautiful, through the countryside the house was located in the middle of nowhere. A beautiful old manor which had been updated recently, it had a long driveway with trees surrounding either side. The whole perimeter was fenced with electric gates allowing extra security all run by Seb. Hallie liked her life, away from the public and tucked away and Seb finally had the one person he had wanted for so many years.

2

It was such a beautiful time of year, Autumn. The leaves changing colours giving a variety of shades, a cold breeze whistling through the trees nearby and everything just looking like something you would see in a famous panting. Wren took this opportunity to surprise his family by coming home early and taking them all out for dinner and a game of mini golf at the local arcade. Wren had a beautiful family, with two children Jessica and Toby who had the most caring personalities.

Jessica was 11 and loved to learn, a tough cookie and strong for her age as she has taken karate since she was three. She was a rare beauty with jet black natural hair which was perfectly straight however her eyes were an ocean blue which made all her features stand out more.

Toby was your typical big brother type. He was fourteen, due to turn fifteen in a few weeks and was a very good-looking lad. Like Jessica he also had jet black hair however identical eyes to Wren, with similar height he was definitely like his father. Toby also took a keen interest in karate from a young age as Wren encouraged them to learn to defend themselves. Toby was due to finish school in the next year and like his father wanted a career in the military, much to his mother's disgust.

Ella. The person who made Wren's life turn completely upside down. Wren met Ella whilst he was on a holiday period when he served for the military. They hit it off almost immediately and Wren fell hard. Wren was a good-looking man but even his friends joked and told him he was still punching when dating Ella. The black hair and blue eyes gene came from Ella and passed to her children; you could see some features of Wren in their children, but Wren was grateful that they had their mother's beauty.

The arcade was one of the most popular locations on the outskirts of town, it was a common favourite for the family to spend time together and have a laugh. However tonight would be one that they would never forget.

Both Toby and Jessica were in a booth playing a zombie game, the aim was to shoot at the zombies to get through to the next level and each one of their laughs got louder than the others. Meanwhile Ella and Wren were close by sharing a pack of freshly made doughnuts. Wren noticed that the building was pretty much empty, they seemed to be the only ones left in the room. Checking the time to see if it was closing hour which to his confusion, closing wasn't for another three hours' time.

"We need to go, something's not right." Wren grabbed both his children and Ella. Hurrying them to the door which was locked. Most kids in a situation like this would begin to panic but Wren kept calm, so everyone stayed calm until all the lights shut off and the music stopped.

"Stay close, stay together and follow me." Wren whispers and each one of them kept close. Wren had his arms around them all as he walked behind, he handed Toby a knife which he knew how to use correctly as had training with Wren. Shots began to fire and all four them crouched behind the air hockey machine. Wren peered above just to see where the shots were coming from as he could see the light from each shot being fired.

"Dad, the fire door is open." Toby pointed over to the door which encouraged them all to head over. However, it wasn't until it was too late, they had been led into a trap. Eight men all armed stood pointing their guns at Wren and his family.

"What do you want?" Wren still stood with his family in his arms keeping them close. Handgun still in his hand but hid behind Toby's back, luckily Toby had hidden the knife his dad gave him in his underwear so he looked unarmed.

"Drop the gun Wren. You're out numbered here." A deep voice which Wren knew all too well emerged from behind the armed men.

Wren's face dropped, "What the fuck do you want?"

"Nice to see you too. And look at what you, produced. Always said you was punching even now."

"This has nothing to do with them, you want me, take me, let my family go." Wren's voice raised and anger filled his face. Never did he think he would ever see him again, he thought he was dead.

"My dear brother, no that would be too easy. You're all coming."

"Brother?" Ella spoke up, she was not nervous or panicking but shocked. Wren had never mentioned a brother, they had been together for over 18 years.

"Not my brother."

"We are by blood. I will always be your brother even though you hate it."

"Thought you were dead anyway?" Wren kept calm however adrenaline was pumping through his body. His family are his life and he would kill to protect them. "How did you find me Tate?"

"It was difficult I can assure you of that one but we both have contacts. Now your little family will be coming with me until you complete a little mission for me."

Wren scoffed, "Over your dead body".

Tate rolled his head back and let out a laugh, "They will all end up dead if you don't cooperate but, you could just come willingly, and no one will be harmed. Come on big brother." Tate looked very similar to Wren but was corrupt and you could see that. He also served in the military however was forced to leave due to being a liability, which Wren disowned him for. Tate ended up shooting someone knowing they worked together to take advantage.

"Wren, just do what he says." Ella looked up to Wren showing him it will be okay.

"Yes, listen to your wife. I see who wears the trousers in this relationship" Tate laughed but was soon cut off by Ella.

"Fuck you." Ella snapped back at Tate which shocked him and his men and made Wren smile.

"Okay, where are you taking us."

"Not that easy." From this comment, four of Tate's men put bags over Wren and his family's heads and all were taken in the back of a van. From this the location was unknown. Wren done everything in his power to not allow work to follow him back to his home life and now it finally had.

3

"Well, that went better than I thought it would." Hallie and Seb had finally arrived back at the manor. It was such a big house for just the two of them but was well worth the space. Every time that they went back to the manor Seb took a different route to ensure that he was never followed. It was late and they were both shattered from the events of the day, a thin layer of dust was scattered around Seb's car from the rubble from the days events.

Hallie and Seb had a tough road to get to where they are now. You would never in a million years have thought that they would be a couple after what had happened. Seb met Hallie originally around 11 years ago when he tortured her in Afghanistan when she served in the military. However, Seb learned in later years that Hallie wasn't involved in the death of his brother, but her previous work partner was. Adam Fowler had worked with Hallie since she was sixteen serving in the army to then work as her partner in the police as Detective Inspectors. Hallie was led to believe that Fowler was the one person she could trust and slowly began to fall for him, until Seb taught her the real truth about him. How his web of lies finally caught up with him. Hallie was thankful that Fowler would never return thanks to Seb. Both Hallie and Seb's relationship was pure and you could really see how they cared for each other.

As they arrived back at the manor Hallie heads straight to shower whilst Seb goes and checks his little guest he has locked up in his basement. Charlie Henderson was someone that had been on Seb's radar for a while as some of the things he has done is not only wrong, but unforgivable. Seb reaches into his jeans pocket and pulls out an old key which hung out of place on his key chain and placed this into the lock. One turn and the door began to creak open. This must have startled Charlie as he began to scream for help.

"Help. Help me. I need to get out of here. Help me. Please. Get me the fuck out of here!"

"There is no one here Charlie so you can stop screaming before I cut your tongue out."

"I won't be silenced. Fuck you. You are a dead man you hear. Dead man." Charlie had a tremor in his voice but meant what he said.

"I don't fear death." Seb stood over Charlie and kicked him into his ribs. Charlie began to squirm and cough up some blood as he already had some internal injuries.

"You must fear something. Everyone does."

"I know all your deepest darkest little secrets Charlie which will now be exposed for the world to see. Your so called little allegiance will be no more. You fear failure, death, not being in control, you fear your little mother will be disappointed in you, so you lie about how you gained your fortune. You are a sick human being Charlie, now we have the names, all will be brought down."

"You really believe holding me here is getting you one step ahead? You are more stupid than you look."

Seb hid any emotion he had. He knew that he was ahead yet had something doubting him. "You have no idea what I am capable of." With that another swift kick to his ribs made Charlie scream in pain. More blood pooled out of his mouth but joined with a smile to which added confusion to Seb.

"That girl. The one that led you all to me. She is what you fear." Charlie began to chuckle. His teeth red from more blood coming up his throat. He spat on the concrete floor. Seb remained quiet waiting for anything else to leave his mouth. "She is something else. She would be sold at a pretty penny. The boss would enjoy her as I can see that you enjoy her." That was it, a switch went off in Seb's brain. He saw red. Hoisting Charlie up, he grabbed him by his throat making his face go redder gasping for breath, Seb's face remained stern. No words just hate.

"You love her, he will enjoy this even more!" Charlie stuttered out which caused Seb to break his grip from around Charlie's neck. As much as he wanted to kill Charlie there and then he needed him alive.

"Who will?"

No response, Charlie was coughing trying to get as much air back into his lungs as he could take. Seb grabbed Charlie again and pulled him up and gave a swift punch around his face.

"Who fucking will Charlie. I will find out one way so better you tell me."

"Best you keep a close eye on her. He will like her." Charlie then began to laugh and Seb walked over to a metal table which had two items on it. A bottle and a needle. Seb drew up the medication and grabbed Charlie by his hair and injected this into his neck. Falling to the floor, there was silence. Seb left him on the floor and began to head back upstairs to check on Hallie. He needed a shower, his mind was going a hundred miles an hour. Hallie was his reason to live, his fear of losing. Before, he had nothing, no one. Now, he has his person. As Seb went into the bedroom Hallie was just getting out the bath, her smell was intoxicating. The fusion from her shampoo, bubble bath and her own scent was something that made Seb want her more. Hallie looked up to Seb and wrapped her wet hair around her shoulder from the towel. All that remained on her was a white towel.

"Well, how did it go downstairs?" Hallie could see a change in Seb and was there for him when he needed as he would be for her. But there were no words that left Seb's mouth.

"Seb? You okay?" Hallie began to walk over to Seb to which he snapped out of his daydream and acknowledged her.

"I am. You're here with me so course I'm okay." Seb grazed his hands down Hallie's arms and kissed her forehead. Heading straight for the bathroom he closes the door and gets straight into the shower. Allowing the hot beads of water to glide down his face he closes his eyes. His mind is spinning, to many scenarios happening, Charlie's comment, *'he will love her'*, who is he? Seb was coming to the realisation that he was in love and in his line of work, this was dangerous. Does he just stop, he has enough money to retire at such a young age, just live a peaceful life with Hallie. Will he be able to stop, Seb has never not worked this could be a change for him. He hadn't realised how long he has been in the shower, eyes still closed he feels a gentle hand on his shoulder which startles him. He sharply spins around to find Hallie stood there with a towel in her hands. Hallie doesn't flinch, she knew he was in deep thought.

"What's going on?" Hallie questions, she wanted answers as Seb was acting distant.

"Nothing darl, I'm okay."

"What was one thing you told me to promise to never do." No answer from Seb, he knew the answer but allowed Hallie to finish. "You told me never to lie as I said the same to you. So, if you don't want to tell me because you are not ready that is okay but know I am here for you when you are ready. Okay?" Hallie gave Seb his towel and smiled, she began to walk away when Seb grabbed her from behind. Hallie enjoyed this playful side to Seb. Seb placed her onto the bed and led on top of her looking into her eyes. Hallie smiled and ran her hands through Seb's wet hair to get it out of his eyes. Seb lent down and kissed Hallie. Kissing her passionately, he then began to kiss down her body then slowly back up again till their lips met again. Hallie wrapped her arms around Seb's neck and her legs around his waist and Seb picked Hallie up then he laid down with her on top of him. Hallie slowly went down on Seb causing him to want her even more. The bed sheets draped over Hallie's back as she rode Seb gracefully, Seb wanted this to last forever as did Hallie. Flipping Hallie to her back, Seb took control and he knew what he was doing. Beginning with his tongue, then himself, Hallie couldn't contain herself which made Seb growl wanting to consume her more. Hallie scratched all down Seb's back as he cradled Hallie and finished. Both sweaty, out of breath, they led under the sheet from the bed as Hallie laid her head to rest on Seb's bare chest. Seb trying to calm his breathing he took a large inhale and whispered, "I can't lose you Hallie."

"What makes you think you will?" Hallie kept her head resting on his chest. Knowing if she looked him in the eyes, he might not finish what he wants to say. "I think I should retire early. Stop doing what I do, just, have a life with you." Seb looked down to see Hallie's reaction and she sat up and looked at him.

"If that is what you want to do, then do it. I will support you." Hallie smiled to Seb to which she received a smile back but just as Seb was going to talk there was someone banging on his front door.

4

The knocks didn't stop and were getting louder. Whoever was at the door, was now using both fists in a continuous rhythm. Seb sat bolt upright and slid on some black tracksuit bottoms. Hallie began to put some clothes on too when Seb stopped her.

"You need to stay here." He demanded.

"What do you mean? Someone is literally beating our door down, I am coming."

"Hallie, please, just stay here." Seb's tone had completely changed, he seemed vulnerable. Hallie nodded in agreement and kissed Seb as he left to investigate. Hallie was too stubborn to listen to his instructions, she would take the telling off later but first she wanted to know who this was. Hallie opened her bottom bedside draw and loaded her Berretta APX A1 handgun which was a gift from Seb and began to slowly creep down the long staircase.

Seb had just got to the door with his gun behind his back, he had checked his phone and looked at the security cameras. However, whoever was at the door had a black jumper on so no sight of their face. Seb began to turn the locks of the door and shouted through asking who it was.

"Seb, open the fucking door. It's Wren."

Seb instantly opened the door and saw Wren was bleeding from his head, sweat covered his body and he fell to the floor when the door opened. Seb helped him up and placed his shoulder under his arm to help hoist Wren up to his feet. Seb went to shout for Hallie however as he looked up, he noticed her running down the stairs ready to help get

Wren inside.

"Hallie, call Katie and Gibb, get them here." Hallie ran back up the stairs to grab her phone and a first aid kit to begin treating Wren.

"Wren, what happened?" Seb had a tea-towel placed on Wren's forehead to capture any blood before he was stitched up.

"They have them, all of them!" Wren was breathless, he had used so much energy beating at Seb's door that he had barely any left.

"Who have? Who are you talking about?"

As Wren was about to speak again Hallie appeared with the first aid kit and a water for Wren to drink. Hallie was stood over Wren and began to clean his head wound before stitching it up.

"Start at the beginning, what has happened?" Seb knelt so he was in eye line of Wren so he could keep eye contact and ensure he could get an answer.

"We went to the arcade, it was quiet, too quiet. I didn't like it. We began to leave when we were targeted. They have my family, and he is behind it all. I will fucking kill him." Wren began to get angry and tried to stand up however was pushed back down by Seb as Hallie was mid stitch.

"Wren, look at me. Who took them?"

"Tate."

"Are you sure?"

"I am positive."

Hallie wanted to interrupt to find out who Tate was but chose not to speak. Gibb and Katie shortly arrived after this and Seb explained what has happened. Hallie still confused with the situation, remains by Wren ensuring all his stitches are tight and covered. Wren looks broken, defeated. Hallie kneels in front of him, wraps a blanket around his shoulders and looks him in the eye. "Whoever this person is, you know that we will get them. You know we will get your family back."

"I do." Wren looked up, it was just him and Hallie. Seb had gone to the hallway to brief Katie and Gibb what to look for when Wren brushed the blanket off his shoulders. "I am so sorry Hallie." Completely unexpected, Wren stood up and grabbed Hallie and began to run out of the manor. Hallie saw red. She was kicking, punching Wren to release her and then she screamed which triggered Seb to turn back quickly. Wren had thrown Hallie into the back of a car and sped off up the long driveway.

"Hallie! Fuck." Seb gets straight in his car and speeds off after Wren. Whatever possessed Wren to take the one thing Seb loves most was the wrong move.

"Wren, what the fuck. What are you doing!" Hallie began to kick and punch the windows but anything she was doing was not working.

"I'm sorry Hallie, they want you. They want me. They will let my wife and kids go if they have us."

"Who the fuck are you talking about Wren. Who wants me. Why would you do this. I thought Seb was one of your closest friends, like family. What have I done that is so messed up for you to do this to me." Hallie had panic in her voice, she had been taken before and she had no control. All memories began to flood back into her mind of not being in control, being held hostage it was happening again.

"I know Seb will find us if we both go, we both have enough training and guts to tolerate whatever they have. They will let my family and kids go. That is what I am thinking of." Wren had defeat in his eyes, he knew there was no going back from this.

"Shit!" Hallie began to punch the back of the seat and started to cry quietly.

Seb was catching up to the car Wren was in to try and save Hallie, Gibb dialled into Seb's car Bluetooth to help. "Seb, what the hell was that?" Gibb questioned and Seb didn't have the answer.

"I don't know, Charlie told me that they would want Hallie because of how I feel for her. Saying how much she would be liked there. I don't know where he could be taking her and I need you both to do history on Charlie and Wren, see if Wren was a backstabber all this time?" Seb then continued at high speed down the road, his heart sank knowing one of his closest friends had betrayed him. It was late and there weren't many cars on the road. Until Wren turned off and vanished. "Katie, where the fuck did Wren go?" Katie was hacking the cameras on the main road to get answers.

"I-I don't know, he's gone." Katie stuttered knowing this was not the answer that Seb was looking for.

"Shit, get all cameras of that car, all history anything. We need to find her, call the team."

"Yes sir." Katie left the room to dial an SOS to Seb's team to head straight to the manor.

"Gibb, I am coming back to the manor, get the system up of the cameras around the manor so I can see who is coming."

"Yes sir."

Seb was not going to accept defeat, he had trusted Wren, and now this. This was another level of betrayal.

Wren and Hallie were in an old car park under the main road. It was dark, cold and no lights insight. You could hear the odd car go over the bridge above but nothing else.

"Why did you do it, we could've found them together. Why take me?"

"I will see my family be let out as we get taken, we can get out I have a way."

"Who is Tate." This triggered Wren, that name sent a cold shiver down his spine.

"Tate fought with me and Seb in the Navy however he betrayed so many, killed his own to gain power and I thought he was dead until I saw him. Tate is my brother."

"What does your brother want to do with me?" Hallie sniffled.

"The same as me, he wants Seb, and we are the way he can get him."

"Are you really going to give Seb up like this? Giving him me? I won't tell him anything. I won't give Seb up. He won't get through me."

"Nor me." This comment confused Hallie.

"What?"

"I want him to believe I am on his side, and then we attack. I have reason to believe he works with Harold Kingston and Charlie Henderson, he could even be the person over seeing it all. I need to prove it, I need to take him down. But I need my family out the way for this. I am sorry Hallie for roping you into it but there was no other way."

Hallie saw a shimmer of hope in Wren's eye. A cars headlights were beaming ahead and stopped directly in front of Wrens car. Hallie hoped at first it was Seb but all she saw was Wrens family getting out the back of the car. A large man climbed out of the passenger seat, he had a nasty slit down his face which looked like it was fresh.

"Have you got her?" The man growled, he had a horrible croak in his voice.

"Let them go and we will come."

"Get out the car and we will send them to you."

Both Hallie and Wren got out the car and stood with the headlights beaming upon them.

"Get in that car and drive, you two. Get in."

Wrens' wife and children ran to him and hugged Wren tightly. Wrens' son handed him the knife he had hid to which he gave Hallie to hide. Wren whispered into his wife's ear, "Drive to Seb's house, tell him they have us both. I love you."

"I love you too."

"COME ON. Get in the car or will take you all back." Both Hallie and Wren got in the back of the car and watched Wrens family drive away.

………

"Seb, someone is at the gate, it looks like Wren's car!" Gibb got Seb's attention instantly and Seb ran to the door with a gun in his hand. His team hadn't arrived yet, but they would shortly. It was just him. A spotlight appeared on the car and Seb was at the door with a shotgun in his hand. "Now slowly get out the car, I don't give a shit who you are, I will shoot." Seb shouted and Wrens family followed orders with hands above their heads. This was a heartbreaking scene for Seb as he saw the fear in Wrens children's eyes.

"Seb, please we are unarmed. Wren told us to come here. Said we would be safe here. They have them." Ella pleaded with Seb. "Please Seb, you have to believe me." Seb was struggling to trust anyone, Hallie was taken, and he wanted her more than anything. Seb began to lower his gun. "Are you alone?"

"Yes."

Seb invited them in and guided them into the lounge to sit by the fire. This night was one that was going to change all of their lives and not in a good way.

5

Seb was pacing up and down in front of his lit fireplace. The only noise was the sound of crackles from the wood being burnt and Seb's footsteps. Everyone was silent, waiting for Seb to talk but nothing, he had no words. Gibb had the urge to speak when Katie nudged him and shook her head indicating that this would be a bad idea.

"So, you were all taken, that is true, yes?" Seb didn't make eye contact with anyone. Both children were asleep on the sofa and Ella was sat upright waiting for what was going to happen next.

"Yes, we have no idea why bu…"

"I know why, what I don't know is why Wren didn't just say what was going to happen, why he just took Hallie."

"He probably wasn't thinking, they gave him a choice and he obviously made it."

"Obviously." Seb's tone was annoyed, he walked over to the bar and poured himself a whisky and shot it in one.

"Seb, I'm sorry but if anyone can find them it is you."

"That isn't the point Ella." Seb's voice was raised slightly, not enough for the children to wake up but enough to get his point across. Ella remained quiet.

"Never was our work meant to end up being linked with our personal lives, but Tate is another level of fucked up and will go to any extreme. I am surprised he let you out, but I don't know why he wants Hallie? Why not just ask for me, I would go with Wren, he did not need to just take Hallie from me. It doesn't add up Ella." Seb didn't believe this story and he was determined to get Hallie back as quick as he could.

"There is a joint bedroom upstairs for you and the kids, you can stay there till I figure out what is going on."

"Thank you Seb." Ella began to stand up and walk over to the children when Seb grabbed her arm and spun her around. Anger filled his eyes, they were dark, he had a tight grip on Ella's arm. "But, if I find out you have lied to me, you will regret it, and you will be dead to me. Understand."

"I wouldn't lie to you Seb. I do not want any part of this situation. As soon as Wren is found, I don't want anything like this to happen again. I'm sure Hallie would feel the same. Now if you don't mind, I have had a very shit evening, I'd like to get my kids to bed, and you are hurting my arm." Ella looked down at her arm then back up at Seb, she was a strong woman who would do anything for her children. Seb released his grip and looked over to the children sleeping peacefully. Walking over to Toby, he woke him whilst picking Jessica up placing her over his shoulder and headed for the stairs. Ella followed close behind and then tucked them both into bed. Seb was quiet, he began to leave the room when Ella called. "Seb, I am very grateful you are letting us stay here. Please find my husband." Seb nodded and then closed the door and headed back to the lounge.

Meanwhile, Katie was nervous. She was tapping on the table then biting the skin around her nail. Gibb noticed this and held Katie's hand and shook his head. "What you thinking?"

"I haven't seen him this mad in a long time Gibb. The way he feels about Hallie, she is his person, I just didn't expect Wren to do something like this."

"Well, he has."

"He must have a reason."

"Yeah, his brother that is the reason."

"Stop that." Katie pulled her hand back off Gibb and looked at him with confusion.

"What, it is true. Why would he take Hallie unless he is already working with Tate. Seb has given that family everything and anything like he has for us and look."

"Wren is not like that. There must be something else." Katie continued biting the skin around her nails.

"Well when you have that something else let me know, but right now, I think he is a selfish coward."

"Jason! Why would you say that."

Gibb stood up and walked over to pour himself another coffee. "Don't Jason me Katie, it's true. He had a choice, allow his family to go but take the one thing that means the most to Seb right under his nose, or come to Seb and we all work together to get his family out."

"Gibb is right, it doesn't add up." Seb had heard the whole conversation which made them quiver.

"But Seb, do you really think Wren would go behind your back in something so fucked up?" Katie still had Wren's back, she believed she had to stay faithful and trust the people who she cares about.

"I don't know Katie, until we get them back, I won't ever know." Seb nodded to Gibb as he poured another coffee. More of Seb's team had arrived and all looked either battered, tired or just worn out one way or another. Seb began to brief his team on what had happened and wanted information on Harold Kingston, Jake Henderson, Tate Kepner and Wren Kepner. When Wren's name was announced all attention was on Seb, his team had a look of disbelief, betrayal, worry.

"Wren has taken Hallie. We are unsure where the destination is as Ella and her children were all blindfolded on their journey. All they know is where the car park was that they got into Wren's car. Driving straight here as instructed by Wren. We are unsure what he is up to and quite frankly I want to know, but my main interest is to get Hallie back. Understand." Seb was usually quite a compassionate person, but he just snapped, his mood could turn at a flick of a switch. He means business and he will not stop until Hallie is found.

6

Hallie and Wren got into the back seats of the car, Hallie made sure she was not making eye contact with Wren, she was so angry at him for doing this and with her history of being abducted, this was an all-time low. Wren turned around to look through the back window of the car to ensure his wife and children were driving away safe. When they were finally out of sight, Wren turned back around and looked at Hallie.

"Hal, I am sorry."

"Fuck you Wren." She spat back.

The two men in the drivers and passenger seats both smirked, they seemed to enjoy the tension of this, the betrayal that had been made.

"Where are you taking us anyway?" Hallie spoke up and began to sit forward in her seat.

"To see our boss. You are two popular people, one ex-military, another ex-military and a cop. You are valuable."

Wren leaned forward also and began to untie the rope which restrained his hands together. Hallie caught sight of this and pulled the knife from her trousers and began to cut.

"What do you mean, valuable?" trying to keep the men talking, a distraction so she could cut herself free.

"You sell to the highest bidder, and you then belong to them. To do what they want, when they want." The large man grunted in pleasure. "I would happily buy you, you pretty little thing" turning around to Hallie which made her grunt in disgust. Unknowingly her hands were free and she took the knife and slit the man's throat. The driver began to swerve around the road as Wren took the rope he once was restrained with wrapping it around the driver's neck, pulling with all force and strength he had, not realising the car was spiralling out of control.

"Hallie, get the wheel." Wren shouted as the other man was still pulsing out blood from his neck, Hallie was getting covered in blood, but she managed to take control of the wheel however the driver had put his foot down on the accelerator and the car began to pick up speed.

"Wren, I can't slow the car down." Hallie knocked the gear stick into neutral and allowed the car to cruise at speed, high revs making the car sound like it was going to blow up. This was their time to jump from the car. Hallie leaned over and pressed the unlock button on the driver's door and both Hallie and Wren jumped from the car. Rolling along the grass at speed until both eventually stopped. The car hit a large lamp post and blew up causing a large fire to emerge. Hallie laid still, her ears had popped from impact. All she could hear was a high pitch scream. Wren climbed over to her to check she was alive when all of a sudden her hearing came back. Hallie gasped for air and sat up right. Wren looked in pain but tried not to show it.

"What the fuck was that about? What have you got into?" Hallie shouted at Wren whist pushing him with both hands. Wren looked down at the floor. "I'll explain it all, but we should start walking back to the manor."

"Sir, there has been an explosion of a black BMW x5 which matches the description Ella has given us of the car Hallie and Wren got in." Katie was typing away to try get into the main cameras and any local cameras in the area.

"Wade, Boris head out there, I will go another route and meet you at the location of where the car blew up. Gibb, log into the police data base see what information you can get or who is on the scene."

"Already on it boss."

"Aaron, stay here, keep an eye on Wren's family and wait for the others to arrive."

"Yes boss."

Seb grabbed his jacket, started up his Jaguar and sped up the drive.

Focused, determined and above all, ready to kill anyone who gets in his way.

It was a very cold night, a frost had begun to set in. Hallie and Wren decided to get off the main road and walk along the back roads in an attempt to get back to the manor somehow. From the impact of that jump, she was sore but could visibly see Wren was in pain.

"Where are you hurt?" her tone was low, no empathy was shared.

"I think my shoulder has come out of place." Wren was holding his arm when Hallie noticed the drop on his shoulder.

"Okay, you need to not hit me when I do this okay."

"Do what?"

"It needs to be popped back into its socket and it is going to hurt. A lot."

"Okay, yeah just do it."

Hallie felt along the top of Wrens collarbone and down the socket of his shoulder to figure out what way she needed to pull or push. Luckily it was to pull his arm as she wouldn't be strong enough to push it back.

"Right, you ready." Wren looked and grabbed the bottom of his jumper and stuffed it into his mouth and nodded.

"Three, Two..." Snap, it was back in the socket.

"Son of a bitch! Where was One Hal?"

"You would of expected it so I went on two."

"Fuck."

"I would say sorry, but I really am not. You deserve that."

No answer from Wren, he just looked up at Hallie. They began to walk when they passed an old Co-Op corner shop to which Hallie realised she was getting hungry, the sooner she was back at the manor the better. The air was cold, after every breath she took, a mist left her mouth, her lips were beginning to dry. The realisation of the cold evening setting in was getting to Hallie. Adrenaline had left her body from the jump from the car and now shivers went down her body. No coat, no warm clothes just a hoodie, blue and grey checked pyjama bottoms and some boots. Hallie had only just left her bed with Seb when Wren came knocking, she didn't have time to even put a bra on which was obvious now as her nipples were hard from the cold. Wren had noticed Hallie was shivering and he offered her his coat to take. Hallie declined this by shrugging her shoulders off, Wren didn't back down though as he placed his coat over her again.

"Seb would kill me if I let you freeze."

"Not if I kill you first for taking me." Hallie kept walking and Wren kept by her side looking around making sure they were not being followed.

"How many times do I need to apologies to you."

"Start by explaining to me who Tate is." Hallie went straight to the point stopping in her tracks to face Wren. Anger spread across her face, she began to square up to him. Hallie was quite a bit shorter than Wren, but she meant what she said. Wren didn't move, he could quite easily hurt Hallie, but he didn't want to, he never wanted to hurt her.

"You. You know something, and you are not telling me. What is it Wren cause I think you owe me an explanation." Hallie stood her ground and looked Wren dead in his eyes. Wren attempted to look down, he couldn't face this truth.

"Look at me!" Hallie shouted which made Wren jump slightly.

"Don't you shout at me." Wren began to snap back.

"I have every right to feel the way I feel, you have not told me shit Wren! What that was about? Who is Tate?" Wren knew Hallie was right, he was angry and didn't want to admit the truth. Before they knew it a car came out of know where and startled them both. Headlights were getting closer and closer. Hallie and Wren prepared for the worse, it could be someone just passing, it could be the people who just tried to take them.

"Stay behind me."

"Don't you tell me what to do." Hallie snapped back, standing tall and ready to be hit with whatever this was about to be thrown at her when the car stops in front of them both. They could run, but neither did. Curiosity got the better of them both, Hallie and Wren were as stubborn as each other. Two men got out the car and stood in front of the headlights, their silhouettes shadowed along the concrete road which laid ahead.

"Wren, Hallie?" A familiar voice, both Wren and Hallie recognised, they both looked at each other and then back at the road.

"Who's asking?" Wren stepped forward and Hallie followed. Hallie pulled the knife which was tucked in between her jeans and underwear and kept one arm by her side just in case.

"It's me, Boris, and Wade is here too. Whatever you guys have got you can lower. Seb sent us." Relief from Hallie when she heard Seb's name, she began to walk up to the car with Wren when she stopped, this could be a trap, who could she trust?

"Call him." Hallie shouted.

"What?" Boris shouted.

"Yeah, what?" Wren agreed with Boris. "Hal, what you doing?"

"I have no idea who I can trust. I am going nowhere till I hear it from Seb."

"Okay, I will call him, don't do anything stupid Hal, I am just reaching to get my phone." Boris leaned through the car window to pick up his phone. "Boss, its Boris, we have Hallie and Wren, but Hallie won't get in the car." Hallie remained still, Wren stayed with her much to her disgust.

"Hallie, they can take us back to the manor."

"I'm sure they could Wren, sure they could." Hallie looked defeated, but the thought of being taken again she was making sure she avoided any traps she could.

"Yes sir, Hallie, it's Seb." Boris shouted back to Hallie raising the phone ahead so it was facing her direction

"Put it on speaker." Boris done as she asked.

"Hal, you there?" Instant relief, Hallie sighed, her shoulders dropped, she began to walk over to the car.

"Yeah, I'm here." Hallie didn't have many words, she knew that she was cold, her voice trembled and the aches from jumping out the car were finally beginning to creep up on her.

"Hallie, get in the car with Boris and Wade, they will bring you back to the manor. Okay. We'll sort all this out when you get back. Please."

"Okay." Hallie knew it was safe, she trusted Seb, the amount he had done for her, how could she not trust him.

"Boris, meet you back at the manor."

"Yes sir."

Hallie and Wren got in the back seats of the car as they sped off back to the manor. Wren was in pain, he made a mistake, thought impulsively and now he looked over at Hallie and saw this regret. Hallie was numb, she watched out the window at the trees speeding past her, the moonlight in the distance. Passing the occasional car on the route back. To ensure that they were not being followed, Wade took a few additional turns before they arrived back at the gates of the manor. It looked like Seb wasn't back yet however as soon as the car stopped Hallie got straight out.

"Hallie, wait." Wren called for her, but she ignored him and continued to storm inside. Ella was at the door, witnessing the whole thing.

"Hallie, I'm..."

"Don't. This is on your husband, not you." Ella allowed Hallie to brush past her and Ella ran straight for her husband and hugged him tightly.

Gibb saw Hallie go straight upstairs and thought best to give her some space. The bedroom door slammed closed and Hallie headed straight for the balcony. Picking up a large red fluffy blanket, she went straight to the lounge chair and curled up in a ball.

A few moments later another car sped up onto the gravel driveway and harshly braked. A slam of the driver's door was enough to startle anyone. "Where is she?" Seb stormed in through the manor doors and headed for the lounge.

"Upstairs. Not a word from her just went straight up." Gibb looked over to Seb who then began to walk over to Wren. It was inevitable he was going to go for him, even Wren knew it.

"I will deal with you later." Through gritted teeth he held Wren up by his collar and spat the words. Wren nodded, he knew he was in for it but to make sure his family was safe, which they now were, he had to do it. Ella looked over to Wren with love and a nod. Wren walked over to Ella and hugged her tightly and kissed her forehead.

7

Dark, peaceful and tranquil the autumn evenings were therapeutic. The leaves on the trees all around had all nearly fallen ready for winter to come but the coldness was settling in. Hallie was hypnotised by the stars and the full moon that evening lighting the scenery around. Hallie closed her eyes, it felt like she was floating away, listening to a fox bark in the distance then the bedroom door began to creak open. Eyes instantly opened but she remained still, waiting for whoever had entered to announce themselves still holding to the knife tightly.

"Darl?" relief ran through Hallie's body. This was one voice she could never be mad at. A voice she had once hated for so long, she'd grown to love. Hallie spun her head around and looked at Seb, emotions were flooding through her body. She wanted to break down into tears, she wanted to remain strong and unbothered but instead all she did was stand up and allowed Seb to come to her. He picked her up and hugged her tightly. Hallie's head cradled into his shoulder, no words, just remaining in each other's arms. Seb began to release his grip slightly and look at Hallie noticing red around her eyes, either she is tired or has been crying, both from what Seb could guess.

"He's a dead man for ever touching you." Hallie noticed anger begin to spread across Seb's face, he had a flush of red flair through his cheeks.

"We need to listen to his reason behind it. He was trying to save his family."

"He could have said something and we would help him save his family, not take you like that." Seb was angry, he didn't want to take his anger out on Hallie but struggled to keep his composure.

"I know that, but we need to hear what happened, the full story and go from there."

Seb began to run his hands down Hallie's back when she flinched slightly in pain. "Did they hurt you?"

"No, we jumped from a car at quite some speed, I slit one of their throats and Wren strangled the other." Seb seemed impressed by Hallie slicing a knife through someone else's throat. At one stage in her life she was so against murder, killing anyone unless completely necessary, yet here she was killing people. A smile appeared across Seb's face.

"Why are you smiling?"

"I am never letting you go, you know that."

"Good, cause you're stuck with me now." From that they shared a kiss and headed downstairs to a room full of Seb's team. Hallie looked over at Wren and headed straight for the bar reaching for the fridge. At first she was going to pour herself a Whisky but instead chose a cold bottle of water. Seb walked over to the fireplace and stood in front of everyone. The flames from the open fire illuminated behind Seb causing a shadow around him. Seb had a tall, muscular build, he comes across very intimidating which is useful in his line of work.

"Right, Wren, Ella, we are all ears. What the fuck happened! And what caused you to do this to Hallie?" Seb kept a calm tone, he knew if he raised his voice this could escalate quickly. He needed to remain calm and composed and if and when the time is right to snap, he would go for it. Picking up the remaining glass of Whisky he had poured earlier and taking a sip from it he kept the glass in his grip.

Wren took the lead in this conversation, Ella however looked very intimidated by everyone here. She knew Seb, Hallie, Gibb and Katie but all these other men were ones she never wanted to meet.

"What I told you was true, we were attacked in the arcade and taken by Tate and his team."

"Explain why Tate has such a vendetta against you?" Hallie spoke up, she was never afraid to speak her truth and quite frankly no one in their right mind would stop her.

"I was the one who turned him into authorities when we served together. Seb and I managed to get all the evidence together. I cut all ties with him, I thought he was dead as he just, he went off the grid. I had no idea he was around, let alone find me and my family."

"Why did he want Hallie, not me?" Seb questioned for the first time he made eye contact with Wren.

"I said I would do what he asked if he let my family go, they had no reason to be involved in this life. Tate agreed and I was shocked by that." Wren went quiet, he looked down at Ella who was sat next to Wren with her hand resting on his lap.

"You've still not answered my question Wren." Seb still calm, composed but not taking his eye off Wren until Hallie spoke up and all eyes went on to her.

"Because you both took something from him, he has taken Ella, he wants me because of you Seb." Hallie looked straight at Seb to which he looked back at Wren.

"Why did you not talk to us, we could have helped, instead you do the one unthinkable thing and take Hallie literally screaming, beating you to let her go and you said nothing!" That was it, Seb began to snap, hearing them words leave Hallie's lips had tipped him over the edge. He was angry, he wanted to blame someone for all of this, and Wren was in the firing line.

"I fucked up okay, I wasn't thinking!"

"Damn right that you weren't thinking Wren, why the fuck did you do it!"

"I was thinking of getting my family out of there, I didn't want them involved in this!"

"And you thought, hmm I will just take Hallie without talking to us before about what was going on."

"I wanted to, but I was running out of time!"

"You were being selfish, you know what she has been through, she trusted you, I trusted you Wren!"

"It's not my fault that the thing she has been through was because of you all those years ago!" That was it, as soon as those words left Wren's mouth, he instantly regretted it. The glass that was in Seb's hand was now launched across the room and shattered into thousands of small shards of glass. Boris and Wade were ready to step in, but Hallie stood up and got in between them both instantly.

"Get out the way Hallie." Seb kept his eyes on Wren but demanded Hallie to move.

"No, this is helping no one so snap out of it, the pair of you. Wren, you fucked up pretty big and shouldn't have done that, but you did so that's that. What we need to do is figure out what he wants with us all and what he is planning to do. Got it!" Hallie was raising her voice throughout the sentence. Still both Wren and Seb stood squaring up to one another and Hallie in the middle.

"Gibb, Katie, you got any info?" Hallie asked to try and ease the tension and get these two away from each other. Never had these two fought before, but this looked pretty close to breaking point.

"Yes, we have a pinpoint on Tate. The location he was last seen he was getting into a car from a pub just on the outside of Andover with a woman."

"Who's the woman?"

"I have done an ID check and her name is Ashlyne Scarsdale."

"You what?" Both Wren and Seb took their eyes off each other and straight to look at Katie who said Ashlyne's name. Hallie was relieved that they were not in each other's faces anymore until it clicked as to who Ashlyne was.

"I thought she was serving life?"

"She was, she is on recall back to prison. We can get an anonymous tip into the police to give them her location if you want?"

"Not yet, let's find her first see what she wants with Tate." Seb began to walk away and look at Gibb's laptop screen to see what he is looking at. "You guys, thank you for coming out here, but I want this to be a top priority. We will get a plan in place when have more info." All Seb's team agreed this was the best outcome and would return in a few hours with the gear they needed to go on surveillance.

"Hallie, wait."

"What Wren." Hallie was still pissed off at Wren and even more so for making that comment about Seb, what happened between them both was in the past.

"I really am sorry, truly."

"I hear you Wren, but you chose a fucked up route about it, we could've all helped and thought of something together but instead you just grab me and take me. Just, give me some time and space, okay?" Hallie began to walk away back to her room, she needed to sleep but first she needed a shower.

Steam began to build across the bathroom, the water was hot and began to sooth across Hallie's aching body. Bruises were forming around Hallie's ribs and across her back from the jump from the car. After washing all the shampoo and conditioner from her hair she just stood still, head under the shower, just quiet. Seb was waiting for Hallie on the bed, she walked out of the bathroom wrapped in a towel and this was a view he could never get tired of. Rubbing her hair in the towel to get any reminisce of water from her hair, she placed an oversized t-shirt on and climbed into bed. Seb grabbed Hallie before she could lay flat and placed her over him. Seb become lost in Hallie's eyes, grazing his hand over Hallie's face and tucking strands of hair behind her ear, her wet hair began to drip onto his bare chest until Hallie placed her hands on either one of his cheeks and began to kiss him. When Hallie pulled away slightly, Seb sat up keeping Hallie on his lap and began to smile.

"What's that grin for?"

"You, just you." This comment made Hallie smile, forgetting everything that had happened this evening she was content, happy, she didn't want this moment to end so she made sure that it would last as long as it could. Still remaining on Seb's lap, she lifted her oversized t-shirt so the only clothing that remained was a lace thong which sat perfectly on the indent of her hips. Seb's hand moved from Hallie's thighs, up her stomach and grabbed both breasts and held them firmly whilst making eye contact with Hallie, neither one of them was going to break this eye contact. Seb's hands then began to move to Hallie's shoulders then slowly down her back whilst allowing his fingers to press hard into her skin causing Hallie to sit up right. Seb smiled, she broke the contact and she knew it. Hallie returned the smile and began to stand up to walk over to the light to switch it off when Seb got up quickly and spun Hallie around pulling her into his body tightly. Their kiss began passionately, both knowing where this was going.

Seb carried Hallie to the balcony and bent her over the railing. This was exhilarating for Hallie, never had she been with someone with so much dominance. Most people would be worried that someone would catch them, hear them but Hallie didn't care. This added more suspense and more drive for her. Her body began to go weak; she was close and Seb knew it, he drove in harder, he was also close but determined to keep it together as he took much pride making Hallie feel the pleasure before. Hallie began to scream Seb's name, this drove him on more making it harder to resist the urge, he was pulsing. He grabbed Hallie's hair and pulled her up to his body holding her and let out a moan in her ear. Everything was still, and beautiful and now it was finally quiet.

8

With minimal sleep and an evening to remember, Hallie felt like she should be feeling a vendetta against Wren for what he had done last night however, she was feeling positive and ready to find this person. Seb was still asleep which was not normal for him as he was the one up at all hours. Hallie took it upon herself to go make coffee for them both and take them back to bed. No one else seemed to be awake which was lovely as she was not ready for the small talk yet. Walking back up the stairs she could hear noise coming from the rooms where Wren and his family are staying. Hallie picks up her pace as doesn't want to acknowledge Wren yet. Trying to be quiet she slowly opens the door to the bedroom and walks over to Seb's bedside, but the floor began to creek below causing Seb to wake up.

"Sorry, I tried to keep quiet. I made you a coffee."

"Thank you, usually it is me making the morning drinks."

"Well, think you deserve to be spoilt a bit." Smirking from this comment, Hallie climbs back into bed and cradles her warm coffee watching the steam rise from the mug.

Seb sits up slightly and clears his throat, "Anyone else awake?"

"Think they are all awake as heard noises coming back up."

"Did you talk to anyone?"

"No, kind of avoided walking slowly." This made Seb snigger, he knew this must be uncomfortable for Hallie.

"Don't blame you, you going to be okay working with him."

"I think I am more concerned that you two don't kill each other judging from how last night took a turn." Seb looked at Hallie and placed his arm around her allowing her to snuggle into his warm body.

"Soon as we find Tate and take care of this little secret coven they have, we can go away." Hallie sat up in confusion, this was Seb's life, he enjoyed being busy and never took time off.

"Where?"

"Anywhere, I'm thinking Caribbean maybe?"

"You wouldn't last sitting around doing nothing, you are the prime example of someone who likes to be kept busy? What's changed?" Seb began to stare at Hallie, his eyes locking onto hers. "Because I love you and never want you taken from me. Before, I had nothing to lose and no one to go home to. Now I have you, and I can't lose you Hallie." Seb seemed sincere in his comment, he wasn't an emotional type however this made Hallie feel so much stronger about him. Hallie put her cup of coffee back on the wooden bedside table and leaned into Seb and whispered, "I love you too." Hallie had never said these words to someone before, never had she been in love. In previous relationships she had strong feelings, but never in love. This moment was one that both Hallie and Seb wanted to treasure but three sharp knocks were hit on their bedroom door.

"When this is over, I am kicking them all out." Seb exhaled annoyed over this moment being interrupted but Hallie just laughed and rolled back onto her side and reached for her mug.

"Yeah?"

Creeping into the room a quiet voice announced themselves. "Sorry, not interrupting, am I?" Gibb entered hesitantly and the look on Seb's face he wished he had waited.

"You're fine Gibb, what's up?" Hallie interjected before Seb could make a comment.

"So, I have done some digging and have come across this photo." Gibb hands the photo to Hallie and Seb looks over her shoulder. "See who looks familiar." Seb noticed straight away, the image below was a group of men all in black suits smiling for a photo and standing next to each other were Tate, Harold Kingston and Charlie Henderson.

"Think I need to go have a chat with Charlie. Thank you Gibb."

"No worries." Gibb had a tremor in his voice like more was to be said.

"Gibb, what's on your mind." Hallie noticed there was something different with him, but he was unsure if this was something they needed to know.

"Gibb?" Seb then challenged which caused Gibb to look back up from the floor to meet their eye line.

"Nothing, just a hunch but I am not 100% sure on it."

"Is it a hunch that we need to know about?"

Gibb was unsure, he wanted to tell them but felt out of place. "No, it's nothing, unless I am sure and I am not so, yeah its fine." Gibb left the room quickly before Hallie or Seb could ask anything and both looked confused.

"Any ideas?"

"Not one. I will talk to him later."

"On that note, I am going to go talk to Charlie. Find out what he knows. Glad I didn't kill him yet."

Hallie heads into the bathroom and runs a hot bubble bath, she knew what she was doing, she wanted to entice Seb into joining her. Knowing that he had work to do she enjoyed being a tease. Seb begins to walk into the bathroom when Hallie places her hands on both his shoulders and seductively whispers into his ear, "You have work to do." Taking a step back she walks over to the bath allowing the black dressing gown to glide down her back as she steps into the bath. Seb walked into the bathroom and knelt behind the large bathtub, gathering Hallie's hair in one hand he pulls her head back gently so she would be looking at him.

"You'll pay for that later." Seb got up and walked away with a smile across his face.

"I look forward to it." This made Seb's smile last even longer, he was enjoying this too much. As he stepped out the bedroom door however his smile soon faded when it was Wren's face that greeted him.

"Can we talk mate?" Wren looked defeated, he was usually upbeat, joking around however Seb noticed the redness around his eyes, the messy hair, which was usually combed back neatly, he was beating himself up over what he had done, and Seb agreed that he should.

"Going to have to at some point but right now I need to go and talk to Charlie."

"Can I do something, anything to help."

Seb wanted him to just go away, leave, never see him again, but Wren was one of the good ones, had stuck by Seb through a lot.

"Just, have a day with your family. Make sure they are okay, probably a lot to go through, especially your kids. We can talk tomorrow?"

"I'm sorry Seb, I am. I should've spoke to you, I shouldn't of just taken her especially after everything. I wasn't thinking. I really regret what I said to you." Seb's blood began to boil, he was bringing up the feelings he had from the night before.

"We will talk later. Just let me sort this. Okay." Before Wren could answer Seb began to unlock the door which led to the basement and locked himself in so no one could follow.

9

The lights flickered on causing Charlie to squirm awake, he had been in the dark for so long that his eyes took longer to adjust as well as having multiple internal injuries.

"Here." Seb placed a large plastic cup filled with blackcurrant squash and a sandwich in front of Charlie. As much as he wanted him dead, he needed him alive at this time.

"Poison? Is the way to go about it now." Charlie wanted this food and drink as he had not had anything in days.

"If I wanted you dead Charlie, I would have killed you already. I want information."

Charlie picked up the drink and drank over half of the pint in one breath causing him to pant of exhaustion. He took a bite from his sandwich and looked up at Seb with his one functioning eye. "What you wanna know?"

"Tate Kepner." Seb paused to get a reaction from Charlie which he got. Charlie stopped chewing on his sandwich and with his mouth half full he responds. "What's he done now?"

"Who is he to you."

"Well, he was working with us, but got too much and when he was told to leave, he just, disappeared."

"So, he is not working with you now."

"Not that I know of. Unless Harold has got him in as I am not there?"

"This photo here, you all looking pretty close, what was this."

Charlie looks at the photo and smiles, "This day was one I will remember for the rest of my life. It was my first day working for them, we auctioned off all those people. We made the highest profit that day which led me to buy my penthouse."

"You are fucking sick, you know that?" Seb needed to keep him talking. "You still close with Tate?"

"Tate? No not since he lost his marbles and thought I wanted him dead. He lost his temper one day with one of the girls I had hired for a night, he beat that girl black and blue. One of her friends comes and finds me to help and I managed to get him off her before he killed her. Then he grabs a letter opener which was on the table and stabs me in the arm before leaving. Since then, haven't seen him." This seemed like a legitimate reason, but Seb didn't trust him in the slightest.

"Okay, final question. Does the name Ashlyne ring any bells?" Charlie then chocked on his sandwich, he had more of a reaction to her name than he did to Tate's. "Take that as a yes, explain."

"You're not working with that psycho are you?"

"What do you know Charlie?" Seb's patience was wearing thin, he wanted answers.

"I know she has multiple screws loose in her head. Fuck if I would ever work with her. Why?"

"Because she was seen with Tate yesterday. Are they close?"

"Fuck no. Tate was the one that put Ashlyne's husband on his death bed, he had been fighting for his life for about eight months before he died. If they were together, he must have something on her."

"Like what?" intrigued Seb moved in closer.

"No idea? But I'm surprised she hasn't killed him! That woman, she scares me. You know she bit off a man's dick cause he called her crazy! Like, who does that!"

"Right, well where would we find Tate?"

"I wouldn't have a clue, unless he is with Harold I don't know."

Seb said nothing, he walked to the wall and turned off the lights and began to head back up the stairs to the manor.

"Wait, wait, leave the light on at least, fuck. Get me out of here." Charlie was shouting as loud as he could to get Seb's attention but was too late, the light was off and the door was locked. Seb headed to his office where he saw Gibb working on the side desk.

"You fancy a drive?" Seb never had taken Gibb out before but Gibb was not one to say no to Seb, any way he could learn from him, he would.

"Sure, just us or?"

"Yeah, I want to go scope something out while Hallie has her appointment at the hospital."

"Hospital, is she alright?" Gibb was fond of Hallie. He went through a lot with her and cared for her in a sibling way.

"Yeah just a check-up she has. We will drop her there and then head out. Sound good?" Seb knew the answer to this, but he wanted Gibb to be comfortable around him and whatever held him back earlier, he wanted to know.

"Yeah, I'll grab my coat." Gibb had been staying in the annex with Katie since his arrival at Seb's manor. For once in his lifetime, Gibb was settled, happy and enjoyed his challenging job. The adrenaline of hacking into databases and looking into camera footages was exhilarating for him.

Seb headed back upstairs to check on Hallie before they left when he entered the room to find her sat on the bathroom floor. Panic set wondering what she had done, if she was okay when she looked up and noticed Seb coming straight towards her.

"I'm fine, took them pain killers and think they just didn't agree with my stomach." Relief for Seb but uncertainty as she had these tablets when they met after her concussion as a pain medication, but Seb tried not thinking too much into it.

"Are you sure you don't want me to go in with you?"

"I will be in there a while, go do a scope around like you decided and if you get tied up, I will find my way back no problem. Will be fine."

"Okay, well ready when you are darl." As they left, they ran into Wren who was looking lost walking around the manor. Seb guided Hallie into the car and walked back over to Wren.

"Where you heading?"

"Taking Hallie to her appointment then scoping an area out with Gibb, see if he can hack a data base."

"Is Hallie alright?" Wren seemed concerned for Hallie's welfare which Seb noticed.

"Yeah just routine check-up. She has asked me not to go in with her but..." Seb paused, unsure whether to trust Wren after the stunt he had pulled before.

"What do you need, anything?"

"Can I trust you?" Sincerity from Seb's face, unsure if he was making the right decision.

"Seb, you have my family here, you could literally do anything yet you are choosing to care for us and I am grateful for you. What do you need?" Hallie looked closely at the conversation that Seb and Wren were having wanting to know what was being said. Hallie had lost more trust in Wren and it would take a lot for it to come back.

"Leave in about 20 minutes. Head to the hospital and just keep a distance but check on Hallie, I'm not sure how long we will be and bring her back here if needed."

"Of course. Yeah that is fine. Do you need me on the scope at all?"

"I will call if need additional back up, but Hallie is my priority right now and soon as this appointment is out the way the better."

"What is the appointment if you don't mind me asking?" Wren didn't want to impose but must be important if Hallie won't see the private doctor.

"No idea, says just a check-up as she has been feeling under the weather but until she has the appointment that is all I know. Guess she doesn't want to worry anyone."

"Stubborn." Both Wren and Seb let out a smile and Seb continued back into the driver's seat of his car.

Hallie looked over to Seb as he began to put his seat belt on and start the car. "What was that about?"

"He asked whether he could help at all and what we were doing. I told him we were scoping an area and taking you to an appointment."

Hallie looked at Seb as he began to speed down the driveway heading onto the main road. "That all?"

"That's all, told him would be back later. He asked to talk to us also but said tomorrow, get today out the way."

10

The Hospital car park was full, there were minimal spaces available however Seb managed to find one close to the entrance. People were going in and out of the main doors like ants, Seb didn't like the idea of leaving Hallie alone however she insisted and would explain all when she got back.

"Darl, you sure you don't want me to come in with you?"

"You will be waiting outside for ages, besides, you have Gibb and intel, get that out the way then we can have a nice meal tonight and relax for once. Sooner we get this target extracted the better. I will be fine okay." Hallie leaned in and kissed Seb, Gibb chose to look down at his phone. As their lips where just parting Seb whispers "I love you" with Hallie replying with "I love you too. See you in couple hours." Hallie zipped up her long black coat and placed her woolly hat on. As soon as Hallie was out of sight Seb started the car and dialled to call Wren.

"I love you eh, never heard her say that before!" Gibb seemed beyond happy to witness their love. Seb just smiled in response and waited for Wren to answer.

"Boss."

"She is inside now okay."

"Yes sir, have eyes will keep you posted."

The phone hung up and Gibb was confused, he had no idea why Wren was following Hallie and didn't like this at all.

"Urm, why is Wren following Hallie?"

"Because we are all walking targets, Hallie is in a public place, somewhere people can hack and see her on security cameras, word of mouth, anything. I want her safe."

Gibb frowned and usually he would keep quiet but instead he asked, "And, no offence on your judgment, you think Wren is the right person for that?"

"No, no I don't, but he is the only hope I got as I have Wade and Boris on another loose end." Seb didn't seem happy with his decision but was the best he could do. "So, tell me Gibb, why did you not want to tell me something earlier?" Silence, Gibb felt a lump form in his throat, nerves began to rise and a slight red blush flared across his cheeks.

"Nothing, its nothing."

"Gibb, what is it, you can trust me."

"Please don't hate me if I am wrong okay?"

Seb looked over at Gibb to see he was uncomfortable with this situation but Seb needed to know, if it could help catch the targets or any intel it needed to be shared.

Gibb took a large inhale and swallowed the remaining saliva that filled his mouth. "I don't trust Katie." Seb was not expecting that, they worked well together, he had worked with Katie for years, what could it be that he doesn't trust.

"What has made you not trust her?" Guilt began to crawl around Gibb's body, unsure if he had made the right choice in telling Seb what he knows. He is the new guy, what if Seb sacks him, makes him disappear. Gibb tries not to let panic override him, but it was proving very difficult. Noticing his palms had begun to get sweat building up in them he looks down and rubs his hands together to try and get rid of some of the moisture.

"Gibb, calm down, nothing is going to happen, I just want to know what you mean that is all." Seb didn't sound angry, hurt or annoyed at Gibb's comment but generally curious.

"I was doing some digging into Tate and what he gets up to, but Katie's name appeared in a coding that I ran. I ran it twice because I was sure I had made a mistake." Gibb went quiet, he didn't want to continue with because he wasn't positive that the facts were correct.

"What did you find Gibb." Seb noticed car headlights appearing closer behind him so he took two wrong turns to make sure he wasn't being followed. It appears that he was being tailed by someone.

"Gibb?" Seb's voiced raised slightly which startled Gibb, he snapped out of his daydream and looked over to Seb who began to speed up the car.

"They were together, I found photos of them both, I know everyone has a past, but their past looks pretty cosy. When I confronted her about it, she denied it all, said she never met him. I knew she was lying because she never shouts or is negative, but she snapped. I just, I don't want to believe she would do this but how else would Tate know where to find Wren and his family, who Hallie was and her relationship with you, just doesn't seem right." Seb didn't answer Gibb, instead he pressed a button on his steering wheel which allowed Seb to ask the car to call Wade.

"Boss."

"Wade, where is Katie? I noticed she wasn't around this morning. Any ideas on her where abouts?"

"Uhh, let me check the trackers, shows she is at Osborne Heights. Want us to get her?"

"Yes, get her and keep an eye on her, I have reason to believe she is the rat letting out all our locations."

"Yes boss, will grab her now, little snake."

"Wade, track this car for me. We are being followed and followed closely. Wren has eyes on Hallie, make sure they get back to the manor. Hopefully can escape these assholes but if not track this car and get a history for me." Seb began to give the details of the car that was following them and just as Seb began to finish where he was heading the phone line went dead. The car had been hit. Seb and Gibb held on tightly as they were thrown around the car as it rolled and ended up on its roof. Seb had blurred vision, all he could hear was a high-pitched squeal, he looked over at Gibb and tried to move him but nothing, he was unconscious. Crunches of glass as someone walked over the debris of the car and began to drag Gibb from the car. Seb was trying to blink hard to regain full vision until he turned around to see a man in the window ready to pull him out.

"Nice to see you again, old friend." With that a swift hit on the head, Seb to lost consciousness. The last face he saw was Tate.

Wade realised that Seb and Gibb had now been targeted, he needed to get Hallie back at the manor safe and begin to find Seb and take Tate down. Boris tried calling Seb back however the phone went straight to voicemail, the same for Gibb, and Katie had disconnected her phone.

"Shit, now what?" Boris began to pace and kept trying to call Hallie. Ella had come down the stairs to see what was happening.

"What's going on?"

"Where is Wren?" Boris looked up at Ella who had looked like she had just got out the shower.

"Oh, he said that Seb wanted him to do something for him. Why?"

"He is with Hallie, I will try him. Ella, where are the kids?" Wade now introjected and this made Ella begin to panic.

"Upstairs, again why?"

"We believe Seb and Gibb's location has been leaked and they have been targeted. Also, Katie has gone and there is no contact or trace from her. Seb believes she is the snake that has been communicating with Tate making him and his team aware of our where abouts."

"Knew I didn't like that bitch for a reason." Ella wasn't a malicious person however she always had a dislike for Katie.

"Wren, we have a situation." Wade had finally gotten through to Wren however he sounded out of breath on the other line.

"As do we? What's up?"

"Seb and Gibb have been hit and believe they have been taken by Tate and his team. Seb believes it is Katie that has been leaking everything. What's your situation?"

"Shit, okay well probably be easier to show you guys. We will be back at the manor in 10 minutes, meet you there?"

"Plan." As both phone lines disconnected Wade began to wonder what Wren was up to and with Seb taking the one guy who knew his way around all things technical with him, this was just a recipe for disaster.

11

Hallie had a gut feeling as to why she had been feeling rough, but the best thing was to get everything confirmed. Finally, she was at a place in her life where she felt full, happy and still a boss bitch. Work was something that always took over Hallie's life and always made it her priority however being able to work with someone she loves was another thing. Seb's whole persona had changed, once out to seek revenge and full of hatred, now, he just cared for Hallie in ways that were indescribable.

The elevator doors glided open as Hallie reached level B of the main hospital, her destination was about halfway up the corridor however as she was walking, she noticed someone very familiar walking out of the Intensive care unit. Hallie immediately begins to speed up, this person is oblivious as to who is following them. As Hallie gains speed next to them, she waits for the right moment to grab them into another room. Taking a turn to look behind her and in front for any people who might witness this, the corridor is empty. Hallie grabs them and tackles them into a large linen room which also seemed to be empty.

"Who the fuck do you... Oh, it's you."

"Don't play dumb with me Ashlyne, who sent you and knows I'm here."

"I could ask you the same thing."

Hallie knew this was the wrong time to be doing this, her appointment was minutes away, but work mode took over again. "Bullshit, who knows and what do you want with us."

"Us, ahh you all happy little fucked up families now Hallie."

"Who knows." With this Hallie grabbed Ashlyne's hair and pulled her head back to make her eyes look up to Hallie.

"Get the fuck off me." Ashlyne pulled away and went to hit Hallie, but she was too fast, she managed to dodge the swift attempt of a punch to the head and her right arm followed through hitting Ashlyne across the left side of her cheek bone. Ashlyne fell to the floor, Hallie knew she could fight, she was a psychopath but somehow Hallie needed to get her restrained. Looking around the room to see if there was any rope, something she could use, she noticed a large amount of torn up scrub tops but as she headed over to them Ashlyne jumped onto Hallie's back and began to hit her around her head. Hallie ducked down causing Ashlyne to fall over her head and back on the ground. Hallie sat on top of Ashlyne and placed her knees and shins to kneel on her arms to try and keep them still. From this she began to tie her hands together when she heard footsteps. Hallie had to work quickly, Ashlyne also heard the footsteps and began to shout.

"Help… help m…" Hallie shoved part of a scrub top down Ashlyne's mouth to prevent her from making any more noise.

"Shut up, you don't play the victim here." Hallie was frantically tying Ashlyne up when the footsteps were now behind her.

"Hallie, what the?" Wren appeared and was in shock with what he was seeing.

"What are you doing here?"

"Seb asked me to keep an eye on you just in case any of Tate's lot got a lead that you were here, looks like I was too late for that." Smiling down at Hallie he admired her strength and tried making light of the situation. Mumbles were appearing from Ashlyne but Hallie was pissed off enough Wren had arrived let alone now she had missed her appointment because of Ashlyne, with that she head-butted Ashlyne to silence her.

"Man, she's pissing me off." Hallie wiped her hair from her face and pulled it up with a scrunchie to a messy ponytail. "You got your car?"

"Yeah, we taking her back?"

"Yes we are, get some answers from her don't you agree?" Wren didn't want to question Hallie, any chance to stay in her good books he was going to do as he was told.

"Absolutely, I will grab a wheelchair, make it look like she is a patient." Wren headed back down the long corridor to go find a spare wheelchair, luckily he had parked close to the entrance. Back upstairs however Hallie was feeling sick again, maybe her mediation she had taken was out of date or some food poisoning, maybe a virus who knows. From this, she pulled out her phone and dialled her doctor's secretary.

"Dr Murphy's office, Candice speaking how can I help?" A very polite voice at the receiving end of the phone, Hallie had visited Dr Murphy for around 5 years, he used to be her general practitioner until he relocated to work inside the hospital however still has the time of day to check on Hallie otherwise, she would see no one and get on with it.

"Hello Candice, it's Hallie."

"Ahh Hallie, didn't you have an appointment today?"

"I did, but I am unable to make it, as I was driving in had to pull over so many times as couldn't control the sick from coming up. I think it is a bug of some sort so have gone back home. Can I reschedule?"

"Because it is you, of course you can. But it is in two days, that gives whatever 'sickness bug' you have to leave your system and come get checked. Understand." Candice didn't ask a question, this was more of a demand which Hallie was happy to meet if it meant getting some answers.

"Perfect, can you send me a text reminder so can put it in my phone?"

"Already sent, see you in a couple days Hallie, you take care."

"You too." As Hallie hung up the phone Wren arrived back with a wheelchair, Ashlyne was still unconscious which was handy. Hallie helped Wren place Ashlyne into a chair and began to untie her, the less it looked like a kidnapping the better.

Both Hallie and Wren tried to make this look like a normal scene where they were just taking a relative out, however this so called relative was beaten, had bruises on her face and was 'asleep' when in reality she was just unconscious. Passers by double looked and it wasn't until they had reached the elevator that there was an elderly couple stood inside. Before both had smiles with one another, but the sight of these three gave them concern. Hallie pressed the ground floor button and waited for the doors to close. Glancing over to the couple she gave a reassuring mile and followed with, "My sister, she has been on psychiatric hold for nearly 6 months and now can come home." The couple smile however don't seemed convinced. Hallie leans into them and whispers "She pretends to be asleep so she doesn't have to talk to anyone. Her home is a residential home as she can't be trusted alone. I do apologies if she is making you uncomfortable." With that the elderly lady relaxed her shoulders and gave Hallie a sympathetic look. "My dear, you must have been through hell and back, bless you for having such a kind soul." Hallie looked back and thanked the lady however, Wren made no eye contact and just smiled. The elderly couple left the elevator first and Hallie and Wren followed pushing Ashlyne as fast as they could to the car park.

Before getting Ashlyne into the car Wren sniggered, "what a kind soul you have Hallie."

Hallie scowled at Wren, "oh piss off and help me get her in."

Managing to get Ashlyne in the boot of Wrens car, they both got in and drove off heading back to the manor. Hallie tried to call Seb but had no luck his phone went straight to an automated voice mail, straight after she tried Gibb, the same message. Hallie's insides began to heat up, panic was settling in, from this she checked the security footage from her phone of the manor to check if they had made it back yet. Nothing. Wren's phone began to ring through the hands free of the car and it was Wade who was on the receiving end. Once the call had ended, both Hallie and Wren had their suspicions that Seb and Gibb were not safe.

12

Arriving back at the manor, Wren and Hallie headed straight inside to figure out what had happened. Seb was the one to usually get them out of trouble and rescue them not the other way around. Wren was greeted by Ella and their children who he was always happy to see however he cared as to where Seb was and what has happened.

"Wade, what's happened? Where are they?" Hallie was still trying to call Seb but the same voicemail kept answering.

"No use calling them Hal, they were hit and taken by we assume Tate and his team." That was it, that word 'taken' sent Hallie down a worm hole. Memories flooding back as to what she had once felt and now she was on the receiving end of it.

"How do you know?" Hallie remained calm, but Wren looked over at her to see she was struggling to hold it together.

"We found the car had been hit, we received a call from Seb and Gibb on route to a potential lead that Katie was one not to be trusted anymore and she was the rat in the pipes relaying messages that we had to Tate. We have been unable to locate Katie since."

"And Gibb was with him?"

"Yes, we believe so. What was your situation." Wade looked straight at Wren who then looked over at Hallie when she realised that she had an unwanted guest still in the boot of Wren's car.

"Can you open the side basement doors please and hook some new chains up, we have someone else to go there. I'm sure we can get answers from them plus, Charlie is afraid of them so will be more entertainment."

The lights were on for the first time in a while for Charlie, maybe this was his time to finally get out. But that reality was thin, and he began to look around see if anything had changed and someone new was tied up next to him however their face was covered. Hallie began to walk up to Charlie and placed a chair in front of him so she could sit and stare him down.

"Ahh, not got your boyfriend on me today I see?"

"Not today, no. My ways of working are, shall we say a little more demanding. We want answers Charlie, but unfortunately for you if we don't get them, then you are no use to me so you may as well be dead. But know this, I won't kill you quickly, it will be torture, I intend on inflicting an immense about of pain on you to the point where you lose consciousness from it. Understand." Charlie listened, for once. He nodded in agreement and sat upright to hear what Hallie had to say. Wren joined Hallie to listen in on what Charlie had to say whilst Wade, Boris and Ella tried to get into any computer systems to track Katie.

"What would your team want with Seb?" Hallie went straight to the point; time was precious and sooner she had answers, the sooner she could find Seb and Gibb.

"His knowledge, him eliminated, you, should I go on?" Charlie smirked but this caused him pain.

"Explain."

"If Seb and his little team are out the picture, that is one less person on our backs to find us and take us down. He got me, but Tate, he works different. Tate takes it to another level and sees double the results, I mean he has earned me millions."

"Paaaa, don't make me laugh, it hurts." Charlies smiled now faded into fear, a voice he recognized too well was now in the same room as him.

"Wh-who is that?" he stuttered and was now Hallie's turn to smile.

"You know me Charlie boy, don't you." Hallie removed the bag from Ashlyne's head and sees her smile straight at Charlie. This caused Charlie to hesitate and scramble away as much as he could, he was still badly injured so couldn't stand well as he kept falling back to the floor but the fear in his eyes made Ashlyne's eyes grow more eager to want him.

"What the fuck is that thing doing here?"

"Thing! What a lovely compliment."

"What is she doing here?" Charlie now shouted which was the first time you could see true terror from him, not from all the torture he had endured but just from seeing Ashlyne.

"What's wrong, didn't you miss me." Ashlyne was enjoying the torment and wanted to push him to the extreme.

"Fuck you Ashlyne, you should be dead."

"Yet here the fuck I am. Chained up, next to you." Ashlyne then looked up to Hallie and straight back to Charlie.

"What's the deal with you two then." Hallie pulled out the apple from her pocket and took a large bite into it. Juices began to spill from the sides.

"Yes Charlie, what's the deal bucko." Ashlyne taunted.

"You are the psycho that made me need surgery and rehab on my dick for months." Hallie choked on her apple from laughter.

"You are the wanker that helped Tate try and kill my husband and then sell me to the highest fucking bidder. You deserve everything that is coming to you." Hallie and Wren were in shock, was Ashlyne on their side and seeking revenge from Tate.

"Right the both of you, shut it. Ashlyne, we saw you with Tate recently, explain that?"

"He found me" she scoffed. "I was as surprised as you are. I have been out of sight for a while just checking in on Henry when I could…"

"Henry! He is still alive?" Charlie was shocked, after what was done to Henry he would have thought he was dead.

"He should have been dead after what you did to him, but I got him help in time. If I ever get my hands on you, I will destroy you." Ashlyne spoke through gritted teeth, she meant every word. "I will let you do whatever you want to me, let me kill him though or let me watch you inflict endless amount of pain on him." A smile appeared across Ashlyne's face when thinking about Charlie being tortured.

"I'm considering it, he is no use to me." Hallie teased and with this comment Charlie's head spun round and looked Hallie in the eye and began to plead.

Charlie began to crawl towards Hallie, "I can help you, any information you need, access to places I can get it. You need me alive. I am the only one who knows where they would be kept and how you can get them out. I can hel-…"

Ashlyne interrupted Charlie mid plead, "Oh stop with the whining Charlie, you absolute pussy. I can help you get them out, but you are both going to want to gear up and prepare for some blood on your hands as this won't be pretty."

Hallie looked back to Wren to consider Ashlyne's request which was risky, she could flee at any moment, she could kill them, but if she knew how to get Seb and Gibb out alive this could be a risk worth taking.

"What do you want in return and how can we trust you?" Wren stepped up and spoke for the first time.

"I want to be the one to kill your brother Wren. I want to kill Tate, Harold, and you." Ashlyne looked straight over to Charlie with determination. Hallie hoped she was one to stick by her word and Charlie was now no use. From what they had done to Ashlyne, Hallie could see why she wanted them dead and the ones to do it. If Hallie could get her talking about her life, her husband she might be able to get a better understanding of her.

Hallie walked over to Ashlyne and released her from the chains, Ashlyne stood up and from what it looked like was squaring up to Hallie. Hallie stood her ground and stood tall and strong; she wasn't afraid.

"I am one to stick by my word Hallie, no harm on any of you will come from me, just let me go on with my piece and will be out of your hair." Hallie nodded in agreement from this, she didn't trust Ashlyne however she wanted to believe her. Ashlyne walked over to the bench which had a variety of tools laid out on, the first one she picked up was a crowbar. Dragging it behind her you could hear the echo of the bar against the concrete floor. Hallie and Wren took a seat against the wall and allowed Ashlyne to do as she pleased. Of course, under supervision.

"Ash, please" Charlie rose to his knees and begged for his life with Ashlyne.

"I have been waiting to do this for a long time." With that she took a large swing with the bar across Charlie's abdomen and a large scream let out. Dropping the bar Ashlyne pulled Charlie up and pulled his head against hers so she could bite down on Charlie's ear which caused him to scream even more. Ashlyne pulled the ear clean off from his head causing blood to pool out from his skull. Hallie and Wren even squirmed slightly; they knew she was psycho, but this was brutal. Next, grabbing Charlie's hand, she knelt on his forearm and began hitting each finger with the crowbar ensuring they were broken. This became unbearable for Charlie to stay conscious from all the pain he was enduring but Wren walked up to Charlie and poured a half bucket of cold water over his head. Gasping for breath Charlie came back, but not for long. Ashlyne knew he would die soon by the amount of blood he was losing. From this she stood up, picked up the butcher's knife off the metal table, walked back over to Charlie and cut his trousers off. Charlie was stirring around, groaning in pain but unable to move much. Hallie had a slight suspicion as to what she was doing but Wren was clueless until he clenched in pain from what she done.

After cutting Charlie's trousers and his Calvin Klein boxers off, he was completely naked to which Ashlyne took the blade of the butcher's knife and glided it down from the top of Charlie's neck down to his torso. Pushing the knife just deep enough it caused a slight bleed from his chest Charlie began to try and plead again.

"This Charlie, this is for all the hell you have given me in my life and for what you have done to my husband. Enjoy hell you piece of shit." Ashlyne grabbed a hold of Charlie's dick and with her other hand made a few swift swings with the knife and slowly cut off his dick. That was it, screams began again from Charlie, but the pain was now torture for him. Blood began to splatter up hitting Ashlyne in her face, she didn't care though, this was pure enjoyment for her.

Finally, it went quiet, no noise. With the amount of blood that surrounded Charlie's body Hallie was surprised he didn't die sooner. Ashlyne stood up holding Charlie's dick in her hand and she threw it at the wall. Hallie let out a small giggle, however Wren still looked mortified at what he saw. Wren had inflicted torture on many people but that, that was another level of fucked up. Hallie threw over a towel to let Ashlyne wipe some of the blood off her face and the only response Ashlyne gave was a nod. Wren gave Hallie a side glance wondering if this was the right decision, but this was probably the only plan they had.

13

Coldness lurked in the room, there must have been a window or a door open at some point as Seb could feel the draft lurking from under the large steel door. Seb's vision was impaired, trying to adjust this by blinking profusely seemed to help. Seb had no recollection of the time, where he was, even the day for that matter and his head was thumping. It had been a very long time since he was put in this situation of being held hostage but was ready to get some answers. Gibb on the other hand seemed to have regained consciousness and was repeatedly asking for Seb, encouraging him to wake up, nerves taking over.

"Seb, come on man, don't be dead. Seb."

"I can hear you Gibb, just be quiet" he groaned, Seb was trying to overpower his thoughts to try forget about the pain he was feeling.

"Oh thank god, you're alive, I was not going to survive whatever this is if you were dead. Any ideas on, well, this?" Gibb was trying to speak normally but his voice pitch kept changing and his body trembling. He too was in pain but the adrenaline from nerves was keeping him alert.

"I have no idea. What do you remember last?" Seb tried to look up at Gibb but it hurt too much, so instead he began to inspect the room, find a way out or any subtle hints to where they were. The room itself was relatively large, looked like it could hold a good three, maybe four more people inside if they were being held hostage and tied like they were. The floor was red carpet like on an old mansion floor, clue one. Focusing on the carpet, Seb noticed the patterns were yellow swirls which conjoined, part of the carpet was faded, maybe sunlight however the windows were boarded up. Closer to Gibb there was a large bleach stain, Seb knew it was bleach as he had used this on many of 'clients' to clean up his work. The wallpaper was dated and had wooden beams from floor to ceiling. A single dark wooden beam centred the room off which hung lower on the ceiling. Seb began to re-focus on what Gibb was saying.

"- and then the car rolled as we were on the phone, and I woke up here hoping you weren't dead as took you longer to wake up. But you're not so that's good, now, what do we do?" Gibb looked hopeful, had belief in Seb but in reality, Seb had no idea where to even begin. Just as he was about to talk, footsteps lurked in the background.

"Gibb, whatever you do, just stay quiet, no matter what. Got it."

"What if I know the answer?"

"Gibb for fuck sake, listen to me, look at me. Don't respond to them, whatever you do. Just let me get a grip as to what they want. Okay?" Gibb just nodded in agreement, and his flood of nerves came rushing back.

"Oh my god, what have they done to you?" Katie walked into the room and closed the door behind her. Gibb's eyes perked up, he learned not to trust Katie and he was right, but he still had a high amount of feelings for Katie.

"Why Katie, why do it?"

"I didn't think it would go this far, really. I am so sorry, the both of you."

"Just let us go, and we will be out of the way." However just as Katie was about to speak again she was interrupted. Tate's build was large, he had weight behind him so would be harder to take down. His brown hair had flakes of ash flowing through it however he seemed to have it slicked back. A prominent scar lies from Tate's ear and goes down to his chest, however this looks relatively new.

"I don't think so, not yet anyway. I'm not done with you" his deep voice was intimidating, had a husk which crept out mid-sentence. Tate ensured the door was closed behind him so Katie couldn't even escape. "You see young Sebastian, Katie thought she was doing the right thing, at least that's what I let her believe at first, but well who could say no to me and to compare myself with him" pointing at Gibb, "I mean, come on, no offence but little techy boy is no match for me." Katie had no words; she hung her head low and looked up to Gibb with empathy in her eyes. Gibb however was hurt and began feeling anger and spite to Katie and to Tate.

"What do you want Tate?" Seb interjected, he could see Gibb was getting angry so before he said something he would regret, Seb needed to speak up.

"You have something my boss wants back." Seb looked up to Tate and stared into his eyes as Tate crept closer to Seb. Seb was sat on a metal chair with his hands tied tight behind his back.

"And who might your boss be huh Tate?"

"Don't play dumb with me Sebastian. DO you or don't you have what he wants."

"Until you define who your boss is, I don't have shit" he spat back, teeth gritting.

"Harold fucking Kingston. You have Charlie, don't you?"

Seb smiled, he knew Tate would give in, he always did. "I do. Now why do you want me?"

"Because you keep getting in the way, you stay out of this business, give Charlie back and we go on with all our lives."

"And if I don't?" Seb enjoyed a little haggle, even if his life was on the line.

"I get your little girlfriend, and torture her till she takes her last breath. Now you wouldn't want that, would you."

A switch flicked in Seb's brain, his emotion was switched off and he was ready to kill Tate for even mentioning Hallie. He remained quiet.

"I nearly had her once Seb, and that was only because my brother was so fucking desperate to see his family out of this situation. But from what I hear, Hallie is a little firecracker, is she not Katie?" Katie looked up in shock, she didn't expect it to turn out like this. Seb's eyes grew with anger, his jawline became prominent as he began to clench down on his teeth.

"Ooooo, have I touched a nerve." Tate began to laugh. He knew what he was doing and was enjoying it far too much. He crouched down to Seb's height to inspect him further until Seb head-butted him causing his nose to bleed instantly. Katie gasped at this fast response and took a step back from the situation.

"Keep her name out your fucking mouth."

No response, Tate began to walk over to Katie and grabbed her wrist dragging her out of the room. As soon as the door closed Seb began fiddling with his hands to try and loosen the rope.

"Seb, you alright?"

"Had headache before, now it is ten times worse. If he touches her, I will kill him."

"I will gladly help." Never in all of Gibb's life has he had vengeance for somebody however today that had now all changed.

14

Hallie knew from the beginning that Ashlyne worked alone, she had a reputation for herself to get into all sorts of trouble, but there was no other way. Hallie led the way up the basement stairs with Ashlyne close behind. As they walked into the lounge Wade looked up briefly from his phone, looked back down then quickly back up again to make sure his eyes were not deceiving him.

"Uhh, what's she doing up here?"

"She is going to help us, as we are going to help her. Ashlyne knows where Seb and Gibb could be, she is our only lead."

"We can find other leads, no offence" Wade looking back at Ashlyne who took no offence.

"That could take days, even weeks Wade, the sooner we find them, the better. Who knows what Tate is planning" Wren interjected as he walked over to Ella and greeted her with a kiss.

Hallie walked over to the bar and offered Ashlyne a drink which she accepted. A large glass of vodka lemonade with two ice cubes which seemed very precise, but Hallie didn't question it.

"I don't blame you for attacking me like that." Ashlyne tried not to speak to loudly over the others whilst they were having an argument as to why Ashlyne was allowed up here.

"Good, cause I don't regret it" Hallie poured herself a lemonade and took a couple of swigs before remaining eye contact with Ashlyne.

"I don't think it is wise for you to go back to look for Seb. Let me take help find him and your tech guy, bring them back to you." Hallie began to wonder why Ashlyne was being so sincere.

"Why?"

"You know where my husband is, which is more than anyone knows, so I am in your debt so you can keep your mouth shut before he is targeted again. In return, let me bring the one person you love back to you."

Hallie placed her drink down and turned to Ashlyne. "No, I mean why do you think it is unwise for me to go find him, don't you think I can handle myself?" Hallie started to become defensive, she didn't like to be taken for some damsel in distress.

Ashlyne took Hallie into the corridor which followed into the large kitchen and whispered, "because you don't want to lose that. Believe me, there is no greater guilt and horror losing something that precious." Pointing to Hallie's stomach Hallie was shocked, how could Ashlyne know that. It is still so early.

"How do you…"

"Because I know the signs, even the short time I have known you. You need to protect this with your life. I know Seb would make a wonderful father." Hallie's heart fell to her stomach, she had tried shutting her feelings about Seb being taken to the back of her mind, how could she raise a child alone without him if the unthinkable happened.

"How would you know?" Hallie questioned wondering what relationship Ashlyne once had with Seb.

"Because once upon a time, he worked with my brother in the military, I know more than you think. I met him a few times before my life took a turn Hallie. Seb was the one that paid for my husband's treatment upfront when he was on his death bed was because of my brother. The only reason he is still alive today is because of Seb. Don't get me wrong I have caused him hell over some time but believe me when I tell you, I owe him. Let me help you." Hallie took a moment to consider this proposal, this seemed genuine and kind which from Ashlyne's history of violence and cold heartiness was a shock. After considering this offer, she thought wise to offer Ashlyne something in return, something she couldn't refuse.

"Okay, all I will say is I will be careful, but I still plan on finding them and bringing them back and not going to be stuck at home because of this. You can stay here in the meantime, but we will bring your husband here too." Ashlyne was shocked, she never had anyone help her before which like Hallie took some getting used to.

Ashlyne took another swig from her cold drink, the condensation was forming around her glass and dripping onto her bare skin. The small water droplets began to fall slowly to the ground. No answer from Ashlyne so Hallie continued with her offer.

"We will get nurses here, convert the outhouse to make his own little recovery centre. I am not sure on his condition but if he is well enough, he is welcome here." Hallie didn't know if this was the right thing to do, they could both be a liability for all she knew, but right now she needed to keep Ashlyne on a close lead and by bringing her husband here, that seemed to be the best thing to do. All of a sudden Wren appeared into the corridor having heard the majority of the conversation.

"What's his condition?" Hallie asked knowing Wren had heard her proposal.

"He is awake but hooked up on many machines, he knows who I am but still hasn't spoken. With the way he is progressing he should be able to leave the hospital soon but would still need 24-hour care."

"Okay, we plan on moving to the location you believe Seb and Gibb are being held in two hours, we are organising the team to set a perimeter." Wren expressed, trying to change the subject in order to not have to many people staying at the manor.

"Wren, I have an idea! But I need to pay someone a visit if it is going to pay off."

Hallie didn't want to bring her past life into her new life but could tie this in with who attacked the police station, have them gun for Tate, get him out the picture. This could work in their favour.

Hallie headed up to her bedroom and began to dial, as the phone was ringing she was taking in the view from the balcony. It hadn't even been a day yet she couldn't stop thinking about Seb and how she misses him. How has she gone from being completely independent and not needing anybody but herself to feeling lost without that certain someone.

A robin landed close by then hopped onto the wooden balcony and pecked around Hallie. Robins were always a sign of someone who had passed checking up on you and Hallie always believed it was Harris, her old teammate who served with her back in Afghanistan. From that the phone was picked up.

"Hello?"

"Sergeant, it's Hallie, how are things?" Hallie tried to sound normal however things were far from normal right now.

"Hallie, it's good to hear from you. All good here how are you. I am guessing you aren't calling me for a catch up though. Am I right?"

"Yes sir. We have a name of who we believe is behind the attack on the station. We are also after him as he has taken two of our team hostage. We have reason also to believe he has someone on the inside helping them get past and not get caught."

"By inside Hallie, you mean within the constabulary?" Hallie speculated this but put all ideas out there and to let Sergeant decide from there.

"Yes sir, I trust your judgment in whoever you put on the case, however there is a rat relaying information back and forth. From what I can gather this person must have some authority or be high up in the rankings."

A sigh breathed heavy down the phone; Sergeant had been through a lot in his time on the force. "Do you have any idea who this rat could be?"

"Not as of yet sir, but if you get the person who is 100% behind this, then we are closer to finding the rat."

"I see, you got a name?"

"Name is Tate Kepner. Has a large team working with him, we are doing our best to..." a brief pause from Hallie, she needed to choose her words carefully to allow Sergeant to not suspect anything. "Sieve through the potential candidates. But this one, he is a tough one to catch."

"Hallie, if we bring him in, I will call and you can come to interrogate. I trust you, always have done. You know what you are doing so if you say he is part of who attacked the station then we will get him. Will keep you posted."

"Thank you sir, the same for you, any updates will reach you on this matter. Oh sir, before I forget, I will be calling you on variety of numbers just keep your phone to hand and be careful who you trust."

"Talk soon Hallie."

With that the call was ended and the Robin was nowhere to be seen. However, in the distance it looked like lights heading towards the manor. Squinting to be certain Hallie then saw the car, one she did not know. From this she ran down the stairs and shouted to the others.

"Has anyone told anyone to come here?"

No answers, confusion around the room.

"That means we have an unwanted guest coming down the driveway." Scrambling to get up from the chairs and sofas, people were reaching for their guns, any weapon they could get their hands on.

Wren went to Ella telling her to go to the bedroom with the children. "Lock the door and stay away from the windows." But before Ella could go up the stairs Hallie called her. "Ella wait! Here, take this just in case. You know how to use one I assume, if not that pin just above the trigger is the safety, push it to the left safety is on, right safety is off. Also, I believe this belongs to Toby." Hallie handed back Toby's knife which she used to kill those men in the car. However, it was no longer red covered in blood but had a stain on the wooden handle where the blood had seeped through.

As Ella went up the stairs, Hallie grabbed another handgun and tucked it into the back of her trousers, also picking up a shotgun she followed the others to the front door. The car was a Black Honda Civic, tinted back windows and no number plates on display. A man took a step out of the driver's side and walked around to the front of the car. Hallie opened the front door and began to walk outside, Ashlyne close behind her. Wren and Boris went out the side door and walked around to the front to catch the mystery man off guard.

15

Stopping abruptly on the drive, hands flung out the window in the air. "Don't shoot, don't kill me. I am here to help!" Hallie recognized the voice immediately and began to lower her shotgun.

"Sarge?"

"Hallie, am I alright to get out or am I in shooting line?"

"You are okay to get out, but you are in shooting range." Hallie chuckled, unsure as to why her old boss had arrived at the manor. Hallie walked down the front concrete steps to greet her old boss. "What are you doing here, and how did you find me especially as you were just on the phone with me?"

"I'm not the only one who can find people Hallie. I want to help, but if there is a rat in the station, I need to be careful who to talk to. Thought I may as well come and see you in person, can relay what information you have and what I have for you. I have known your location for a while now so thought best to come here." Hallie was intrigued. Wondering what her old boss has that she needs, she needs Tate taken care of and the police were a good way to grab him. But she needed to listen to what Sarge had to say.

"Could have mentioned on the phone you wanted to see me in person as we just hung up?"

"I could have, but you would have declined knowing you, or left here putting yourself at risk."

Hallie invited Sarge in and sat close to the log burner. The winter nights were getting colder and the amount she had been sick these past few days her immune system wasn't the strongest at the moment.

"How did you find me? I am careful in where I go and how I get back. I am curious what I need to change to go off the radar." Handing Sarge a bottle of Corona beer, Hallie didn't sit down but remained by the fire. Ashlyne watched closely in the distance and Wren had eyes on Ashlyne.

"I've wanted to see you for a while, and for you to call me was the perfect chance to come see you away from the station. After you telling me this, I began to rack my head around who could be the rat in the station, I mean we have a couple people I could suggest but not be certain. I know you are one to do background checks so before I entrust people with this information, I need to know what I can and can't say." This was unusual for Hallie, for the majority of her adult career she had reported to this man, had been handed instructions to deal with from him and now he is asking her what to say to protect her. "No offence Hallie, but we both trusted someone who was a killer and a first-class psycho." This made Hallie's eyes perk up, she hadn't heard of Adam Fowler in a long time mainly because of Seb, his name was never to role of Hallie's tongue ever again. Seb and Hallie had managed to frame Fowler for three murders Seb had committed and a potential kidnapping of Hallie, which Seb actually did. But Fowler's true colours shined brightly as a compulsive liar and a murderer back when he served with Hallie in Afghanistan.

"I'm sorry Hallie, that name must still haunt you, does me. Where is your partner?" Hallie felt a lump form in her throat, nausea began to take over and Wren noticed as well as Ashlyne. Wren stepped forward and began to talk. "He has been taken by Tate, with Gibb." Hallie seemed relieved that she didn't have to say that allowed.

"And who is this man?"

"My brother, he served with myself and Seb, he is one to take things too far. Dismissed from action in the military for killing his own. We have reason to believe he is working with one of our targets in a, well, a very fucked up business." Wren didn't want to disclose too much, Hallie knew Sergeant well, but he didn't. Sergeant was speechless, he didn't expect that. "I see, okay and Tate is the one who targeted the station?"

"Yes sir."

"I see, okay so I can pin some info together to make him seem like the suspect but when I catch him, I will call you Hallie, I want you there to look my team up and down see if you can smell the rat, you always had a knack for that." Hallie laughed, she did miss her old life but would never go back. All she aimed for now is to get Seb and Gibb home.

"I have a new number Hallie, solely for you to contact me, if my phone gets bugged or anything, I will be able to keep you hidden if you contact. Will be in touch." Just as Sergeant stood up, he finished off his bottle of beer and looked around the room to see a handful of people stood around with guns in their hands.

"Remind me Hallie not to visit you unannounced again, seems like you're safe. Take care."

"You too sir." Sergeant walked off and drove back up the drive. Wade enters the room with his phone grasped firmly in his hand. Nodding to Boris and Wren he then looks at Hallie and finally speaks up.

"Hal, the team have eyes on the building, it's time to go."

Hallie turned to Wren who was ready to gear up. "Wren, your family are here, you need to stay here with them, make sure it is safe."

"Hal, no way. Seb is also family, I am coming."

"Wren. Look at me, please stay here. Someone needs to stay here, be with your family, keep your phone close and I hate to ask you to stay but get near a computer to hack something if we need you too."

Just as Wren was about to speak up a young voice spoke from the staircase. "I can hack into the systems." Toby was listening in this whole time, Hallie looked at Wren then back at Toby. Wren was confused, "How do you know to hack?"

"Uncle Seb. I would also watch Gibb and Katie, I just took it in really." Hallie smiled, impressed by the kid's intuition.

"Perfect, you can help your dad. If that's okay with you." Looking up to Wren waiting for his approval to allow his son to do some very illegal hacking.

"Sure, do not tell your mother what we are doing though." Everyone knew who wore the trousers in that relationship. As Wren headed back upstairs with Toby to begin to try and access the security footage and track the others, Ashlyne led Hallie and the team to the building where Seb could possibly be.

16

Hallie never thought this would be the situation she'd end up in. As Wade and Boris took the front two seats this left Ashlyne and Hallie in the back, Hallie had nothing to say, no words. Just trying to figure out a plan in her head as to what they may come across. The state the boys might be in, who they might end up facing. Hallie thought of every worst case scenario in her mind, somewhat kept her calm thinking the worse, preparing her for what may come. Ashlyne spoke up to direct Wade and on where to go, this description got Hallie's attention back into the car, her mind no longer wondering.

"I'm sorry, where did you say we were going?" Hallie's voice was strained, battling the thought of nausea mixed with slight travel sickness.

"It was an old psychiatric hospital, got closed about a year ago, big house. When I saw Tate one of his team let slip the name, I have put two and two together thinking what better place to hide people than somewhere this remote and unknown." However, in Hallie's eyes, this place was not unknown for her. Everything kept coming back to this manor. Her past was flashing before her eyes, all the sleepless nights, the visits to St Catherine's to try and solve her last case, those three murders all linked with that place, her mother was sectioned here, then Fowler came to her mind, his last words to her.

"Hallie! You alright?" Ashlyne shouted which took the attention for Wade and Boris up front. Boris kept his eyes on the road however looking in the rear-view mirror whereas Wade spun around shaking Hallie's leg to get her attention.

All the colour had drained from Hallie's skin, she was pale, words tried to escape her mouth, but a short exhale left her. Her heart was thumping out of her chest, thinking Fowler was out of her life was beyond the truth. He may be dead, but still haunting her. Looking around to see all eyes were on her, Hallie took a big breath, closed her eyes for a moment then answered. "How long till we are there?"

"2 minutes. You good?"

"Yes. I know this building well, we will need to split up if we are to find them both, they are likely to be kept separate to make a rescue harder for us. Is the team set up?" It is like Hallie's panic attack never happened, Wade and Boris knew Hallie was able to shut her emotions out easily, but Ashlyne had never experienced what Hallie was like. Noticing Hallie was hiding something, Ashlyne said she would go around with Hallie which both Wade and Boris were hesitant with. Hallie picked up on this and she didn't like the idea, but showing fear in front of Ashlyne was a bad idea. "If she was going to kill me, she would have by now. Even if you two don't trust her, just try." Ashlyne had only ever had her husband to stand up for her, a small smile came across her face until the car stopped, and her game face appeared.

Boris parked a couple streets away and they walked the rest, Wren had called which linked to everyone's earpieces, Ashlyne was not used to working with a team, but she wanted her husband safe, so this was something she had to do before they could both escape.

"Well, this is strange seeing you from this side of it." Wren jokingly laughs down the earpieces to the team.

"You managed to figure it out then." Generally curious as Wren knew his computers but wasn't completely clued up on it all.

"He had no idea, most he done was open the door and turn the computer on." Toby scoffed; he was Wren's double but had his mother's sarcasm.

"And what have you told Ella you and Toby are up to?" Wade enjoyed stirring the pot, he was the type to sit back with his popcorn and eat it but not be involved in the drama.

"She thinks I'm on the play-station in Uncle Seb's office while dad keeps tabs on you, when kind of feels like the other way round." Toby's voice had not long broken, learning to adapt with his new deeper voice it was almost unrecognisable. The team laughed at his response, he was going to make a good member of this team no matter his age.

"Well, just ensure you don't lie to your mother, it's not just your dad who's scared of her." Boris introjected causing both Hallie and Ashlyne to let out a small laugh.

"Yes sir." Toby was a very well-mannered young lad, he was raised to show respect and when he had a funny five minutes like any child, he always apologised if he was in the wrong but stood up for what is right.

"Perimeter set up boss." A deep voice echoed through the earpiece, one of Seb's team who was a trained sniper had his team set up around St Catherine's. No one on foot had any idea where they were which was the idea, just in case the communication frequency became compromised.

A few moments of silence when no one answered, "All set on this end as well, boss." Hallie seemed confused, maybe it was just a habit for the team when out with Seb on a job. Until Wade spoke up and spoke directly to Hallie, "All ready to go boss?" Hallie's confusion continued to grow, without Seb was the team instructed to consider her next in line. No time to think too deeply into that now, they needed to get the real boss out.

"Let's go."

Instantly the team on foot headed to the back entrance of St Catherine's. The door was boarded up however looking closely at it the wood was on hinges making it look like it was not in use, you could see a worn part of the door where it gets pushed open meaning it is still in use. As the team enter the building, the building hasn't changed since the last time Hallie visited it, however the power was on which seemed strange as this was supposed to be abandoned. Hallie listened and heard a humming in the background. Hallie whispers, "Wren, see if they are using some sort of generator to power this place up, no way they would use the mains if they didn't want to get caught." They continued into the first room, Hallie and Ashlyne entered whist Wade and Boris kept a look out until they were not able to enter the room. The large steel door had slammed closed and no one was able to get it open, they were trapped.

"Hallie, Ash can you hear me?"

"Yes, still have signal for now, if they didn't know we were here before, they do now. You both need to continue to search for Seb and

Gibb just..." that was it, their signal was cut. Looking down at her phone, Hallie saw she had no signal and just hoped Wren and Toby could get into the mast tower to regain a signal before it was too late.

"Looks like just the two of us." Ashlyne was looking around the room at all the photos which hung on the wall, most were crooked, then walking over to the bookcase to observe the books.

Hallie didn't respond and joined Ashlyne at the bookcase and started to grab the books and pull them off the shelves. Ashlyne was unsure what Hallie was up to, but enjoyed making a mess so joined in until Ashlyne found a book that she could not pick up, tilting it backwards the bookcase began to open. "Looks like we have our way out." Both walking through the entrance they are not letting their guard down. The room is dark, cold, and somewhere neither one wanted to be. This was until Hallie turned around and she was hit across the back of the head. Falling suddenly, she was still conscious however had no strength to get up.

"Welcome to Hell Hallie. Hope you enjoy the ride."

17

Seb was trying to figure a way out of this mess, he had no idea where Gibb was being held or where he could be, the place seemed familiar, but he had only seen this room. Trying to keep quiet to hear any distinctive noises, a car passing, wildlife foraging around, a conversation between people, but nothing, there was nothing for Seb to grasp on which led to his imagination running wild. This was until he heard footsteps coming towards him, he began to hold all remaining strength he had, to show no emotion at his captures, to remain silent. But that was until the door opened and it was Hallie. She was being held up by Tate, a gun pressing into her spine to ensure she doesn't do anything that could get her killed. Tate was alone, no one with him, Ashlyne was nowhere to be seen nor was any of the team. Hallie still had her earpiece in which was very well hidden, hoping a signal would come back up soon so she could inform that she was now held captive.

   Seb remained quiet however began to sit up as straight as he could without being in too much pain. His eyes looking over Hallie, wanting her in his arms as tightly as he could. Hallie's eyes began to fill up with tears, she took a deep breath and closed her eyes briefly. Thrown to the floor, she was unable to stand, pain was spreading through her body like wildfire. Trying her hardest to show no emotion was proving difficult as this felt like she was being carved internally. Seb tried to pull his hands from the rope which restrained them together, marks forming around his wrists from the constant pulling he was doing.

   "You lay a fucking finger on her you are more than a dead man

Tate." Anger flooded all around Seb's body, he watched the woman he loved barely moving from the pain Tate had inflicted on her. "You want me, you don't need her Tate."

"Oh how the tables have turned Sebastian. Never in a million years would I have thought you would show a shed of emotion for someone other than your dead brother. Shame, I liked you when he died, you turned, what's the word. Cold. But this. Her. Well, this another level. You're right, my business is with you, but I am sure she will make me very rich." As soon as Tate made that comment Seb spun his legs out in front of him and grabbed Tate in a lock with the force from his legs. His legs wrapping tighter around Tate's throat whilst his body thrashed around, gasping for air. Tate tried to use his arms to allow Seb's grip on him a bit of room to slip out of it, but this was no use. Hallie crawled over to Tate and knelt over his body, sitting on his chest she ripped open his shirt and slid her knife which sat in between her laced thong and her bare skin. Looking up to Seb with love she began to carve into his chest with the knife, gliding down his stomach screams bellowed from Tate. Seb made sure he didn't allow his grip to become too tight so he remained conscious for this. This was until Ashlyne ran in close behind with Wade and Boris and pulled Hallie from Tate.

"We need him alive Hal, he has people hid all over the place, for them to stay alive he needs to be alive." Hallie was confused by Ashlyne's comment, out of everyone here she was the one who wanted this man dead. Ashlyne helped Hallie stand whilst looking her up and down, whilst Wade and Boris untied Seb, he wanted nothing more than to get out of this rope and pull Hallie in tightly. Wade handed Seb an earpiece and his spare handgun. "Any ideas where Gibb could be Seb?"

"Along this floor somewhere, I heard a door sla..." Seb paused, his eyes were focused on Hallie, "Hallie, you're bleeding?" Instantly, Hallie reached to touch her head thinking it was from there but that pain she was feeling inside, that was the reason she was bleeding.

"Hal, we need to get you to a hospital, like now." Ashlyne looked down at Hallie then back at her eye line.

"We need to find Gibb and get out of here." Hallie didn't want the attention on her, the last thing she wanted to do was answer questions. Seb was now walking over to Hallie and pulled her into his arms, this hurt them both from the amount of pain they were both in, but it was needed. Whispering in her ear, his voice made Hallie feel so comfortable yet so emotional.

"Seb, I can't stress enough she needs to go to a hospital now or…" Ashlyne didn't want to share Hallie's news aloud but knew the severity.

"Or what?" Seb snapped and then concern went back to Hallie. "Darl, what did he do to you?"

Hallie sighed, she thought this was going to be a good thing to tell him, but the trauma she had just endured as well as all the stress from the past few days must have taken its toll on her body. As soon as she was about to walk a pain like no other hit her stomach, feeling like she was being stabbed continuously her body began to keel to the floor. Seb crouched to the floor with Hallie holding her in his lap.

"Ash, what the fuck did he do?" Ashlyne knew the answer, as soon as she was about to say it, no words left her mouth, she was speechless.

"I think I'm having a miscarriage." She cried, Hallie's vision was starting to become blurry, nothing was focusing.

That one sentence, one that has changed the course of everything. The room was silent. Hallie tried to stand again when another flash of pain spiralled through her body causing more blood to fall down her legs. Seb was in shock. This pain was one that no one should ever feel. The amount of blood Hallie was losing was not safe, colour began to drain from her face and it wasn't only Seb that noticed this. Ashlyne knelt to the floor next to Hallie, looking Seb dead in the eye, "she needs to go straight to the hospital now, we will find Gibb and get Tate. Get one of your team to take her if you…"

"I will take her, otherwise I will end up killing him." With this, Seb stood up cradling Hallie in his arms, she was drifting in and out of consciousness from the amount of blood she was losing.

"Boss, let one of us carry her out."

"Just find Gibb, get that prick locked up so we can deal with him later. I am not letting her out of my sight." With this the team helped guide Seb and Hallie out without being caught, leaving Tate tied up in one of the abandoned rooms so they could find Gibb without lugging his body around. Signal had now come back on and the earpieces now had communication with the snipers and Wren back at the manor.

"We are back, T hacked the mast, what's your ETA."

"I need a car outside now to take Hallie to the hospital." Wren was shocked to hear Seb's voice.

"What's happened?"

"Just get me a fucking car now!" Seb was one to keep his cool but Hallie could die from the amount of blood lost, something wasn't right and this was something Seb couldn't just patch up and help heal the wound.

"I'm outside boss, black Audi A1 reg ending TPT." With this Seb clocked onto the car instantly as the driver was flashing his lights at him. He placed Hallie on the back seat and ran around the other side and joined her in the back allowing Hallie's head to rest on his lap. He began to stroke her hair to try give her some comfort, but Hallie was too weak to notice anything.

"How far?"

"Will be there in 4 minutes boss." Seb trusted his team, they knew not to ask questions and just do the job they are asked and for them to come help find him when he was in danger. Shows he has some people he can count on.

"He is one dead man, they all are." Seb was filled with anger, adrenaline was filling his body causing his hand to shake, the pain he was feeling from being beaten was fading from the anger.

"I don't doubt that." Hallie groaned causing Seb's vision to divert straight back to her, a smile formed and gently kissing her forehead.

"Why didn't you tell me."

"I was, after the appointment, was the plan, but you got taken."

"I am so sorry Hallie. I just…" his head fell, shaking in disbelief as to what was happening. Hallie used all the strength she had to hold his hand and tried to smile.

"You have no reason to apologies. I am the one who needs to be sorry." Seb instantly took her hand and squeezed her gently, however just as he began to respond Hallie's eyes closed. Her body became heavy, and her hand that was holding Seb's fell to the floor. Shock took over from Seb and with this they had just arrived at the hospital. Running out of the car and picking Hallie up he tried to go as fast as he could to the emergency department. Shouting to anyone who could hear him, he was not about to lose the one thing he loved more than anything, but the uncertainty filled his body, the what ifs.

"I need some fucking help. I need a doctor!" A doctor came running towards them, directing Seb to carry Hallie to one of the beds which was labelled Resus 2. Seb placed her on the bed and a swarm of doctors and nurses were around her like an infestation. Before Seb knew it, she was hooked up to the ECG machine, cannulas entering her body, monitors beginning to beep around. Everything was turning into a blur for Seb, placing his hands on his head he hated that he couldn't help Hallie but the next words that left the doctors mouth made him fly forward to try be with her.

"We have no pulse! Start CPR." It took two doctors and three members of security to get Seb back and into a room nearby. Security stayed in the room with Seb, they knew who he was, but this was no place to make small talk. Hallie's life was on the line.

"Sir, we should get you checked out." One doctor noticed the injuries that Seb had, but no answer from Seb.

"Sir?"

"I'm fine, just save her. Please."

"Can you tell us what happened to her, her head." Seb had to think carefully as to what to say to this doctor, usually he would have his personal doctor fix him and his team, but this was beyond his expertise.

"The same man that done this to me also hit her but knocked her out. She is pregnant, that amount of blood, that's not normal, is it doc? Has she lost it?" his voice began to crack when saying this. Only suspecting that Hallie could be pregnant to now her potentially losing their child as well as her life. No words could describe what Seb was feeling.

The doctor looked down then back at Seb, "may I join you?" Seb nodded and waited for an answer to come from this doctor. "You are right, that amount of blood is very dangerous. We still would need to run few tests, but it is likely she has lost the baby. I am so sorry sir." A short pause from the doctor to allow all the information he was giving Seb to sink in. He continued, "Now, I am going to be completely transparent with you, but you need to not lash out like you did before, stay in this room till my say so. Is that okay with you?"

Seb looked up, he didn't want to leave Hallie but this was serious, and he wanted answers. Agreeing with the doctor, he continued with the update on Hallie.

"As you heard, we lost her pulse, we had no rhythm from Hallie and no heartbeat. We performed CPR as well as using the paddles and managed to get a heartbeat back. She is stable however the CT shows that we need to take her to surgery as soon as possible as she has fluid filling up in her brain. Whoever did that to you must have kicked or hit Hallie hard to cause her to bleed like that. The surgery has minimal risks however judging on how she arrived it is uncertain. Now before she goes to theatre, you don't have too but if you want to see her, now is the time." With this Seb was already standing up heading out the door.

As they walked together into the resus bay, Hallie had tubes all over her, her clothes now cut and scattered across the floor and Seb still had her blood all over his clothes along with his own. Seb went to her side, security still staying with her and Seb. He grabbed hold of her hand and leaned in and kissed her forehead. A tear began to fall down his face from seeing Hallie like this. Whispering to her "I love you, so much and you stay strong. Please, don't leave me." Placing his forehead on hers, machines were helping Hallie breathe and a team of surgeons arrived.

"Sir, we need to take her now, we have a doctor available to check your injuries over and we will keep you updated throughout the surgery." Seb nodded not wanting to let Hallie go. As she was taken away by a team of doctors, Seb remained in the Resus Bay. Blood was all over the floor, clothes torn and ECG stickers stuck to monitor near. Reality began to set in, what life could be like without the one person who makes his life worth living.

And just like that, everything was about to change.

4 months later

18

Spring was such a beautiful time of year. The time of year when new life would enter the world, lambing season is upon us, wildlife is growing fresh leaves and flowers to add colour to the world and the sun begins to shine brightly again.

This time of year was truly beautiful, however the past few months have not been easy for Seb, especially not being able to celebrate Christmas the way he had planned with his one true love.

Hallie had been hospitalised for over three months, however this past month she was able to be released from ICU and to a ward, that ward being Seb's spare bedroom he had converted to fit all of Hallie's needs. He had hired a team of nurses to check on her when she needed as well as his own private doctor who worked alongside a neurologist consultant to do the checks necessary on Hallie. As well as having a miscarriage due to the trauma that was inflicted on Hallie, she unfortunately suffered with a Subarachnoid Haemorrhage. This is an area of the skull between the brain and the tissue covering the brain which is an uncommon type of stroke. Due to Hallie's previous medical history, she had sustained her fair share of head injuries but this one was the icing on the cake. Having coded twice whilst being in hospital, Seb thought he had lost her for good. Never in a million years would Seb have thought he would be in this position, even with the manor being full of people, he never felt more alone. Every night Seb would put on Hallie's favourite sitcom show for them to watch together as well as her favourite songs throughout the day. Anything he could do to entice her to wake up, he was trying.

Unfortunately for Seb, he had also received some injuries after being taken by Tate and was being treated by his doctor on strict home visits. Seb didn't let this stop him, but to everyone around him, he seemed like a changed man, he seemed broken. Seb put his mind to work trying to capture Tate after what he had done to Hallie. When Seb rushed Hallie to hospital, the team stayed behind in search for Gibb, which was successful. What wasn't successful is that they tied Tate up and hid him but when they returned to get him, he was gone. This did not go down well with Seb.

Seb spent most of his days in the room with Hallie, laptop in hand working whilst spending as much time with Hallie as he could. Every day she slowly started to look better, but anything to get the image out of his head of her hooked up to machines was good. No one dared to disturb Seb when he was with Hallie, he had a tendency to lash out over small things, he was hurting, everyone knew it, but he didn't confine in anyone.

Whilst Seb was upstairs, the rest of the team were working in the lounge, debating who's turn it was to interrupt Seb and get him down there. Ashlyne took it upon herself to go and get Seb, out of all the men in the room, she was the one who had the most balls.

Ashlyne's life on the other hand couldn't be better, her husband Henry was discharged from hospital and only had to return to hospital every two weeks for physiotherapy. Henry stayed with Ashlyne at the manor at Seb's request until they got rid of Tate and his team which Ashlyne agreed too. Ashlyne was no longer on recall back to prison as all eyes now led to Tate, another one of Seb's crafty curve balls, making the killings Ashlyne committed look like Tate so all eyes were now on him. Seb had time for Ashlyne as she has been in this situation before with her husband, the unknown of when or if they will wake up. All she knew was that time and space was a great healer.

Three knocks at the door and Seb's eye line rose to see who it was. Ashlyne peered her head through and stepped inside. "Sorry to interrupt, how you doing?" Seb closed his laptop and looked to Hallie, she looked peaceful like she was just in a deep sleep, wondering if she could hear their conversation.

"Good as can be I suppose. Yourself?"

"I can't complain, can we borrow you, we have some intel need to ask your opinion on?"

Seb hated leaving Hallie, but he hadn't been with his team properly in a long time. He looked back at Hallie and didn't answer Ashlyne straight away.

"I know the others don't see it, but I do understand what you are going through." Ashlyne was empathetic towards this situation, because she had done it, and for years she never knew what would come of it.

From this Seb stood up and kissed Hallie on the forehead and walked out the room with Ashlyne, no words just silence as they walked down to the conference room, everyone was already in discussions with each other but as soon as Seb entered, silence hit.

"Don't stop on my account."

"Sorry sir, we have an update on Tate, he was spotted leaving Harold Kingston's manor at 1:52am, we tried to track his whereabouts but was unsuccessful when he hit the tunnels. However, now we have proof of Harold and Tate being together we thought we take Harold and…"

"I will stop you right there. Harold is a very high profiled man, the minute he is reported missing it goes national, on the news, police everywhere the lot. Taking him yet is not an option. Is there a way we can get these images you have of them together to the police, Tate is a wanted man with them as well as us, if Harold has links, get the police to arrest him. Call Hallie's old boss, he will get it done. Anything else?" Silence again fell across the room. Seb's whole persona was now so dark and different no one knew when he would crack. He never was one to use the police for help let alone to capture one of his main targets.

"We have some leads but just need to tie them to be certain before hands."

"Okay, thank you all." Just like that Seb began to stand up to leave when Wade spoke up.

"That's it? That is all you have to say. We are working our fucking ass off on this case, and barely any input from you and that is all you have to say!" Seb remained looking at the door, he closed his eyes and took a deep breath in and slowly turned around to face Wade.

"I am doing my part to catch him, as are you."

"You keep yourself locked up there all the time Seb, least you could do is socialise with us instead of ignore us." A switch flicked in Seb's brain and rage came out as an answer.

"I wish to fucking god that I wasn't there twenty-four-fucking-seven, but I am, because I don't know if Hallie will take a turn for the worst, she might wake up and if I'm not there for something like that I won't EVER forgive myself so back the fuck off. You are in my house, I pay ALL your fucking wages, you all knew what you had signed up for. It was supposed to be ME that got hurt, ME who was targeted, instead she was the one who got it. So, in answer to your question, I don't give a SHIT what you think about me. Understand!" Seb was squaring up to Wade with Wren and Boris standing either side, it took Ashlyne to get in the middle of them both and shout louder than they were.

"This is helping no one, Wade you need to learn your fucking place, Seb you are angry, upset but don't take it out on the ones who care for you!" From this Gibb walked in, he was needing a walking stick to aid him to walk after his leg was shattered by Tate's men. "I have something." This was perfect timing for Gibb to enter, otherwise this would escalate to a fight very quickly. Gibb took it upon himself to carry on talking and not caring who was listening or asking what had happened. "Have a location on Katie, she has just entered a flat close to the town centre. Have the address here."

From this Ashlyne had a smile over her face, she wanted to inflict pain on anyone of Tate's team and this was one she had eyes on doing. Seb noticed this and looked back over to Gibb and nodded. "I will happily go get information from her!" Ashlyne perked up.

"You can but take someone with you."

"That will look more suspicious, I will be fine. Someone can drive me though." Looking over to Wade to try get him out the manor. Agreeing that he will drive Ash to visit Katie they grabbed their coats and left the manor. But just before they leave Seb calls Ashlyne back, "Don't kill her straight away. Least get some decent information from her."

"My pleasure!" A devious grin stretched across Ashlyne's face, she enjoyed inflicting torture onto others, Wade was yet to witness this in person.

Without being prompted, Ashlyne headed straight to the door and grabbed her coat and the first available car keys throwing them back to Wade who was following close behind. Everyone worked well with Ashlyne, but she could go off the rails at any moment.

19

The drive to the location from Gibbs's lead on Katie's whereabouts was 10 minutes away from the manor. Wade thought best not to make conversation with Ashlyne, the least he knew about what was going through her head the better. Ashlyne opened the glove box pulling a yellow microfiber cloth out and stuffing this into her pocket. Confusion spread across Wade's face which Ashlyne noticed. "To put in her mouth to keep her quiet till I want her to talk." Wade just nodded, he had inflicted pain on many people before but usually alone, not working with a psychopath. As they pulled up at the address Wade unfastened his seat belt which Ashlyne looked up quickly wondering why he was leaving the car

"What are you doing?"

"Coming with you, make sure the place is secure then waiting outside till you're done."

Ashlyne was confused, she was not used to having help but she didn't disagree with Wade allowing him to follow, she was no longer able to just follow her own rules. Rules which she never had anyway, only thing Ashlyne worried about was not getting caught. The area was built up with houses and flats surrounding in the town centre. Ashlyne was observing the area to ensure her face was covered so she wouldn't get picked up on any cameras meanwhile Wade was more worried about getting Katie, eyes were on the mission and he needed to put all feelings aside for this as Katie and himself were reasonably close. Thankful that Ashlyne was the one to get the information from Katie ensuring he would not have to lay a finger on her if he could help it.

The entrance to the flat was simple, Ashlyne walked up to the call buzzers and pressed her hand at the top and smeared it all the way to the bottom ensuring every call buzzer was pressed, someone was bound to answer and luckily one buzzed the door to open so no conversation was needed. Katie was staying on the third floor, flat 12 b. Sharp knocks on the door, Ashlyne stepped to the side to ensure that neither her nor Wade's face was in the peephole of the door. From this the door opened slowly and Ashlyne barged in with Wade following behind. Ashlyne grabbed Katie by her throat and guided her down the long corridor, her arms frantically waving around and trying to grab Ashlyne's hand in an attempt for her to loosen her grip. Katie stumbled and fell to the floor. Ashlyne knelt on top of Katie, grabbing both her arms and tucking them under her knees to ensure she is unable to use them. Katie was kicking and screaming however Ashlyne was ready for this and pulled out the cloth she had from the car and stuffed it into her mouth. Katie was gagging as the cloth was hitting the back of her throat.

"Wade get me something to tie her legs up with." Wade saw a curtain tie close by and helped Ashlyne tie Katie's legs, making sure they were tight Katie let out a scream which was muffled by the cloth causing her to gag again.

"My god, you would be shit at giving a man a blow-job girl." Ashlyne joked which Wade let out a snigger.

"Yeah she is." Regretting saying that aloud instantly Wade's face dropped, Ashlyne turned around to him shocked at what he had just said.

"You what?"

"Yeah, we slept together, you know as something to do. She had that innocent vibe about her, you know." Ashlyne started to worry, did Wade have any feelings for Katie, was Ashlyne in trouble, she remained calm and on top of Katie.

"So, she made her way around the team then? You are a little slut after all."

"She is, plus is shit in bed anyway, least I get a better shag now." Wade laughed and walked to the door and attached the chain along with locking it. Ashlyne looked up to the ceiling and took a large deep breath in. This was the reason she trusted no one, they had too many secrets. Looking back down at Katie, her mascara was beginning to smear down her face from the tears which formed in her eyes, the look of desperation and the sheer need to fight was key but Katie had no idea if she had the fight in her. Ashlyne stood up and grabbed Katie under her shoulders and tied her to a dining room chair, pulling the cloth from her mouth, Katie was gasping for air and began to plea.

"Oh please, save the begging. I want answers. The right answers might even be the reason you stay alive. Understand." Katie nodded, beyond scared of her outcome she did what she was told.

"Why did you go behind Seb's back?"

"Tate found me at a bar one night, promised me the world if I would help him. I asked what he wanted; it was to find some men who betrayed him in the past. I said of course I would help him, I mean he was my first love, he told me he still loved me and would do anything for me in return. Gave me this flat if I helped him too."

"Seb gave you everything, why Tate?" Wade queried but Ashlyne already knew the answer to this.

"Because you are in love with him. You slept with every man you could or who would be gullible enough to, but Tate gave you false promises. Right?"

Katie nodded.

"And you went and worked for Seb knowing you were still trying to contact Tate, when he came back you were ready to drop them and crawl back to him. What I don't get is why you outed Seb and made Tate aware of Hallie and the rest of the team?"

Katie looked down at her lap and sniffled, she began to cry which is when it clicked again for Ashlyne and she walked slowly to the kitchen to find something alcoholic to drink.

"You had feelings for Seb, didn't you?" Wade looked up shocked at what Ashlyne had said. Ashlyne found a bottle of vodka, a glass that was on the draining board was now in her hand and began to pour herself a neat vodka.

"You didn't, did you?" Wade asked when neither one began to talk.

"He didn't want me, said he wanted no one, then she came along and he was hooked, obsessed. Had me help track her and take her, she fell for him too and now look at them. It should be me." Ashlyne glanced over to Wade then back at Katie. Tapping her glass and pointing back to Katie. "Ding Ding Ding, we have a winner. You were jealous, you told Tate that was Seb's weakness." Ashlyne placed her glass back on the breakfast bar and walked over to Katie. Katie began to shiver, adrenaline taking over her body from the fear and panic. She was scared, and so she should. Ashlyne walked behind her and closed the curtains, took a large section of Katie's hair and pulled her head back. "Oh, I am going to have so much fun with you. Think we should take her back, just in case we get any unwanted visitors, don't you agree?" Wade smiled and nodded heading into her bedroom to look for something.

"Please, you don't have to do this, I'm sorry okay, I will tell you anything!"

"Oh I know you will, but you see, I am the type of person who works alone, trusts no one, but I have taken a liking to Hallie, we are more similar than people think, and what you have done, I can't wait to fucking take you." From this Wade walks out with a large black suitcase. "This will do, don't you think?"

"Perfect! Ready for your holiday?"

"Ho-holiday? What holiday?" she stuttered

"Oh silly, one you will never forget." From this Ashlyne grabs a lamp base and hits it straight over Katie's head. Stuffing Katie into the suitcase, they left the block of flats wheeling her behind.

"Where are we taking her?"

"The manor, that basement is the perfect place to take someone." She smiled and looked out the window at the night sky gazing at a plane flying in the distance. Fixating on the red lights blink on and off on the wing Ashlyne's mind was wondering.

20

Back at the manor, tensions were still high, emotions on breaking point and one thing missing was lack of communication, it was only a matter of time before something was going to blow.

Ella manages to grab Wren when they leave the board room and she was not happy, which Wren noticed straight away, he would much rather deal with the awkwardness of the board room again rather than deal with whatever Ella had going on.

"What's wrong?"

"Our son." Instantly Wren's heart dropped, had something happened to Toby.

"What's happened? Is he okay?"

"He's fine, what I'm not happy with is how our son now has a new hobby of hacking and learning coding. What the hell were you thinking?" Ella was pissed. Wren knew she would find out sooner or later, later was a better option for him.

"He is good at it Ella and enjoys it. Why would I want to stop him in doing something he enjoys."

"Because he is just a kid Wren! A child, and you have him doing illegal shit, it's not on, I won't have it."

"It's no different to him playing those assassin and war games, this he can help us with." Ella wasn't agreeing with Wren at all and voices were beginning to raise.

"And what if he gets caught, goes to prison for hacking, what if the people that are after you all find him and take him. I won't have it Wren!" Ella was now shouting in Wren's face which caught the attention of Seb and he began to walk over.

"Everything alright?" asking calmly.

"Oh I'm sure this was your bright idea teaching him all of this."

Seb had no idea what Ella was on about and looked over to Wren for some guidance or insight as to what this was about however Wren answered before Seb could.

"This had nothing to do with Seb, I asked for Toby's help when were looking for Seb the night it all happened."

"That still doesn't make it right Wren, I can't be dealing with this right now! I'm taking the kids till this is all figured out!"

"Where?" Wren demanded, he was not happy about this situation.

"My mums probably as I can't go home can I!"

Seb introjected, "Wherever you go, you will be monitored twenty-four hours a day and you will be putting your parents lives at risk going there." Ella's face changed suddenly, the fact is that sounded like a threat, her mind started to spiral.

"What are you trying to say?"

"I am saying, it is Wren's brother who has taken you all once, someone who has it out for the both of us, as we do for him. Soon as he is taken care of, go wherever you want." Seb remained calm, he had no energy to shout or argue with anyone.

"Yes love, and we are safer here together till this is sorted."

"You don't fucking get it do you? I want my kids safe and this, whatever this is, this is not safe! I would not put anyone's lives at danger if I stayed with them! I don't want my children involved in this!" Ella had lost her temper, her voice raised and you could hear the pain in her words.

"You would be putting a death sentence on your parent's heads Ella, along with you and your children if you leave. Your kids don't have to be involved, but if Toby asks me something, I won't lie to him as to why he can't help any more. What your son has done so far saved lives, you should be proud not punishing him!" Seb still was calm, he had walked over and poured himself a whisky, cradling the cold glass in his hand.

Ella stormed over to Seb with Wren close by holding her back.

"You have no fucking clue what it is like to put a child in danger let alone your own! I hope you don't have children as you would have NO idea how to keep them safe!"

"Ella!" Wren shouted at her which caused Ella to snap out of this. Her facial expression had completely changed, her anger was no longer showing, but instant regret. Wren had no idea what to say, no words.

"Seb, I..." Ella tried to apologise but Seb placed his glass on the bar and walked over to them both.

"Lucky for you, we lost our child." Seb began to walk away, Ella was frozen, regret crawled over her body and Wren couldn't look at her. Seb continued, "Wren, you and your family can still stay here till it's safe to leave. But you Ella, you stay the fuck out my way." Seb slammed the door closed and began to head back up the wooden staircase to check in on Hallie.

Seb had barely slept since she was taken, he missed Hallie, she was his person, his purpose, his life was Hallie. As he entered the room, Hallie was still in the same position as she was when Seb left her. Heading straight for the shower, Seb began to strip off his clothes and step in. The steam building around the room, Seb just allowed the water to hit his head and glide down his face. No movement, just the sound of the water hitting him then onto the tiled floor. Tears began to form in his eyes, he was broken not knowing if Hallie would pull through. As he turned the metal dial to shut the water off from the shower he heard knocks on the bedroom door. Pulling himself together, he wrapped a towel around himself and walked to the door.

"I am so sorry Seb, she was out of fucking order." Seb didn't respond, he allowed Wren to enter the room while he dried himself off. Wren made eye contact at Hallie, with a sympathetic look, he looked back over to Seb as he noticed the look of defeat. "She wants to come and apologise to you."

"There is no going back on words like that Wren, and she knows that. Just keep her away from me for a while otherwise I will do something and not regret it." Seb made eye contact with Wren, Wren would usually do anything to stand up for his wife, especially when someone has just threatened them, but he knew Seb was just hurting and he could have snapped then but remained calm for Wren. Knowing Seb meant what he said, Wren nodded agreement.

"Only reason you guys are still here is because of you. If that was any of the other team's partners who would have said that, they would be gone. I care for you and your kids Wren, they are safe here."

"I know that and I can't thank you enough especially from the circumstance."

"Well, I think we have gone for worse people, but after we get Tate, that is." Wren looked up confused, Seb remained looking at Hallie.

"What do you mean that's it?"

"She has put her life on the line to many times, I can't ask her to do it again, I can't go through this again."

Wren was shocked, he knew he loved Hallie, but to give up his life for her is another level of love. "So what, pack up completely?"

"Not sure, not thought of the ins and outs yet, it will be something I decide in the future, but you need to be aware. After Tate, take your family away on a holiday, somewhere nice, make memories. Then, when we are all back, we can re-evaluate things and go from there."

"Sounds like a plan." From this they heard a car pull into the driveway. Ashlyne and Wade had both walked to the boot of the car and stood there staring into it. Seb and Wren knew exactly what they had done. Seb looked back to Wren and asked, "Fancy dealing with whatever that is for me, I am fucking knackered." Wren smiled and nodded, he agreed with Seb, he looked like crap and needed the rest, beside Wren enjoyed his job especially when it involves a bit of torture.

As Wren closed the door to their bedroom he had Ella on the receiving end, "I need to apologise to him, I didn't mean that!"

"Well you said it Ella, I would stay away from him for a while." Wren began to walk away from Ella showing his annoyance on her. "I have work to do."

"So, you're pissed off with me too."

Wren spun around and faced Ella, her body froze as she saw anger fill his eyes, "Yes Ella, I understood you were angry with me about letting Toby help me, but I needed to get my best friend out alive and our son is a fucking genius! You had no right to say anything like that to him after what those two have been through! He has taken us in when he could have let us find our own way as it is my own fucking brother who is after us as you well know! So please, go and sort the kids out, let me go do some work so I can calm down too and will see you at dinner. Okay!" Ella nodded, she knew she was in the wrong but had no idea how to fix it. Wren kissed her on the forehead and headed to the driveway to figure out what Ashlyne and Wade had done.

Meanwhile, upstairs Seb had got under the duvet next to Hallie and propped himself upright and began to watch the TV with Hallie by his side. His eyes began to slowly drift in and out of sleep. A couple of hours had passed without Seb realising he had been asleep, he sat back up and rubbed his eyes and tucked his hand behind his head. Unknown to him Hallie was slowly waking up.

21

Hallie had to blink a few times to try and regain focus, slowly looking around the room she was finally able to focus on the TV, not moving her head too much as she was in a huge amount of pain.

"My favourite part." She mumbles.

"I know it is darl." Without realising that Hallie was awake it took a few seconds for Seb's mind to notice Hallie had just spoken. Seb sits up and looks over to Hallie smiling, stroking her hair back beyond happy she is awake.

"How are you feeling darl? My god I have missed you!"

"I've always been here, my head feels like I have been run over by a truck, it is throbbing, but I don't care." Groaning through the pain but a smile ended her sentence.

"I care, let me get some pain meds for you."

"Seb, I'm so sorry." Tears were building up in Hallie's eyes, trying to keep herself composed Seb came back to her side and cradled her in his arms.

"What are you sorry for?"

"I wanted to tell you, I wanted the doctor's appointment to be the surprise for you to make sure I definitely was pregnant." Seb's head dropped and rested on hers. "I am supposed to be the person who can protect their child while they are growing inside them, be the armour, the one to fight but I lost it, didn't I?" Hallie looked up to Seb as tear fell down her cheek. Seb's hand raised to her cheek and wiped the tear away gently.

"You have no reason to be sorry, I knew deep down what was going on, I saw the test weeks ago and all the sickness you have had, but I wanted to wait for you to tell me when you were ready. I am the one who should be sorry, for getting you involved in this. I hate to be the person to tell you but yes, we lost the baby." Those words hit Hallie and her pain in her head was now numb, even though she was still early in the pregnancy the emotions she was feeling were making her stomach sink. Seb continued to hug her tight and not leave her side.

"Hallie, I am just grateful you are still with me, I couldn't imagine my life without you and that man who has done this to you, I will kill him."

"Can I at least watch." Trying to make light of the sad moment Seb smiled back and nodded in agreement. This was the first time Seb had smiled like this in a long time. Seb laid back down next to Hallie and allowed her to cuddle into his arms, he felt warm again, his love was okay.

"Darl, I need to call the doctor to let them know you're awake, my phone is in the office. Are you going to be alright for a minute."

"I'm a big girl, I think I will be fine. Can you ask him when I can have a cup of tea, I am beyond looking forward to that!" Seb laughed and kissed her gently on the lips, slowly pulling away he whispers, "god I've missed you." Hallie smiled back and slowly places her hand on the back of Seb's head, fighting the pain to do so but determined to move. "I'm going nowhere."

Seb heads to the office and runs into Wren and Ashlyne in the corridor, however Ashlyne once again is covered in blood. "Boss, we have information…"

"Not yet." Seb didn't want to be rude, but Hallie took top priority at the moment. Both Wren and Ashlyne were confused. "Not yet but boss we…"

"Can it wait!"

Wren was still worked up from what had happened earlier with Ella he began to lose his temper. "You get us working none stop to find information about Tate and his team, we get something which is probably more important than anything right now and you say can it wait?"

Seb snapped and hit the wall next to him in anger, "nothing is more important than what I am dealing with right now!"

Wren hit back, "What else is more important?"

"Hallie is. She is awake so I need the doctor here to check her over. Work can fucking wait right now. If this is information that needs acting upon immediately then it will still have to wait. Understand." Ashlyne stepped in between Wren and Seb and most of the manor had heard the shouting. Henry came around the corner to check on Ashlyne and slowly approached the situation. "Well, can it wait?!" Both Ashlyne and Wren shook their heads agreeing and Wren stepped back. Seb turned around and headed back to the bedroom, he was not wasting anytime away from Hallie.

Henry looked Ashlyne up and down and smiled, "I've run you a bath, figured you might ache a bit after that."

Ashlyne walked up to Henry and wrapped her arms around his neck, "Only if you are joining me?"

"Me and you bathing with someone else's blood on you, count me in!" He laughed, he had the same psychotic tenancies as Ashlyne which was more of a turn on for Ashlyne. For Wren on the other hand, he wasn't sure whether he was cringed out from the situation he just witnessed or scared.

As both Ashlyne and Henry headed back to their room, Wren's body shivered with disgust at the situation he just witnessed. Walking back downstairs, Wren wanted to stay close by to let the doctor in when they arrived. Ella joined him with freshly washed hair and in a lounge wear set, tying her dressing-gown around her waist as she sits close to Wren, not caring about his smell, she was used to this by now.

"Hallie is awake." Ella sat bolt upright when she heard these words and a smile across her face.

"Really! Is she okay?"

"No idea, Seb went back in the room, just waiting on the doctor to arrive to do the checks on her."

"Are you okay?" Ella sensed something was wrong.

"I, I am just relieved she is awake, if I'm honest. If Hallie didn't make it, then I think Seb wouldn't either. That is the worst I have ever seen him get." Ella agreed. Not knowing when the best time to bring up her little outburst she had earlier, all Ella wanted to do was apologise to Seb for what she had said.

"You know what I said was in the heat of the moment, I do regret it." Wren turned to Ella as she looked down at her knees, raising his hand to her face to tuck her long black hair behind her ear. Ella looked to Wren with tears forming in her eyes, one slowly falling down her cheek. Using his thumb, Wren wiped the tear away and then cupped her chin to guide her head up.

"I know, we have both said things to Seb we regret, just give him some space and he will come to you."

"But he hates me!"

Wren laughed and shook his head, "believe be Els, if he hated you he, one, would not be letting us stay here with our children, and two, he kills the people he hates. I know from experience as I would do the same." Ella seemed shocked at how easy the word 'kill' rolled off Wren's tongue. Ella never used to ask what Wren got up to at work because what she didn't know wouldn't hurt her, but since living here and seeing it firsthand she began to understand what they do is for good. Three loud knocks at the door interrupt their conversation and Wren stands up and kisses Ella and gives her a reassuring smile.

"Ahh Wren, good to see you. Hear someone is finally awake."

"Sure is doctor. I will walk you up."

22

Seb heard the doctor pull up in the driveway but remained by Hallie's side. Time was valuable in his eyes and too much time had been lost. Staring deeply at her as she took sips of her cup of tea, he began to analyse her face, counting each freckle that spread across her nose to then looking up at her hair, even being in a messy bun she still looked incredible. Hallie could feel Seb's gaze upon her and slowly turned her head to face him. Responding with a smile he had no words but also a thousand words he could tell her. Instead, he remained quiet and stared into her eyes.

"You know I could hear you, before." Hallie reaches for Seb's hand, unknown as to how he would react to this news.

"What do you mean darling?" Anytime Seb would call Hallie darling her stomach would fill with butterflies.

"Before, when I wasn't awake, I could hear you. When you spoke to me, when others came in, when the doctors were here. I could hear you. It was strange, almost like I was trapped on the outside looking in. Or like it was all a big dream, I mean it could have been all a dream. But there was one day, one day in particular I knew it wasn't a dream and all I wanted to do was be there for you Seb. Hug you. Just be in your arms to tell you that I was okay." Seb shifted his focus to the television as he couldn't re-live that day. Hallie continued, "I knew I was going to be okay, but for them to tell you I was likely to die, it scared me and to hear you—."

"Stop" he snapped. Hallie ignored his demand and continued,

"Seb, I will always be with you." Hallie had never witnessed Seb vulnerable but what she heard that day, the look Seb had now, she knew that she didn't dream it. Seb stood up and walked over to the window.

"It has taken for me to nearly lose you to realise how much I love you. I have always loved you Hallie but now, I can't lose you." Seb didn't look at Hallie when those words left his mouth, he remained at the window looking out at the beautiful scenery of trees and wildlife. Shocked when he felt arms around his waist, Hallie should not be moving let along walking, Seb reached his hands around her waist to keep her balance and Hallie just smiled.

"Don't you trust me that I can walk." Hallie breathed.

"Not when you look like Bambi on ice right now." He smirked, knowing he should get Hallie back into bed, he wanted to enjoy this moment a little longer. Hallie went to step in a little closer, but her legs felt like jelly, she was struggling to stay upright. Seb noticed this, looking her up and down he scooped her into his arms and he placed her back into bed. All with good timing as the doctor was knocking at the door, he would have lost it if he had known Hallie had gotten out of bed without his all clear. Seb stayed in the room as the doctor completed all the relevant checks he needed to on Hallie. From simple remembering names, hand placement tests, to testing reflexes. Hallie's worst one was when the doctor had to check the reflexes on the sole of her feet, running a cold pen up the centre of her sole she moved quickly from this response as she was incredibly ticklish when it came to her feet. Making Seb laugh from this moment even the doctor looked over at him and smiled in return. "You know Hallie, this is the most emotion I have seen from Seb since I started coming here. It is nice to see." Hallie was still holding her breath when the doctor was still touching her feet and breathlessly said, "yes well I am glad my ticklish feet make him laugh but right now I want to hurt you for touching my feet!" From this the doctor pulled his pen away and placed it back in his medical bag smiling.

"I am happy to say that I am shocked at how well you have responded to these tests giving the amount of time you were unconscious for Hallie. You have surprised me. That is a good thing. I still don't want you to do anything too strenuous or high activity. Even going up and down the stairs will need to take time and need to have supervision. If you notice anything different, even if it is a headache of some sort you call me. Understand, I don't care how minor it is, if you get a numb toe, you call. I will still come and do weekly checks but I am happy with what I see." Hallie smiles back to the doctor then to Seb.

"Does this mean I can finally have something decent to eat, I am starving!" Seb laughed and looked over to the doctor to answer Hallie's question.

"You eat to your hearts content Hallie. But I need your word that you will call me if anything changes, okay."

Hallie nodded, "I will call you, if not, I'm sure Seb will." Giving Seb the side eye she knows that she is going to be watched more intently than ever before.

"You better, or else I will be doing more tests which involve your feet." Hallie squirmed at the thought of this leaving Seb and the doctor laughing, Seb walked the doctor back to the front door thanking him for all the work he had done. Meanwhile Hallie wanted to get out of this room, she hoisted herself up from the bed and slowly walked into the bathroom, she glared at herself in the mirror and felt like she need to take the longest shower to feel clean, but she had no energy, that short walk from the bed to the bathroom had tired her out quicker than she thought. Turning on the tap she grabbed a hold of her toothbrush and began to clean her teeth, even this was tiring but she needed to do something to make her feel clean and this was a good start. However, she heard someone in the room, keeping the toothbrush in her mouth she slowly walked to the bathroom door and stood behind it peering through the gap of the door and the frame to try and see who it was. There was a candlestick holder on the shelf next to her, she reached up and grabbed it to use as a weapon. Knowing it wasn't Seb who had walked into the room as he would have announced himself, no one else was welcome in her eyes. The bathroom door began to creak open. Hallie's legs were starting to go like jelly again, she tried to fight past this and use whatever strength she had to keep herself upright. A man walked into the bathroom, still not announcing who he was, Hallie stepped forward and began to swing, however Seb came up quickly and caught this swing along with Hallie. Seb was angry.

"Gibb, what the fuck are you doing?" Hallie was shocked, she nearly hit Gibb with something very hard that could have killed him.

"I wanted to see Hallie, see if she was okay! Didn't expect you to try to kill me Hal?"

"You didn't even announce yourself. Normal people would knock, say someone's name or I don't know shout 'are you decent' before walking into their bathroom." Seb helped Hallie back into bed, but instead of her getting into the bed she remained perched on the side. Seb headed back into the bathroom to pick up her toothbrush from the floor and clean it up before placing back in the holder.

"I'm sorry I made you jump, I wasn't thinking." Gibb looked deeply sorry, Hallie knew he didn't mean it and thanks to Seb's quick actions there was no injuries.

As Seb walked back into the bedroom he walked over to Gibb and tapped his shoulder. "You hungry, I'm ordering take out seeing as someone has a huge appetite over here." Tilting his head in Hallie's direction, Seb tried to make light from that moment.

"Who wouldn't be hungry if you had been asleep for... wait how long have I been out for?" Seb hadn't told Hallie how long she had been unconscious for, Hallie turned to look out the window to see the spring sun, yet summer was approaching. Seb asked Gibb to see if the others had already eaten if not get their orders and get someone to deliver it here. Gibb left after giving Hallie a small hug, "it's good to see you, well, alive Hal." Hallie laughed and agreed with Gibb, it was good to be awake.

"Seb. How long?"

"4 months."

"What!" Hallie was shocked, she thought it was only a couple weeks, if that. Having no idea she was unconscious for that long she began to lift her arms to her head to feel if she had any scars to her surprise she did. Seb explained everything to her, from when he took her into the hospital, what surgeries they had done to when he was able to bring her home yet still to be on twenty-four-hour observation. Looking defeated, Seb then explained to Hallie that Tate got away, they are now on the hunt for him.

"Are there any leads yet?" Hallie was still invested in work regardless of how she felt.

"That doesn't matter right now. Let's get some food in you and we can go day by day darling." Seb's voice was calming, soothing yet Hallie still had so many questions.

"I will grab us some plates ready and…"

"Oh I am eating downstairs, need a change of scenery by the sounds of it for you especially."

"I don't care where I eat."

Hallie began to stand up, however head rush got to her quickly, pushing past that feeling she began to slide some fluffy slippers on her bare feet and put on the closest dressing gown. Seb didn't say a word, it would be a losing battle for him to argue with Hallie especially with her being so determined to go downstairs.

Seb placed his arms around Hallie to assist her to the banister, crutches or even a walking stick would be useful for Hallie right now, but she did not want to feel any less worthy than what she already felt. Distraction was what was needed given what they had both endured and emotions were still high for Hallie. Reaching the top of the stairs Hallie was ready to tackle them one at a time but Seb believed this was too soon for her. Placing one arm under Hallie's legs and another across her back he carried Hallie down the stairs.

"I can walk."

"I know, but I have no idea how long it would be till we reached the bottom." Seb joked, Hallie smirked and was in a way relieved she didn't have to tackle that obstacle yet. Seb looked back to Hallie and smiled, "one step at a time baby and only steps forward from now. Okay?" Hallie nodded and when they reached the bottom of the stairs Seb gently placed Hallie back on the floor, her legs still weak but having Seb by her side meant she could walk aided for now. Hallie turned back to Seb and placed her hands on his face guiding him to her lips. Hallie needed this, it was somewhat like a boost of energy flowing through her body as she kissed Seb, slowly pulling away they remained close to each other, their foreheads touching and the tips of their noses brushing against one another. A smile appeared on both of them, they were content.

"I am so bloody happy you are okay!" Ashlyne walked up to Hallie and gave her a hug, neither one of them were affectionate. Hallie returned the hug before grabbing Seb's arm again to lean on. Ashlyne noticed that Hallie wasn't ready to walk but knew her stubbornness would not back down. Ashlyne assisted Hallie on the other side so Seb didn't take all the weight. Not that it was a problem for Seb as Hallie was half his size, but Seb liked to see that Hallie had somewhat of a friend.

23

Seb walks slightly ahead to grab Hallie's chair and pull it out for her, then tucked her in.

"True gentleman, you giant softy." Ashlyne jokes which Hallie smiles in return. Seb takes his seat next to Hallie at the head of the table, only Ashlyne and Gibb are the others in the room. Hallie turns to Ashlyne, "so I hear your husband is here, is he well?" Ashlyne smiles nodding, "Yes he is, he is pretty much back to normal." Both Gibb and Seb let a little snigger to which Ashlyne shoots them both a look that shuts them up instantly, Seb continued to smile. "Darl, you can practically hear that they are back to normal." As he stands to go get himself and Hallie a drink, neither of which is alcohol which was a surprise to Ashlyne and Gibb as that is all he had been drinking beforehand.

"Will he be joining us Ash?" Hallie asks to try and save both the boys from their deaths.

"He is asleep, had a late night so letting him rest." Again, both Gibb and Seb let out a laugh to which Hallie shoots them both a look, this time the look shuts Seb up. Ashlyne liked having someone who has her back. Wren enters with the bags of Chinese in his hands, Ella close behind smiling seeing Hallie's face, but her smile soon fades when she sees Seb's face is stone cold. Hallie notices her change of expression and looks to Seb.

"You wanna tell me what that is about?" Hallie demands.

"Nothing that you are thinking of darling." Seb assumes Hallie is thinking the worse like something happened between them both. In some ways, something did happen between Seb and Ella, but it was something Ella said and nothing else.

"Well then tell me." Hallie was stern in her voice.

Seb leaned into Hallie and whispered in her ear. "Darling, I can promise you, it is not relevant right now. This is something that she needs to apologise for to me. I told her to keep her distance from me for now. You are my priority." Hallie had a subtle smile appear on her face. She loved the way he called her darling. But if Seb said it isn't important right now, Hallie believed him. They trusted each other. However, both began to approach Hallie and went in to hug her. Hallie stood with a smile and open arms for Wren and then Ella who followed closely after. This caused Seb to stand up and give a look that he was not happy. How someone could say these words and then act like nothing has happened to them behind their backs. Wren noticed Seb's reaction as his eyes began to darken and tapped Ella on the back.

"Come on, let's sit down. I'm sure Hallie is starving." Trying to make light of the atmosphere in the room and to ensure that his wife remains alive until Seb has cooled off was priority for Wren.

Hallie was tucking into her chow mein and enjoying the variety of Chinese food laid across the table. This was more of a banquet and Hallie's eyes were certainly bigger than her belly.

It really was a magical evening, everyone was in food comas and jokes flying across the table. All because one person is back. Seb was truly his happiest when he was with her, and everyone now could see that first hand.

Wade then appeared, all red faced like he had ran here. "Sorry I'm late, lost track of time, is there still any food." Hallie laughed and offered a plate over to him as he took a seat next to Ashlyne. Ashlyne grabbed a napkin and wiped the side of Wade's face which had a small amount blood smudged across. This caused Hallie and Seb to both frown from this, looking at each other than back at the two of them of course Wade and Ashlyne didn't bat an eyelid. Wade thanked her and tucked into his meal. No one else seemed to notice these two and their closeness, Hallie had clocked on though. Hallie leaned over to Seb and whispered into his ear, "is her husband real or are they a thing now?"

Seb laughed and whispered back, "they had an extraction recently, guess they are 'bonding' from that. But her husband is very much real, if not she must do stuff to herself pretty loudly." Hallie had just taken a mouthful of her lemonade which she very nearly spluttered all over the table from laughing. This made Seb let out a laugh which made everyone smile. As he reached for a napkin he wiped the side of her face. Ella leaned over to Wren smiling, "She really is his person, isn't she!" Wren nodded and gave Ella a kiss on her head.

"And you are mine." Ella met Wren's gaze and smiled.

"These past few months have been hell, I hope it is all upwards from now." Ella looked hopeful but when she didn't get a response from Wren, she knew he didn't want to jinx anything.

Back at the other end of the table, Hallie wanted to get her own back for Seb making her nearly spit all her drink over Gibb. So she leaned over to Seb with her hand under the table and began to graze up and down Seb's leg. Seb tried to keep a straight face as he was mid conversation with Wade. Hallie enjoyed being a distraction, so she made each stroke a little harder. Then when Seb met her eye line, she looked up to him slowly and had a small smile spread across her face, her small dimples became visible. Seb leaned into Hallie, "If you want to distract me, all you have to do is plead." Hallie's insides were doing somersaults. She knew she could play Seb even better at his own game, she pulled her hands up from the table and used her finger to get Seb to move his head closer to hers. As he did, she slowly went up to his ear, exhaled slightly and breathed, "Sebastian, please. Take me." Hallie's head was tucked behind Seb's so no one was able to read her lips, only Seb's facial expression.

"You know I will carry you straight upstairs right now if you carry on." Seb enjoyed the tease, he had missed this.

Hallie was one to also fight, she knew he would give in, but what lengths could she go before he snaps. "Either that, or you fuck me on this table. I think our bed is more, suitable for now. Don't you?"

"That depends, how bad do you want me darling?" Seb wasted no time in leaning back into his seat, contemplating whether Hallie will take the bait or if she will fold.

Hallie stood up slowly and placed herself on Seb's lap, she didn't care who was watching. In her eyes, it was just the two of them in the room. "Well, judging on how hard you are right now, I think you want me just as bad." She whispers causing Seb took stare into her eyes. Murmurs from around the room, no conversation was relevant in his eyes.

Ashlyne however had kept her eyes on them both, smiling as to what was going on. Wade on the other hand was completely clueless.

"Ash, what's going on there?"

"They are making up on lost time." She giggles. From that, she stands and announces "right, I'm off to bed, busy day tomorrow, and I am sure these two have some, let's say, catching up to do." She laughs as she walks out the room and begins to head up the stairs. Seb bows his head into Hallie's chest as Hallie laughs loudly, "cheers for that Ash!"

"Anytime Hal, never let me be the one to interrupt when people need to have sex." With this Hallie's laugh was louder. She looks back to Seb, "was our conversation that loud."

"No, that woman has some sort of superhuman hearing I'm sure of it. However, she's not wrong." Seb stood up with Hallie in his arms, they began to leave the room and Hallie shouted to everyone, "lovely seeing you all, see you in the morning. Would love to stay and chat but… Well… You know." Her voice got quieter as they headed up the stairs. Gibb's laugh was infectious from this causing the remainder of people to laugh. As Gibb's laugh slows down, he smiles looking up the stairs. "It is crazy, you know. How just one person can change everything. She really is the light. Don't you think." As the others looked around the room, they all agreed. Having Hallie back, was the best thing that could have happened. Now all that was left was to capture Tate, end that alliance and that would be the end of it.

As they entered their room, Hallie insists she can walk now. As Seb slowly lets her down, he remains close to her body. Hallie could feel his chest as he breathes slowly. Exhale. Inhale. How was him breathing turning her on so badly. A part of Seb's hair fell over his forehead, Hallie's however is tucked behind her ears, where Seb likes it. Looking up to Seb, practically begging him with her eyes, Seb brings his hand slowly up Hallie's back and begins to grab all her hair that falls elegantly down her back into his hand. "You're going to have to use your words darling." Hallie looks down then back up at him slowly, "I don't need to." Smiling as she knew she had Seb wrapped around her finger but right now, she wanted him to make her beg.

"Fuck Hal, what are you doing to me." His hands were all in her hair as Hallie removed her dressing gown. Slowly unbuttoning her pyjama top to reveal her chest, nothing completely on show but enough to entice Seb in. As Seb looks down, he bites on his lip, shaking his head, he was always good at the games, but with Hallie he lost more times than he would care to admit. Hallie began to lift Seb's t-shirt over his head, gliding her hands down his body, then slowly back up to rest on either side of his face. "I need you." Hallie whispers. This was the begging he was after, and it worked. From this, he picked her up with her legs wrapping around his waist. Placing her on the bed he laid on top of her and kissed her, kissed her like he had never done before. As she began to help him unbutton his jeans, she slowly pulled down anything that was in her way, whereas she already seemed to be completely undressed. Seb moved from her mouth and down her neck slowly whilst still paying attention to her in certain areas. Hallie moaned, "Seb, let me. Fuck." Hallie couldn't even get her words out. Seb was now in full control, he took more than enough pleasure ensuring Hallie was completely satisfied, until he would slowly climb back up her body. Hallie tried to catch her breath, but she quickly became breathless again, Seb was enjoying making Hallie beg. But he enjoyed it more because Hallie deep down thrived for this. Seb needed to make sure to not push Hallie to far as she was still recovering, he pressed his body closer to Hallie's whilst his hips did all the movements, until he couldn't hold on anymore. Letting out a moan that breathed heavily in her ear, she smiled at him. Pulling his hair away from his face, Hallie placed her hand at the back of Seb's neck and pulled him in for a kiss. This kiss was soft, their lips fitted together so perfectly.

"You, you darling are just too perfect for me."

Hallie smiled and slowly sat up to meet Seb's eyeline, "I couldn't imagine my life ever without you Seb."

Seb sighed and tucked a small part of Hallie's hair behind her ear, "I have, and it is not a life worth living."

"But you won't lose me, and I don't want to lose you."

"Darling, you would never lose me. Besides, if you did, I would just take you again." He sniggered and Hallie let out a laugh and pushed Seb to lay down so she could sit on top of him. With just a sheet to cover her, she allowed the sheet to fall down her back which made Seb look her up and down and lick his lips.

"You not have enough of me before?" he jokingly groaned.

Hallie leans down to be close to Seb's face and kisses him, "I could never have enough of you."

24

One week later

Hallie had made incredible progress in such a short amount of time. Seb had helped in any physiotherapy he could which mainly included her cardio sessions being sex with him. However, when the doctor begins to ask what she has been doing to keep her fitness levels up and heart rate elevated slightly Seb's mouth opens before hers answering for her.

"Me doc. Just so I can keep a closer eye on her." Seb smiles whilst Hallie's face becomes flushed, her cheeks showing a small amount of red flourishing through them. Seb notices this and makes his smile grow. His dimples now become more prominent. The doctor on the other hand lets out a small laugh and quickly changes the subject.

"Well, I don't think I can write 'has sex often' in Hallie's work up, can I." Before any other comments were made there were three knocks at the door, however no one entered. Seb takes this as his chance to leave, not without leaving with another comment for Hallie to have to answer. "I mean you could doc, but if you need details, I'm sure one of us could re-live it for you." And winked at Hallie as he left the room. Hallie's blush had now spread across her face, she was shaking her head at Seb as he kissed it, "I'll be back in a second darling" he whispered. Stepping outside Hallie shouted, "you take your time." Which made Seb laugh more as he walked out. He was greeted by Wren and Ella and his face soon dropped.

"Everything alright." Seb's tone had completely changed, the happiness had drifted away from his face and Wren saw this.

"Sorry Seb, I told her now wasn't a good time to chat with you but-"

"Her?" Ella snapped. "I just, we haven't spoken in a few days and I…"

Seb introjected, "there is a reason we haven't spoken Ella, I told you, you and your family can stay here but YOU need to stay away from me." The 'you' was said slightly louder than all the other words, anger began to spread through Seb's body, blood beginning to boil from re-living the words leaving Ella's mouth. Wren stepped forward to try ease the situation, he did not enjoy this one bit, but he still had to defend his wife even though she was the one in the wrong.

"Look, this is not the time. Seb, can we have a word somewhere later just us, try and hash this out somehow. Please." Seb noticed the pain in Wren's eyes, but he tried to dismiss this. He was not just going to roll over and let her think she got off lightly, he wants Ella to pay for what she said, make her realise that she needs to think before words leave her mouth. Ella looked up to Wren then to Seb with that same plead in her eyes. However, before Wren could answer Hallie had opened the door to see the three of them standing there. Confused by the situation she remained by the doorway allowing the doctor to leave.

"Will see you next week Hallie, make sure you are not overdoing it. Understand." However, that 'understand' was aimed at both Hallie and Seb, this made Seb's lip curl up with a snigger.

"Yes, thank you again." With that the doctor made his way out the door and let himself out. Hallie was still confused as to the tension she had witnessed. "What's happened? Could cut the tension out here with a knife." Seb began to storm back into the bedroom without answering Hallie's question. Looking back and forth, she noticed Ella looked like she was going to burst into tears.

"Hey, what's happened Ella? Are you okay?" Hallie was concerned and Wren went to put his arm around Ella to comfort her. Sniffling she blinked back the tears as best as she could. "Yeah," sniff, "I'm fine, just need to fix something that's all." Hallie looked to Wren confused as to what she had missed.

"Right, and the thing you need to fix is with Seb?"

No words, just a nod.

"He has been very off when you guys are around. Come on, we are fixing whatever this is now." Ella's eyes snapped up, she doesn't want Hallie to know what she said.

"No no, he wants space, I need to allow that."

"Ella, we have no idea how long you guys will be here. We are squashing whatever has happened now. In." This wasn't a question, this was a demand. Ella looked up to Wren who gave her a remeasuring nod and they stepped into the bedroom.

Seb walked out the bathroom and the rage soon came straight back to his face. "What are you two doing in here?"

Hallie walked over to him and placed her hands on around his neck and looked him straight in the eyes. "Whatever has happened, this gets squashed. Now." Seb knew Hallie didn't know what had been said. He had been protecting her from hearing this but now, it was all coming into the air.

Wren and Ella placed themselves on the large futon that was near the dresser and also close to the door for an easy exit. They didn't know how this was going to go, but if needed they had a quick escape.

"Right, for starters, whatever this is I need to know what started it as right now I am very lost." Seb walked over to where Hallie is sitting and made her look straight at him.

"Darl, you don't want to know."

"Oh but I do, as we are living together and now working together to end Tate. So if we are going to do that, no secrets. Now, was this before or after I woke up this little, situation?" Hallie crossed her arms, she meant business and was a pro at interrogations so this should be a piece of cake getting answers.

"Before." Ella cried.

"So, what was said, because worse things have probably been said to us all. So for you to be all shitty and riled up whenever Ella walks in must have not been nice. Am I wrong?" Looking between Ella and Seb, Ella nodded, Seb remained his eyes fixated on Ella looking like he wanted to rip her throat out.

"Before I go to in-depth, if you flirted or kissed him I will rip your tongue out Ella, understand." This made Ella's eyes look up in terror and Seb smile. "I don't know what you're smiling for, if you'd done the same to her, I would be doing worse to you." The look of determination on Hallie's face, Seb knew all too well, he knew she meant what she said.

"Hallie, no. Absolutely not. Nothing like that. No offence." Relief flowed through Hallie's body.

"Good." She smiled. "So hate to be that person, but Ella what did you say. And go straight to the point."

Ella began to stutter, "Hallie, I, I can't repeat it."

"Wren?" Wren looked up, he did not want to be involved in this, but he could not leave Ella alone in this situation.

"Ella said something she regrets, I explained that it will take Seb time to forgive but it will get easier."

Hallie rolled her eyes, "okay, well that wasn't what was said, Seb?" Seb didn't look at Hallie, she knew she would get the answer from him even if he was trying to protect her.

Seb remained looking at Ella but she couldn't make eye contact with him. "Cut a long story short, Ella was pissed that Toby helped with getting me out of there and how Toby has a talent for hacking and computer work. She threatened to leave, I then explained wherever she went was a death ticket and I won't let Toby get roped into this kind of work but if he asks to learn some bits I will happily help." Seb then cleared his throat and Ella's eyes were burning into the back of her leg, she couldn't look up. "She then said 'You have no fucking clue what it is like to put a child in danger let alone your own! I hope you don't have children as you have no idea how to keep them safe!' I said she can stay here but stay the fuck away from us." Seb was beyond angry for reliving that, now he shared that anger with Hallie. He looked down to her as Hallie was still staring at Seb, her gaze slowly drifted to the wall. Seb was caught up in so much anger and that anger was only building up when he saw Hallie's eyes well up.

Ella looked up to see Hallie's vacant stare. "Hallie I am so so-"

"Did you mean it." Ella went to answer but Hallie answered for her. "Of course you did, you said it." Hallie sniffed. "Well, it was actually me who asked Wren for Toby's help. I would understand if he said no and gave a reason, but he didn't. So, your anger should have been at me, not Seb. And now, well guess what you said kinda came true." Hallie looked down at her hands, she rubbed her fingers together whilst Seb placed his arm around her.

"Think you need to leave." Seb aimed this at Ella, he didn't care where she went, she now hurt Hallie, and no one is to hurt her.

"No." Hallie stood up and walked over to Ella, Ella's body became stiff, afraid to move.

"I meant what I said, we are squashing this now. All I want to do right now is put your head through a wall. But that will solve nothing. We will move past this eventually, Seb has had a bit more time to process everything, I am still, well, trying."

"Hallie, I am so sorry, I cannot express how sorry I am for what I said. Knowing the circumstance and still saying it, it was out of order. If putting my head through a wall will help, then do it." Ella's shoulders began to tense, trying to prepare her body for any impact she would sustain. Seb stepped forward as did Wren.

"Ella, everyone says things they don't mean when they get angry, sometimes emotions take over a little too hard. But right now, we all need to be on the same side. So, I am happy to push past it for now. Seb?" Hallie turned to Seb and he noticed tears in her eyes, she wanted it all to be over, no fighting, she was too exhausted for all of this.

"For you, anything." Seb remains looking at Hallie. Wren looks at Hallie's hand and sees it shaking slightly. He places his arm around Ella and gives her a reassuring nod. Ella's body eases, shoulders slowly dropping. "Thank you" she pleads.

"We will see you both downstairs bit later, yeah?" Wren looks to Seb who agrees. As they leave the room, Ella is overcome with emotions and is thankful her face wasn't used as a punching bag. Laughing down the corridor to head back to their kids, she finally felt somewhat back to normal. However, on the other side of that door, Hallie was now wrapped in Seb's arms. Tears falling down her cheeks. Seb knew she was crying but kept her close to him. Guiding her to the floor he sits her down and kneels beside her. Using his hand, he cups the bottom of her chin and guides her head up to look at him, using his other hand he wipes away the tears to prevent them from falling. Placing both hands on her cheeks he softly asks, "what are you feeling?"

"Just, feeling sorry."

Confused by this answer, Hallie tries to look down again, but Seb pulls her head back up to make her look at him. "Sorry for what?"

"I, I just know, it was early days, but I was actually exited for that. Even though it made me sick quite often, I knew you would be an incredible father." What felt like a rock pound into Seb's chest he tried to remain strong. However, the words 'incredible father' implied to him, just hit hard.

"And you would be the perfect mother. It doesn't matter how early days it is darling, it is still a loss, and it is a loss that will affect you slightly more because you had a different connection. You lost-"

"We lost" Hallie introjected.

"We lost something. But we will be the best fucking parents one day." Hallie's tears were still filling up her eyes, but she was smiling at this thought.

"I fricking love you."

"And I love you Hallie." Hallie wrapped her arms around Seb and he slowly stood up with Hallie. As Hallie pulled away from the hug, she kept her hands fixed in his as she saw a thought go into Seb's mind, his face had changed. A smile that he only shows when he is doing something else.

"What?"

"Marry me."

"I'm sorry?" She questions.

"Marry me Hallie. I want you. I'd kill for you, I'd lie for you. I would die for you Hallie Jones. I want my last name to be yours. You are my main reason to live and breathe in this world and it would sound even better calling you my wife. I want to hear my last name roll off your tongue when you introduce yourself." Hallie's tears had slowly disappeared, she was never chosen, never loved by anyone until Seb came into her life.

"I could not think of anyone else I would want to be with, I have never loved anyone before I met you Seb, and now I can't imagine a life without you."

"So, will you be Hallie Chandler?"

"I would happily be your Hallie Chandler. Yes!" Excitement filled the room, Seb spun Hallie around and placed her on the ground and planted a kiss before he walked over to his dresser. Hallie was confused what he was doing in his underwear draw until he pulled out a ring box and got on one knee. Making it official. The ring fitted beautifully on Hallie's ring finger, as if it was made to measure. There were small stones which were up the band and intertwined into a large diamond stone. It is as if the moment of sadness had slipped away and gave Hallie hope to live on knowing Seb wanted her for life.

25

That evening, everyone gathered for drinks and a meal unknowing why this felt like a celebration. Hallie asked for Seb to move on from Ella's comment which he promised he would, but still had lost his liking for her. As Seb and Ashlyne headed into the basement due to having some questions for Katie who was now a toy for Ashlyne to play with. Hallie on the other hand was enjoying a well-deserved catch up with Gibb.

"So, when did that happen." Gibb was the only person so far to notice the ring, he looked down and raised his eyebrows at the ring then back up to Hallie with a smile.

"I would say a few hours ago." Hallie's smile still has not gone from that moment.

"Well, congratulations, about time we have something good going on don't you!" As they both cheers to that Hallie remained on lemonade were as Gibb on whiskey which at first was a surprise for Hallie but judging from what he has been through it's understandable the change.

"Isn't it crazy how we got to where we are now." Gibb laughed.

"Yeah, from being kidnapped to now marrying the person who took me!" another loud laugh projected from them both. From this they were now not alone but Henry had joined them.

"Don't you think it is funny how well fitted we are here though. Like I fricking love my job, except the new walking stick." Gibb tapped the solid wood stick against the tiled floor twice.

"Well, that's only temporary like most things, think I'm excited for all of my hair to grow back." Another swig of their drinks.

"On that note, need the bathroom." Gibb hobbled up and headed to the closest bathroom leaving Hallie and Henry alone in the dining room.

Hallie looked up to Henry to notice he was already staring at her. "You okay there?"

"Huh, sorry. Daydreaming." His deep voice echoed through the empty dining room. Hallie felt unease with Henry and couldn't quite put her finger on it as to why.

"That's alright. Realised haven't properly had a conversation yet have we." Hallie remained in her seat hoping Henry would sit opposite. Instead, he chose to sit right next to her which made her feel slightly uncomfortable.

"You're right we haven't. Haven't been able to get you alone as your always with him." Hallie's face scowled, this man was living here rent free and he cannot even use his name.

"Who Seb, well we spent quite a bit of time apart, I don't want to miss any more."

"So where is he tonight then. It is nice to see you without him joined to your hip." Hallie pulled her chair out slightly so she was able to swing her legs around and get up quick if she needed to. Having no idea where this conversation was heading, she tried to end it.

"Like I said, would happily spend time with him." However, Hallie didn't know that Ashlyne and Seb were in the corridor listening in to their conversation. Seb instructed Ashlyne to wait to go in to see how that conversation will develop.

"Well, I must admit, your beauty is just breathtaking." Hallie's face curled up cringing at those words, that wasn't a compliment, that was a chat up line. A very bad one.

"I would say your WIFE is breathtaking, I am just ordinary." Seb shook his head knowing this was not true, but Ashlyne smiled at the thought of someone complimenting her.

"Meh, nothing on you." That was it Hallie stood up and began to walk to the other side of the table.

"Meh! What is wrong with you. That woman had been by your side everyday while you were recovering, paying your bills, fighting your battles and that is all you have to say is 'meh'"

"Well yeah, she's alright. But I wouldn't mind a taste of you." Henry had taken it upon himself to grab Hallie's arm and try to pull her close. This was a bad move all around. Seb and Ashlyne had already started to barge in, but Hallie was one step ahead, she had grabbed Henry's arm and twisted it over her to get his body to crash to the floor. Pinning both hands behind his back Henry had nowhere to go.

"Ash, I am so sorry, he was saying all this crap then tried to touch me it was either this or stab him." Ashlyne looked down at Henry with sympathy.

"She's lying babe, think that concussion has gone to her head, she was all over me. Fucking slut." That was it, Seb's eyes darkened and he was storming to Henry. He grabbed him from the floor and dragged him to his feet. His hand grabbed hold of Henry's throat as he pinned him to the wall, the other hand now in a fist, and that fist meeting Henrys stomach causing him to wince. "You fucking liar, you say one bad word about her, and I will cut out your tongue. Understand me." Seb dropped his grip and Henry fell to the floor. Walking over to Hallie he pulled her close. "I could've taken care of him."

"No one gets to say a bad word about you. Understand." Seb looked over at Ashlyne walking over to Henry. Seb whispered for Hallie to go and get Wade as he has an idea. Hallie done as she was told.

Breathless, Henry was trying to talk but was winded by Seb's punch. "Baby, please, come on, you know she was lying. Right?"

Ashlyne shook her head, for the first time since Henry being back, she looked defeated, broken and like she could cry any minute. "I know you were lying. Why?"

Henry looked confused. No words. Ashlyne then grabbed him by his hair to get his head to look at her. Whist a fist full of hair in her grip, each strand of hair was pulling slightly harder against Henry's scalp causing him to squirm in pain. "Fuck this, Seb I-" But before Ashlyne could finish her sentence Seb had Wade standing by his side along with Hallie.

"We will take care of it. Wade." From that they zip-tied Henry's arms and legs and both Seb and Wade grabbed Henry and carried him to the basement. Hallie took it upon herself to keep Ashlyne in the dining room with a large vodka in her hands ready for her.

"Thanks. I know he was hitting on you, Seb and I heard the whole thing." Ashlyne's tone was deep and sombre.

"I'm sorry Ash, he's a pig and you deserve so much better." Ashlyne nodded in response before swallowing her drink whole, luckily Hallie had brought the bottle. Gibb however had just entered from being in the bathroom.

"The fuck did I just miss?"

"My husband being a pig." Gibb had no words, he looked at Hallie and widened his eyes. Hallie responded with a nod then looking back at Ashlyne.

"Well, least you can use him as your human punching back now."

"Oh I am going to use him more than a punching bag, I intend to cut his dick off and make him swallow it. Gag on it for all I care. Then cut out his tongue, for all the slimy words he has said to who knows, then I want to shove a pin into his brain causing him to be paralyse before slitting his throat and allowing him to slowly bleed to death." Hallie looked back to Gibb and his mouth had dropped open. Both their eyes widened, they knew Ashlyne had some crazy tendencies, but now she was going on a war path. The one man she loved more than anything has now turned his back on her, there is no stopping this woman's warpath.

26

You could hear the echoes from each step as Seb and Wade dragged Henry down to the basement, even if he was kicking and attempting to be released from their grip. Seb pulled Henry's arms tight behind his back and kicked his legs out so he was on his knees. Wade grabbed the loose chains which lie on the floor ahead and as he walked back to Henry he dragged the chains along the concrete floor, a smile across his face.

"I am going to enjoy this." Wade sniggered which to his surprise made Henry smile. "What you smiling for, your soon to be dead."

Henry let out a laugh, Wade looked up to Seb then back at Henry, his eyes began to darken. The sound leaving Henry's mouth was making Wade's skin crawl. "I see the way you look at Ash. I know you want to fuck her, she won't let me die. She will let me off the hook soon enough, she always does." From this Seb's grip tightened and Wade's fists began to tighten, Seb shot him a look to try and calm him. Wade's eyes remained on Henry until the basement door swung open. Wade slowly turned around to see Ashlyne walking slowly down, dragging a metal bat behind her. Every step Ashlyne took her metal bat would hit the step previous with a bang every time. Ashlyne was humming a tune aloud and Seb looked up to Wade then gave him a nod allowing Ashlyne to be able to approach Henry.

"Caught in a Bad Romance." Quietly singing, each step Ashlyne took, the song she was singing was getting louder. Wade looked to Seb in confusion, "is that Lady Gaga?"

"Sure is." He responded, still keeping an eye on Ashlyne. Henry was now chained up, his arms hung from the ceiling. Katie was sitting in the corner, her arms wrapped around her legs making sure she didn't make a sound.

"Baby, please. Come on, you know me Ash, I only have eyes for you." Ashlyne scoffed at Henry's comment. She knew his lies and felt sick that she didn't see them sooner. Wade stepped up and stood close to Ashlyne, "Want me to take care of him?" his voice calm, soothing. Hallie had since quietly crept down the stairs and hugged Seb from behind, she didn't want to miss out on the fun. However, from Wade's ask, Ashlyne dropped her bat and wrapped her arms around Wade's neck and kissed him, both their tongues fighting to get in each other's mouth. Hallie's jaw opened whereas Seb just laughed. Neither one of them were expecting that. However, this kiss was passionate, fiery, well they may as well strip off and have sex right there right now, it was like no one else was in the room. That was when Henry found his voice from the initial shock and started to shout at them.

"I knew you were a fucking slut, you just can't help yourself can you. You may as well have sold yourself back then, least you know your worth, to think I fucking defended you against Tate, he should have sold you to the highest fucking bidder you tramp." Their kiss ended, Ashlyne remained looking into Wade's eyes, the lighting wasn't great in the basement, but he could see Ashlyne's eyes forming tears. He tucked her hair behind her ear and looked her in the eyes, "now can I kill him." He asked making Ashlyne smile. Before she could answer Hallie stepped forward.

"Let me get this straight, you worked with Tate, before. You knew he was behind the taking of innocent people and selling them on, how he nearly sold Ashlyne. Yet you were married to her the whole time? Something doesn't add up?" Seb looked back to Hallie then down at Henry. Hallie continued.

"You only married Ashlyne to get her close to you, Tate knew this, he had no idea how to get a hold of Ash and you were the key. Only you took the hit and ended up in that coma. It was an act, the whole time, your whole marriage together, Ashlyne believed you and you were with Tate the whole time?" Henry was silent, Ashlyne had anger filling around her body, a red blush spread across her face and she bent over and picked up her metal bat. Hallie knew it was best to get out of her way or she could take a hit too.

Ashlyne lifted the bat and swung it across Henry's torso, "answer her fucking question you pig!" Grunts left Henry's mouth, the smack from the metal bat across Henry's bare skin slapped and echoed the basement.

Just as Henry caught his breath he answered fearing he would get another hit. "Yes, I worked with him, but when I told him he couldn't have you, he turned on me. I couldn't let him sell you to that fucking man. You were mine."

"I was NO ONES." Another hit across his stomach, this time more anger filled Ashlyne and the hit was harder, you could hear something crack inside Henry. As he coughed, blood began to appear from his mouth.

Seb walked up to Hallie and placed his arms around her neck and pulled her into his chest, she could feel his warmth in such a cold environment, making her feel more at ease. Hallie was still adjusting to this life however she had plenty of practise in the torturing part.

Wade interrupted Henry from talking, "What man, who wanted Ash?" concern from Wade as to however wanted her then, might still want her.

"Harold, Harold Kingston. He wanted Ashlyne as his little, toy." Ashlyne began to feel sick, she turned away and walked over to the metal table and began rummaging through the draws. Wade turned to Seb and he nodded, still no words left Seb's mouth, but he kept Hallie close. Hallie kept the back of her head resting on Seb's chest however her eyes fixed on Ashlyne. Wade took it upon himself to try get some more answers from Henry before Ashlyne got her hands back on him.

"What else don't we know about Tate?"

Henry sniffed drawing up some phlegm from his throat which he spat out, only it was not phlegm but blood. "Know idea, been here since, no phone or access to the outside world."

"Bullshit." Wade crouched down to Henry's height and got close to his face.

"What, you have taken out his main man already, take out the top two and then what, what do you think will happen, it will all go away. Someone else will just take it upon themselves to take over. Besides, I fucking miss the thrill of it all." Silence. Ashlyne had stopped rummaging through the draws to listen closely. Henry continued, "I miss hearing the screams, the pleas, those girls would do anything to be free, it was exhilarating seeing what someone else would do to save themselves. The way they beg, makes you feel, superior and the way their mouths just-." But before Henry could finish his sentence Ashlyne was already storming back to him, a rag in one hand and a large knife in the other. Wade stepped back not interfering with this one. Henry began to squirm, he had a feeling what she was about to do and screams began to rip from his chest. Ashlyne had pulled his trousers and boxers down to his ankles and pressed the knife close to his dick.

"Ashlyne, don't do anything stupid. Get that knife off me."

"Or what Henry, you are a sick human being and you deserve to be stripped from your so called manhood." With that the knife slowly pressed firmer into Henry causing him to try and wriggle away, he couldn't go anywhere. Ashlyne used the rag as a tourniquet and pulled it tightly around the top of his dick.

Wade and Seb looked in discomfort the thought of that pain as Ashlyne began to hack his dick off. Every swift movement she had with her butchers' knife made blood spray all around her. The mess was indescribable. Henry's heart was beating wildly causing more blood to circulate around his body faster which meant, more blood being lost if Ashlyne had not tourniquet it off. She didn't want him to die straight away but suffer like he made others suffer. Ashlyne then went back with her knife and cut his dick clean off. Screams bellowed around the basement, Ashlyne was getting fed up with Henry screaming in pain, so she picked up some duct tape and placed it over his mouth, his screams still there but not as loud.

Seb whispered down into Hallie's ear, "wanna go back upstairs think she has this handled, don't you." Hallie sniggered raising her head up to Seb,

"What? This make you slightly uncomfortable?"

Seb smiled and pulled Hallie to the stairs, leaning into Wade on the way up, "you staying down here?"

"Yeah, make sure she's alright. Plus want to let off some steam in a bit." Seb laughed, Hallie already walking up the stairs.

"Well remember whatever 'steam' you let off down here, you have eyes in that corner." Wade had forgotten about Katie, he didn't care though, she deserved what she got for working with Tate also.

Just as Seb began to make his way upstairs to join Hallie, Ashlyne called after him,

"You still got that woodchipper?" Seb nodded and looked over to Henry then back at Ashlyne.

"Can I use it when I am done?"

Seb breathed out loudly and smiled, "Knock yourself out, let me know if you need me. Just make sure you clean up your mess." Leaving the room not waiting for a response. Seb didn't care what they got up to in his basement, he was more looking forward to what he was going to do with Hallie.

27

Henry's skin started to drain in colour, his eyes struggling to stay open as he drifted in and out of consciousness from the pain. Ashlyne had wrapped a rag around where his dick once was as a tourniquet to stop the blood from pooling out and to ensure he stays alive until Ashlyne is ready.

"Ash, please. You know I love you. Just let me go. Please." Henry groaned, his voice deep and husky. Wade walked over to the works bench and grabbed another rag and began to walk over to Katie. Fear took over Katie's body, she had no idea what was in store for her, her first instinct was to fight, run, hit Wade any way she could to escape. All of these thoughts rushing through her head but instead of acting on them, she froze. Her eyes began to fill with tears, her pupils large from the darkness she sat in. Wade knelt to her level. Katie's breathing increased as panic flooded her body.

"I need you to put this around your mouth, cover your screaming from what you are about to see. If either of us hear you, our need to kill you will come around much faster. Understand." Wade whispered, his voice made out that this was not a question, Katie just nodded her head as Wade placed the rag around her mouth tying it from behind. Wade stood up and headed back to Ashlyne as she had laid out a variety of knives. Her hand resting on her chin as she contemplated what she wanted to use. The room was quiet, the odd groan from Henry but they both drowned out that sound.

Ashlyne looked up to Wade with a smile, "you can go if you want, this is my mess to fix." Wade half smiled and placed his hands on

Ashlyne's long hair, he took the hairband from her wrist and began to tie her hair back in a loose ponytail.

"Don't want any of that lovely hair to get matted up with his blood." Wade leaned in close to Ashlyne's ear and whispered, "I'm going nowhere."

"Fucking SLUT!" Henry shouted which made both Ashlyne and Wade look over to him, sweat began to fall in beads down his forehead. His breathing had increased, the thought of this made Wade smile, he wanted to add fuel to Henry's anger, he enjoyed a good game.

Ashlyne slowly walked over and knelt to Henry's head, leaning in close to him she could hear him struggling to breathe. "You are going to fucking suffer."

With this Ashlyne took Henry's hand and with one swift movement pulled out the hammer she had tucked behind her back and slammed down onto his little finger. Screams bellowed the basement, and with every hit on each finger that Ashlyne was breaking, more croaks appeared in his scream. Wade was surprised he had not passed out from the pain. Pulling a metal chair from the corner of the room, Wade took a seat next to the work bench as he wanted Ashlyne to enjoy inflicting this pain, to give her some closure from her failed marriage.

With Henry's dick just lying close next to him, Ashlyne took it upon herself to cut it up into small pieces and placed it into a small ziplock bag which once contained Katie's sandwich she had for lunch. "I'm bored of him now." Ashlyne looked over to Wade and he nodded in agreement. Heading to the opposite side of the basement he typed a code which unlocked the large metal door. Walking back over to Ashlyne he untied Henry and re-tied him so his arms and legs were bounded together hoisting Henry up over his shoulder, he carried him outside. Ashlyne followed closely behind. Wade then placed Henry on the ground, however Henry was in too much pain to realise where he was. With the push of a button the motor kicked in. The vibrations from the machine began to shake the ground which then made Henry look up and begin to panic.

"St-stop please, no you can't do this. Get me fucking off of this thing. Now. Fuck."

Wade then stepped aside and gestured to Ashlyne to the machine, "care to do the honours Ash." A smile went from ear to ear on Ashlyne's face, considering she was just about to send her husband to his death she seemed pretty happy about the situation. Walking up to the woodchipper Ashlyne looked up to Wade and nodded. With that Wade picked Henry up and placed him in line of the inlet table. Reaching around into the truck which was hooked up to the trailer the woodchipper sat on, he pulled out some headphones.

"It's going to be noisy." As he handed Ashlyne some headphones, he climbed up to the chipper and placed the outlet chute to point towards the river ahead. All remains would then be flushed back to the ocean or eaten as some fishes bate.

"Ashlyne, please." Henry groaned, he was breathless and close to dying from blood loss, so Ashlyne was ready to allow him to feel every bit of pain from the woodchipper.

"See you in hell, you piece of shit." Not allowing Henry to answer, Ashlyne pressed the button to initiate the woodchipper to start and begin the cuts. Screams bellowed across the forest, it echoed. They were fortunate that there was no neighbours or footpaths nearby for anyone to hear the pain Henry was enduring. As his body slowly entered the chipper, blood began top spill out of the outlet and the bits of flesh from his legs, then the screams stopped, Henry was dead from the amount of blood he had lost however his body still began to spill out of the outlet chute and fall into the river turning the once clear blue water into a deep red. The stream tide was flowing quickly, and when the chipper was done with Henry's body the water soon turned back to its original colour and all traces of Henry were now gone. A tear fell from Ashlyne's face, not from sadness but from anger. Had she seen his intentions sooner she could have got on with her life a long time ago instead of sitting by his bedside waiting for Henry to wake up. Wade noticed this and placed his arm around her and pulled her close.

"If I'm honest, is it selfish of me to be happy he is now out the picture." Wade looked down at Ashlyne and smiled.

"Not at all, if anything it is a relief." Ashlyne then grabbed Wade's hand and pulled him towards the truck. Climbing into the backseat she laid down while Wade stood by the doorway. Licking his lips he climbed on top of her and began to kiss her. The door swung closed behind them and steam began to appear on the windows.

28

Meanwhile, upstairs Seb had taken full opportunity of an empty manor. Wren had taken his family out for a change of scenery through the forest whereas Gibb was at Physiotherapy for his legs which he enjoyed attending for the beautiful doctor he had. As Seb headed up the basement steps, Hallie was nowhere to be seen. He remained still, trying to hear out for a sound to which his phone pinged with a message.

"Let's see if your hunting skills are still any good."

This brought a devilish smile to Seb's face. He enjoyed a little game, especially if Hallie was the reward. That is how he got her in the first place, by hunting her down, taking her and allowing herself to fall in love with him. Only this time, she was the one in control. Seb began to respond to her message.

"I've taken you once before darling, let's play."

From this Seb put his phone on silent and tucked it in his back pocket, ensuring no noise left him, he slowly slipped off his boots and began to walk around the house. Checking all of the rooms downstairs, they were empty, he glanced up the stairs and smiled before taking each step one at a time. His phone vibrated in his pocket once more.

"What makes you think I won't sneak up on you for once."

Looking around Seb's heart rate began to rise slightly, the adrenaline from this was taking over. He knew Hallie wouldn't hide in their room as that would be too easy, so he tackled the spare rooms first, nothing. Then the library, the side door was open slightly. Instead of heading through the side door he went out of the library and into his office. Looking around his office that same side door was now closed. He knew where she was from this, time for him to wait for her next move.

Hallie tried to calm her breathing so she wouldn't give anything away. Seb enjoyed the odd game and Hallie now had full excitement of being the one in charge of this game. Hallie crept out from behind the bookcase once she heard Seb enter and leave the room. Knowing she left the side door open on purpose to make him believe she was in his office she crept out and headed for the hallway to find another room. Listening closely, she heard Seb close his office door, this was her chance to sneak into his office through the side door and then creep up on Seb. Carefully opening the door, she slid her body through the gap. Creeping through the halls of the manor Hallie thought she had the advantage here, that was until the lights went out across the manor. Perhaps they had tripped the electric in the basement. Little to Hallie's knowledge, Seb wanted her in darkness.

Seb heard one of the doors closing in the room nearby, taking his time he slowly took to the darkened hallways, until he heard her hit herself on the cabinet ahead. Seb stopped in his tracks, and a smile appeared across his face. Hallie was within a few feet of him yet unknown to her knowledge, she had no idea he was behind her. From this, Hallie stood still for a moment, trying to hear any sounds around her. Nothing. Seb remained still. Hallie then began to walk, suddenly hearing footsteps behind her adrenaline kicked in and she ran for the stairs. Seb followed quickly behind keeping up her pace. Hallie ran down the stairs, panic yet smiling from this rush going through her body. As she reached the bottom of the stairs she turned to head for the kitchen, however Seb took the route through the open lounge which leads into the kitchen. Hallie was sure Seb was still close behind her, however her heart stopped when arms reached around her body.

Seb spun Hallie around and pulled her close.

"You seemed to enjoy that." He sniggered.
"I could say the same for you." Breathless yet still smiling. Until silence fell again and both stared into each other's eyes. Hallie's gaze remained on Seb's eyes whilst Seb's eye line dipped to Hallie's lips then back to her face.
"I.."
"What's wrong darling, taken your breath away." Cocky yet certain he knew the answer.
"Not at all." Hallie went to step back but Seb's arms pulled her in closer, his head was close to Hallie's ear.
"Then let me do just that." He whispered. Before Hallie could do anything, Seb had lifted her up so she was sat on the kitchen side. Hallie met his gaze, wrapping her legs around his body she pulled him close. As their tongues met with another, Hallie moaned quietly which made Seb pull her closer to him. Already taking off whatever clothes were on Hallie, Seb picked her up and placed her on the island which had some mugs on from earlier that day. Seb climbed on top of her already having taken his clothes off and allowed himself to fit perfectly onto Hallie. Her legs lifted around Seb's lower back to which she pulled him closer into her. Reaching down to her neck, Seb began to kiss each bit of skin that he could access whilst each thrust let out a small moan until he put every inch of himself inside her causing Hallie to not contain her silence. No longer did she care if anyone were to walk in, both were in the moment and enjoying this far too much. Noise began to fill the manor however, Wren and his family had walked in through the back from their journey through the forest and Gibb followed close entering the front of the manor from his appointment. As soon as the first door opened Seb picked up all the clothes which lay on the floor and hoisted Hallie over his shoulder and quickly entered the second lounge, one quick turn of the old-fashioned key they were locked inside. Laughter spread from Hallie as she reached down for her clothes in an attempt to put them back on. Seb however had other ideas.

"Who says I was done with you yet?"
Hallie raised her eyebrows, "didn't get enough of me then?"
"Darling, I would never have enough of you. Now let me finish this

game you started."

Hallie and Seb joined the others in the kitchen and to Hallie's horror Gibb had just begun making himself a sandwich where she was once laying. Realising she didn't wipe down the area she chose to keep her mouth shut. Seb however noticed how mortified Hallie was and let out a laugh.

"What's so funny boss?" Wren asked looking confused. Wren looked over at Hallie and met her eye line which was focusing on the surface Gibb was making his food, then looked back to Seb who just raised his eyebrows and smirked. Wren put two and two together and laughed along. "Ahhh, now I see." Ella looked still confused and just as she was about to ask, Wade and Ashlyne entered looking like they had both been dragged through a hedge backwards. Ashlyne's hair was all over the place and Wade still had a flush of red over his cheeks. All heads turned to these two which made Hallie slightly more relieved all eyes were off them.

"Well, you guys look like you've been busy, get that inconvenience sorted?" Seb asked however Wren and his family had been out the whole time when Henry was being tortured.

"Yeah, I saw the chipper outside, anything I need to know?" Wren turned to Seb then back to Ashlyne and Wade. Ella took this opportunity to take the children upstairs if they were about to talk about dead bodies.

"Henry is now gone, and I would avoid using the truck for a bit. Especially if you're taking your family out Wren." Ashlyne said calmly while walking over to the fridge and pulling out a bottle of water.

"Don't tell me his body is in my truck rotting away?" Wren looked pissed off and was about to shout when Wade answered soon after.

"No, no dead people or bodies are in the truck, just, well some bodily fluids I guess." Seb smirked at this response and Ashlyne winked back at Wade for the answer. Not saying anything else Ashlyne then turned to Seb and Hallie.

"Looks like you two have been busy too, and recently by the looks of it." Hallie smiled and Seb reached around her and picked up his drink. Gibb had now begun to eat his sandwich but stopped mid mouthful when he saw Hallie and Seb's faces.

"What?" However, Ashlyne was already one step ahead.

"Well Gibb, judging by the smirk on Seb's face and that look on Hallie's I would say they done it right where you made that sandwich." That was enough to make everyone laugh except Gibb.

"Tell me you cleaned down after?"

"You guys walked in, didn't have time." Seb sniggered.

"Man, I'm trying to eat my sandwich. Fuck it, I'm not making another." From that Gibb picked up his sandwich and walking stick and began to leave the kitchen. "And this is another reason I can't wait for all of this to be over so I can get a place of my own where no one has sex where I make my sandwiches."

"I mean don't knock it till you try it Gibb." Hallie responded causing Seb to choke on his drink and laugh. No response from Gibb as he left the room. Hallie then moved her gaze to Wade and Ashlyne waiting for them to explain what their situation is. Ashlyne took this opportunity to speak up as Wren was still not in the loop about Henry.

"Cut a long story short, my husband, well ex-husband, made a pass at Hallie before she put him to the floor. Then turns out he worked with Tate but Tate lost it one day and that's how he got his injury and put in a coma, course I was none the wiser. So, we took him to the basement, I kissed Wade, cut Henry's dick off and he ended up in the chipper then I fucked Wade in your truck. There, think that is everything." Speechless, no one made a sound. Wade continued to drink his water whilst Hallie remained smiling at Ashlyne. Wren however was looking back and forth to Wade, then Ashlyne then Seb, back to Ashlyne.

"So, you two, like you two a thing now?"

Wade spoke up this time, "I mean no one else is going to lay a finger on her if I can help it so yeah, guess we are." A smile spread from ear to ear across Ashlyne's face and Hallie was pleased to see this. It was about time someone embraced Ashlyne's fucked up side and Wade has an even messier thought process on things.

Hallie now walked over to Ashlyne and put her arm around her shoulder, "Well remind me not to piss either of you two off, that death would be, well fucked up!" Hallie smiled and Ashlyne returned this smile. Hallie picked up two cold bottles of water with a bar of Cadbury's chocolate, and slowly walked back to Seb handing over one of the water bottles. Rolling onto her tiptoes she placed her lips close to Seb's ear and whispered, "I'm off to shower, if you care to join me" and began to walk away. No time to give a response, Seb gave a smile, turned around and caught up to Hallie lifting her over his shoulder. Giggles echoed throughout the hallway as they scurried off to their room. Wade and Ashlyne followed to the other side of the manor shortly after leaving Wren to head off to find Ella. The children would be settled down by now so he could spend some quality time with his wife.

29

Within the next week things were finally coming together. A plan on how Seb and his team were going to tackle this situation without causing too much of an uproar and exposing themselves. Their line of business was discrete, only a certain few people knew about the establishment and others just guessed, but no one except Seb and his team knew the full extent of their line of work. With Hallie being back in Seb's life his whole mood had changed for the better. Everyone was working well together and each person had their own little thing to bring to the team. Seb was working from his laptop at the dining room table alongside Wade and Wren, loaning his office to Gibb which he enjoyed. Toby would often sneak into the office to spend time with Gibb and learn what he got up to. Ella knew this and was okay with it as long as Gibb showed him things that would not traumatise him or send him to prison. Hallie had just come back from a walk with Ashlyne and much to Seb's surprise, the pair of them had a look on their faces which could cause trouble.

Seb peered over his laptop screen and scanned over them both, "I don't like where this is going already." Wade's attention had now shifted and nodded in agreement with Seb.

"We have an idea." Still smiling but concern and uncertainty was still on Seb's face.

"We?" Looking to Ashlyne then back at Hallie.

Ashlyne then spoke up, "yes, we. We both thought it was a great idea." Wade then closed his laptop screen and leant back into his chair. Seb still had his screen open.

"I'm listening" Seb murmured.

Hallie then pulled out a chair opposite Seb and leant over the table. "We know that Jacob Mendes works closely with Harold, they have done deals in the past. What if we set up a little run in with Jacob, get some information from him and he might let slip of a location or what Harold has planned." Seb then looked up to Hallie and closed his laptop. He crossed his arms and looked deeply at Hallie. Taking this opportunity of silence, Hallie continued. "What if, we see where he has a dinner, or a late-night drink and either myself or Ash can get chatting with him, get some answers."

"You both want to flirt with him to get answers?" Wade spoke up, Seb still kept his eyes on Hallie, no words yet.

"Yes, he is a man who likes his fair share of women. If one of us run into him and can get him talking, maybe slip something into his drink and go from there." Ashlyne was smiling from this plan, Hallie however was trying to read Seb's facial expression.

"Boss? I personally don't think this is a good idea. Do you?" Wren now spoke and all eyes were on Seb. His eyes still did not move.

"You both can do it, you will be watched by us all though. Anything slightly unsure you leave. Understand." Ashlyne smiled to Hallie and then nodded to Seb.

"Of course, best go find my smallest dress." With that Ashlyne then headed for the stairs and Wade then got up from the table. Wren noticed Wade leaving the room quickly.

"Where do you think you are heading too?"

"Did you not hear that, her smallest dress. Absolutely not, too many eyes on her for my liking." Wade then stormed upstairs to assist Ashlyne in finding a suitable dress. Wren laughed from this comment and then excused himself from the awkward situation to get another drink. The tension between Hallie and Seb had increased and he had no idea what it was about.

Hallie then smiled and then stood up slowly, placing her hands on the table and leaning forward ever so slightly and whispered, "so you wanna help me choose something to wear, or am I just going to have to go wearing the bare minimal to get his attention." Seb rose to his feet quickly and grabbed Hallie pulling her close. Hallie always seemed shocked by his strength however this just made her smile.

"You are mine and mine only, understand."

Hallie laughed and looked back to Seb, "As you are for me." His jaw tightened as he held eye contact with Hallie.

"I'm serious, one wrong move, one finger that anyone lays on you and they won't live another day." Hallie didn't answer, she just smiled and began to walk upstairs to get dressed. Seb didn't follow instantly, instead he continued typing away on his laptop, trying to keep focused and remain working. Wren arrived back in the room looked over to Seb then back at his screen then back to him.

"So, you not going to follow?" Wren cautiously asked.

"Nope"

Wren not convinced, closing his laptop and leaned on the table and remained looking at Seb.

"What?" confused Seb tried to keep typing.

"Nothing, just seeing how long this lasts." He sniggered

Seb frowned, "What lasts?"

"This, you'll be upstairs in no time. I can see your brain eating you up inside wondering what dress she is going to choose to flirt with another person that is not you." Wren smiled, he enjoyed winding Seb up. A vein on Seb's forehead began to appear from his increased blood flow from anger. Inhaling Seb then looked back at his screen.

"No one will touch her."

Wren laughed, "yeah right, no offence but with Ashlyne by her side, someone will have eyes on her. I'd be feeling the same if it was Ella, thankfully she wants nothing to do with this line of work." Seb then looked up to Wren and saw the smile. Closing his laptop, he picked it up and began to storm out the dining room.

"Fuck you Wren." He laughed as he left which caused Wren to shake his head and laugh along.

Seb walked into his room and to his surprise Hallie wasn't wearing something too revealing. Her dress was off the shoulder however the sleeves covering her arms, her collarbones were prominent as her hair was tied back into a low messy ponytail. The dress covered just to her mid-thigh so if she were to bend over nothing would be revealing.

"This okay?" Hallie asked as she placed a necklace on, the chain getting caught in her ponytail. Seb strolled over to Hallie and took the necklace from her to attach the chain. As he clasped the chain, he ran his hands from her shoulders down her arms leaning into her neck. He whispered, "You always look perfect." Hallie looked up into the mirror with a smile and slowly turned around to meet Seb's gaze.

"Now before I rip this dress off of you, I will meet you downstairs with Ash and talk business." Seb tried to distract his mind from Hallie. Opening his laptop screen, he showed Hallie a picture of the man who would have information on Harold Kingston. This was the man who they needed to try and flirt with in order to get intel.

30

Lights were flickering around the street, multiple colours illuminated the pavement ahead. Hallie and Ashlyne had walked past the long queue of people who looked like they had been waiting hours for access to this bar. Gibb had managed to get the access to a VIP section which qualified them to be able to skip the queue and go straight into their own section. In a van outside, Gibb remained on his laptop hacking the club's security footage alongside Seb, Wren, and Wade in the back seats all on laptops. Boris remained in the driver's seat ready just in case they needed to get away quickly also keeping an eye on any unexpected visitors.

Ashlyne chose a black mini dress which barely covered her ass, black strap stiletto heels and a gold clutch bag holding her good knife. Hallie took no bag with her but had a knife on her garter under her dress. Both walked straight over to the bar and ordered a shot, fortunately for both, all eyes landed on them including their target.

Jacob Mendes. Well known for his good fortune as a successful lawyer. Jacob managed to target wealthy people to have as clients, people who would pay him a high amount of money to help make their problems disappear. Jacob was just under six feet tall and wore a blue tailored suit which looked too tight for fitting. His eyes dived straight for Ashlyne and Hallie, curious as to how they got access there, he took a swig of his drink and waved the bar man to get them both a drink. Brushing the girls' legs that were already on him, her face looking confused, but she just stood up and went to the next table. Hallie noticing this without making direct eye contact, she picked up her drink and leaned close to Ashlyne.

"He is coming over." Ashlyne nodded and took a swig of her drink.

"Good evening ladies, it's safe to say I have never seen you here before." Jacob's voice was deep and had a slight accent which Hallie couldn't quite make out.

"Yes, well we had been recommended this place so thought give it a try. Yourself?" Ashlyne brushed the hair that was draped over her shoulder to her back to give full view of her low-cut dress showing her cleavage. Jacob's eyes couldn't even focus on her face. His eyes glanced down then back up again. Hallie smiled and took a sip of her drink, trying not to laugh from the boys' comments she was getting through the earpiece.

Clearing his throat, Jacob continued, "This is a regular for me, nice place to just, unwind. No what I mean. How did you two get into this part." Hallie then interrupted.

"Like it's hard. Just got told to say our names at the door and get straight in."

"Are your names as beautiful as you both?"

"Is this guy serious, how the fuck does he get laid?" Wade scoffed causing the others to laugh.

"I'm Maeve."

"And I'm Lola. Yourself?" Hallie responded she didn't enjoy small talk, but she needed to get this guy talking and using fake names was a start.

"I'm Jacob. Pleasure to meet you both." Jacob invited them both to sit in his booth with a couple of his friends. Agreeing, they ensured every drink they got they kept close just in case one was to be spiked, but making sure they got Jacob very drunk to start to get him talking.

A couple hours had passed and Jacob was beginning to get a bit hands on with Ashlyne and Hallie but nothing they couldn't handle. Both of Jacobs friends had left with other women making this the perfect opportunity to get the information from Jacob.

"So Jacob, you were telling us about this auction. I am sure we would pay a pretty penny for what they are selling. How do we get access?"

Jacob was slurring his words but placed his hand on Hallie's leg. "Well, I will be there so I would want both of you to come. It is at Victoria Manor, one of the manors owned by Harold Kingston." Ashlyne slid another shot to Jacob which he took in an instant. Hallie tried getting more intel.

"Do we need an invitation or just turn up?"

"It is invite only as there are some important people going however judging that you both are part of the royal family you could get invites easy! Just contact the manor and tell them you want an invite for August 5th. Do not say what as they will think you are police. I look forward to-," But before Jacob could finish, he stood up and fell backwards instantly. Hallie and Ashlyne looked at each other and then back at Jacob.

"Gibb, you able to get us in."

"Already got you all an invite."

Hallie breathed in relief, nodding to Ashlyne they both exited the club swiftly and walked to one of the black cars parked across the street which Wade had already parked.

******

The preparations leading up to August 5th were draining. Sleepless nights working on guests lists, how to stay under the radar, what teams needed to be in place and most importantly how to stay hidden when many people working with Tate knew Seb's team by their face. More information was being uncovered as the days went on. Gibb was working tirelessly on a new software to ensure that they would not be hacked and go un-detected. Hallie was putting her detective skills to good use and working out a timeline on missing people who could be potential victims that are being sold to the highest bidder. Hallie had never in her line of work dealt with something this intense. Many murders, missing people, robberies you name it, but sex trafficking was another level of messed up. Deep in thought Seb appeared with Hallie's phone in his hand.

"Think you need to get that." Passing the phone over Hallie didn't even hear it go off. It was Sergeant and looks like he had been trying to call a few times.

Dialling back the phone didn't even ring once before it was answered.

"Sarge, sorry not had my phone on me. Everything alright?"

"I need you to come to station just to give a follow up statement on the day the station was targeted. Just need something on file." Hallie's eyes looked to Seb, she didn't like the idea of going back to the station, facing her old demons. Seb gave her a reassuring look and nodded.

"Yeah, we are on our way." Hanging up the phone, Hallie exhaled loudly, her shoulders had been tensed and Seb pulled her close feeling her tense slowly release, and her shoulders relax. Seb's callused hands rested on Hallie's cheek and guided her eye line to meet his.

"In and out. It sounds like it is just a protocol that needs following up with." Hallie knew they needed everything on file especially if they have leads, everything had to add up and Hallie was on the scene she was just surprised she hadn't been called in sooner.

31

Pulling into the visitors bay outside the station, Hallie just remained still not wanting to get out of the car. Seb placed his hand on her lap and squeezed it slightly to be able to get Hallie's attention.

"Let's get this over with." Hallie sighed. She disliked this place the more she thought about it. Once her safe haven and the place she used to spend all hours of the day was one that made her stomach curdle with the lies she was once told.

Walking straight through the automatic doors, Hallie had both hands clenched into fists, her knuckles began turning white, Seb however noticed this and took his hand gliding his fingers through hers. Instantly he noticed Hallie's relief knowing she wasn't alone. Seb didn't make eye contact with anyone as they headed to the elevator. Pressing the floor they needed to go on, nobody questioned Hallie as to why she was there, and Hallie made sure she was not making eye contact with anyone for them to ask questions.

Arriving at Sergeants office, Hallie knocked a couple of times before entering. Sarge rose from his chair along with a detective Hallie did not recognise. Hallie kept calm and made sure her face showed no emotion.

"Hallie, thank you for coming, this is Detective Roberts who is assisting me." Before Sergeant could finish, Detective Roberts was walking over to Hallie. His stocky build and dirty blonde hair stood out for Hallie. She had never met this man before and was curious as to where he came from.

"Pleasure to put a name to the face." His deep voice was inviting, something Seb did not like.

"Can't say the same about you. How long have you been here?"

Sergeant took the opportunity to answer, "Detective Roberts has been here since you left the station."

Hallie nodded, "ahh so you're my replacement." Seb took a step closer to Hallie still hasn't said a word.

Detective Roberts sniggered, "I guess I am, big boots to fill though." Seb remained keeping eye contact on Roberts, he noticed that he was trying to flirt but making a poor attempt from it. "And this is?" Roberts eye line now moved to Seb.

"Sebastian Chandler." Seb's hand met with Roberts shaking it firmly with a nod. Hallie looked over to Sergeant, "Right can we get this over with." Sergeant nodded and gestured for Hallie and Seb to take a seat. Surprised that this was not taking place in an interview room, but Hallie remained quiet.

"So Hallie, I lied to you. I didn't need a statement from you about the station. I just needed to get you here somehow." Hallie straightened and leaned forward. Confusion spread across her face.

"Why?"

"I asked." Both eyes now on Roberts, even more confusion for Hallie. Seb however introjected.

"That doesn't answer her question."

Sarge and Roberts both looked to Seb, straightening their posture, both unsure on Seb as they knew nothing about him.

Sarge continued, "Now it wasn't all a lie, I just needed to you write a statement I don't need a verbal one, but Roberts asked to meet you in person as… well best you explain, but Hal you are not going to like it." Hallie looked to Seb then back to Roberts and waited for him to talk.

"So, as you know, Adam Fowler had led a double life. Has a wife and a child as well as previously seeking something with yourself before taking you and killing those people. Fowler's wife has been reaching out to the department to try and get in contact with yourself." A lump had formed in Hallie's throat, her hands were once again clamped into fists.

Seb leaned forward and diverted his eye contact to Sergeant but before Seb could speak Hallie stood up. "You mean to tell me, you got me to come down here, so I could speak with his wife, tell her what she wants to hear, give her closure. Are you for real?" Hallie's voice began to raise. She turned to Sergeant, "I thought I could trust you, why the fuck would I want to speak to her?"

Sergeant stood, "I knew you wouldn't want to, but Roberts made some good points." Roberts tried to talk but Hallie cut him off again.

"Bull shit he made some good points. I'm leaving."

Roberts went to block the doorway so Hallie couldn't leave to which Seb stood very close to his face, "I suggest you move before I make you."

Roberts's lip curled, "Is that a threat?"

Seb smiled, looked him up and down before getting back in his face, "No, that is a fact." Roberts looked to Sergeant and reluctantly stepped to the side. Seb opened the door allowing Hallie to exit first not until she was stopped on her path by a blonde haired, petite woman.

"Excuse me, are you Hallie?" Hallie stopped in her tracks and Seb knew exactly who this woman was. No answer left Hallie's lips.

"I'm Megan, my husband used to work with you and, well I just wanted to talk to you." Hallie froze, she had no idea what she had walked into. Roberts and Sarge began to walk close behind to which Seb stood tall and shouted to them both, "What is this an ambush or something?"

No answer from Sarge or Roberts. Seb looked to Hallie and leaned to her ear. "Hal?" Hallie looked up to Seb, pleading with her eyes to help her get out of there. Seb knew this immediately and took her hand to help guide her from that situation. However, her wrist on the other hand was being pulled back. Megan had tried to get Hallie to stay. Hallie however saw red and grabbed Megan's hand twisting it and pulling it to behind her back, restricting her from any movement. Hallie then spat through gritted teeth, "Touch me again and I will break this fucking wrist, do you understand me." Realising her grip, she pushed Megan away from her and began to turn away.

"I just want to know why he lied Hallie? I want to know why Adam Fowler, the man I thought loved me would do that to you and those other people." Hallie stopped and turned around slowly, she walked back over to Megan, her eyes were filled with tears whereas Hallie's were filled with anger.

"I don't know why he lied. I don't know why he killed those people as well as people I cared about in the army. I don't know why he never mentioned you or your child. I don't FUCKING KNOW. So, leave me alone!" Hallie was close to Megan's face, shock was over not only hers but Sergeants and Roberts's faces.

Megan stuttered, "You can't even say his name, can you?" a singular tear fell down her cheek.

Hallie then looked Megan up and down, "That name will never roll off my tongue. And you should not shed a single tear for that monster." No response. Hallie looked over to Sergeant and Roberts then turned to walk back to Seb and place her hand in his.

Back at the car, Hallie exhaled loudly. She had so many emotions building up however before she could even talk or get in the car, Seb had pulled her close and kissed her. Ease filled Hallie's body as she stepped in closer to his body. As Seb pulled away, he remained smiling at Hallie.

Hallie tilted her head to the side and smiled in return. "What's that smile for."

"You, using my choice of wording all that time ago, nice to hear."

Hallie frowned, "Well least I can take orders and remember them. Looks like we have an audience." Hallie looked up to the second floor to see that Sergeant and Detective Roberts was looking down at them. Seb took this opportunity to kiss Hallie again, this time he placed his hand behind her head pulling her in tightly however as Hallie placed her arms around Seb's torso this displayed his gun he had tucked into his belt. Sergeant and Detective Roberts focused on this then were in conversation with one another.

Arriving back at the manor, Hallie felt somewhat betrayed by her old boss. She trusted that man and he knew her feelings on the station let alone on Fowler and to be ambushed like that was out of order. Seb placed his arm around Hallie as they walked through the manor doors, "I don't trust that new detective they have. Something about him just feels odd." Hallie nodded in agreement. "I'm going to do some digging into his past, see if anything sticks out. I think it might be best if you keep contact with Sergeant to a minimal darling, just till after this all settles." Hallie understood where Seb was coming from, she didn't like that someone she used to trust did something like that. Agreeing with Seb, he kissed her on the top of her head before heading up to his office to try and get some dirt on Detective Roberts. Hallie however took it upon herself to head to the basement and have a little chat with Katie. Any day now she would die, so least Hallie could do was try get as much information from her that she knew.

32

The basement lights flickered on, the strobe lights took a bit longer than most bulbs to illuminate the room quickly as they needed to warm up. Katie was sat in a ball, her arms wrapped around her knees which were tucked in tightly into her chest. Her right eye was the only one which was open, the other had swollen shut. Hallie joined Katie on the floor crossing her legs and leaning forwards placing a drink and a Mars bar in front of her. Katie looked hesitantly at this and then back to Hallie before taking anything. Hallie nodded to Katie acknowledging her permission to eat. Katie crouched forwards and unwrapped the chocolate bar slowly eating it with a painful jaw.

"Katie, why did you sell us out?" Hallie sounded empathetic, like she cared. Deep down she did care for Katie after she helped her however seeing her in this state was not nice.

Katie looked up and a tear fell from her only open eye, "because I love him, I thought he loved me. He has done this before, but I thought it would be different." Hallie nodded and continued.

"So, he has led you down a false path before? When?"

Katie swallowed her small mouthful before picking up her drink to help wash it down. "That is why Ashlyne dislikes me so much, I helped Tate get Ashlyne, befriended her before he took her."

Things were starting to piece together, that was why Ashlyne volunteered to capture Katie, she was taking revenge. Hallie couldn't blame her. "So why go behind Seb's back, the amount he has done for you? Why tell Tate?"

Inhaling slowly, Katie's face changed as if she was possessed by a demon, the once empathetic look she had had vanished. A smile spread across her face, "because Seb is not Tate. Tate sees me for me, and I do not care. I will always choose Tate. But now I am stuck here I am sure he has got her by his side." Instantly shock, Katie's mouth fell open and her eyes widened. She made a mistake, let slip that Tate had another person helping him capture people.

"Katie, who?" Hallie leaned closer.

Katie was shaking her head, hitting herself with her own hands, she picked up the drink and launched across the room. Hallie had to think quick, a way to help calm her down and get information.

"Katie, stop. Look at me." Hallie pinned both her arms to the ground and was close to her face. Remaining calm she looked Katie in her eye. "If you tell me who is helping Tate, I promise you I will unchain you so you can escape. You are not to tell anyone. Tate obviously likes you as he has been looking for you." Katie's eye lit up, a small smile beamed from her face.

"Re-really. He does care."

Hallie nodded, "He does, now I am a sucker for helping and I think what you did was so brave." Katie nodded in agreement. "Katie, you did what anyone else would, you helped the man you love. That takes balls to do. Now help me so I can help you. Who is helping Tate." Katie then looked down to the floor shaking her head, unsure whether to trust Hallie.

"Katie, let me help you get rid of the woman who is trying it on with your man." Hallie demanded causing Katie to look up, her eye filled with anger.

"Her name is Jessica. She has always wormed her way in with Tate. She has people on the inside and in the police to help make sure her and Tate are not seen. She isn't very smart, but she has her looks to help her get what she wants. Bitch." Katie spat, Hallie was surprised Katie would break that easy. She needed a full name or a description.

"What's her full name?"

"I don't know, she had so many identifications I was never able to track her full name down. All I know is her initial is J.R. which is what she used to sign messages off with."

Hallie sighed, she needed to get this information to Seb and Gibb. "Thank you Katie, for being honest with me at least."

Katie smiled, but her smile soon faded when Hallie began to walk away. She had a description of Jessica and an initial, Katie was no more use to her. "Hallie, you said you'd let me go."

Hallie turned slowly at the end of the stairs, "One thing I learned the hard way, trust no one. You're dead to me Katie. Pressing the light switch Katie was now in darkness. Screams bellowed from Katie's lungs, screams which led into cries for help. Hallie bolted the basement door closed and was greeted by Wren on the other side of the door which startled Hallie.

"Jesus Wren, made me jump." Hallie could feel her heart rate had risen from being startled.

Wren sniggered, "I heard most of the conversation, nicely done."

"Not my first rodeo." Joining Hallie for the walk back to Seb's office both were trying to figure out how to find Jessica. However as both entered the office Seb and Gibb were deep in conversation and pointing to monitors which surrounded them. Seb noticed Hallie had walked in and as she approached him, he still acknowledged her arrival and greeted her with a kiss on the top of her head.

Hallie pointed to the screens around, "What's all this?"

Gibb screen shares what he has on his laptop screen to the TV ahead, "Getting as much information on this new detective and the more I dug, the more interesting he got." Seb gestured to Hallie to take a seat which she accepted, Wren rolled his eyes, "I'll stand, thanks for the offer though bud." Hallie chuckled and Seb looked to Wren and gave him the finger to which both laughed from.

Gibb continued, "Detective Casey Roberts. Became an apprentice as soon as he left high school, slowly worked up the ranks until he went to take his Detective Degree Holder which he passed with flying colours. Has a somewhat normal family, both parents still together enjoying retirement on the Isle of Wight and has a sister who doesn't work but has lots of contacts high up judging by these photos." The photos showed a petite woman with long blonde hair, her ocean blue eyes were captivating however most photos showed her with minimal clothing on, whether that be a dress that enhanced her fake boobs or that she was on a yacht somewhere in a very skimpy bikini. Hallie however looked straight to Wren who nodded in agreement with Hallie's eyes. Seb noticed this nod to Wren.

"Do you two know her?"

Hallie stood up, faced Seb. "We don't but Tate sure as hell does."

Gibb took a pause from looking at his laptop and focused on Hallie. "How do you know that?"

"Because Katie just described that very person to me, including her name. This woman apparently signs off all her messages with the initials with J.R. That is how they have not been caught, because her brother works as a fucking detective here." Seb then loaded his laptop and pulled up another image to which Hallie was beyond surprised with.

"What the..." Hallie rose from her chair and walked slowly to the screen.

Seb spoke softly, "looks like they took their detective degree together and became each other's friends." The photo showed a group of people holding their degree certificates in their hands, and standing next to each other was Casey Roberts and Adam Fowler and on the side lines was Sergeant. Sergeant looks like he was their awarding the candidates of their achievements.

Hallie spat out, "so that's why they ambushed me at the station, that is why Roberts got my job, cause they all know each other. That is why Roberts knows Fowler's wife. It all makes sense."

Wren walked to the screen and pointed, "and if they all knew each other, and Jessica is working with Tate, then one thing is for certain. Roberts is protecting his sister or."

"Or he works with Tate." A silence filled the room, pieces of the puzzle were adding together and now, they needed to attend this auction and shut it down from its core. Kill everyone involved and most importantly, trust no one.

5th August

33

The day had finally arrived. After much anticipation, planning and sleepless nights to make sure the plan was perfect, this was it. This was the time to take down this establishment, take Tate down and all of his sick team with him.

Seb had ensured he had as many of his team available and in the best positions possible. This was unlike any other mission he had endured. This auction was well thought of and planned to ensure no one could crack it.

Gibb had managed to get the location of the auction the day before it was due to be released to give them all a head start. The location was a country manor located near the south of England on the outskirts of Lymington. Gibb had managed to get the floor plan of this manor and any secret passages. Fortunately, due to its historic age he managed to find out that it had a substantially large basement which was once a wine cellar. This led the suspicion that this was where the prisoners were being kept. The estimation of numbers was unknown, until they were inside, they had no idea the level this establishment was at. Judging by the guest list, this had to be one of the biggest operations they would hold. Seb had managed to get a track on Jake Henderson, Charlie's brother, however instead of capturing him they just kept tabs on his every move these past few weeks. It would look too suspicious if he were captured.

The peak of summer had definitely arrived, the evenings were light and warm which made it the perfect evening to have a gathering or in this case a secret auction of human slaves. Hallie was upstairs for most of the day preparing physically and mentally. First starting the day off in the gym training with Ashlyne ensuring her fighting skills were up to scratch. Each hit Ashlyne took she attempted to get one back, but Hallie managed to swiftly dodge.

"What type of concussion did you have to give you this superpower?" Ashlyne laughed as she pivoted quickly on the ball of her foot and swinging the other leg around to kick Hallie in her torso. Hallie however saw this move and reacted quickly grabbing Ashlyne's leg and swiping out her other causing her to fall onto her back.

"The type where you get four months of sleep to recharge." Laughing breathlessly, she let go of Ashlyne's leg and reached her hand out to help her up, sweat beading from both their bodies. Unknown to them Seb and Wade had been watching on the sidelines, both with smiles on their faces.

"I reckon your fighting is up to scratch, I guess." Ashlyne breathed winking back to Hallie to ensure she knew it was a joke. However, before Hallie could reply Seb spoke up,

"Think both of you can call it quits now, don't want you tired for tonight."

Hallie laughed and breathed out, "what don't think I could take another round?"

Seb chuckled and Ashlyne wiped her towel across her forehead to capture as much sweat from her head, "well I reckon she could take you down." Hallie looked over to Seb with a grin, she knew Seb would not fight her, but she was up for the challenge.

"I'm not going to fight you Hal so wipe that grin from your face."

"What's up boss, afraid she will kick your ass." Wade pulled Ashlyne close and wrapped his arms over her shoulders so they both were watching.

Seb looked over to Hallie as she had her arms open accepting this request to fight. "Fine, but don't overdo it Hal." Hallie smiled and kissed Seb on the cheek.

"And don't you go easy on me."

From this Seb pulled his t-shirt off over his head and threw it to one side. Hallie took a swig of water and was ready. She had practised with Seb fighting but was more he wore the paddles and she punched like crazy. Never had she fought him like this, knowing it was practise she was happy it was Seb as she would be taking out a fair few men tonight.

Seb sighed and placed his hands into fists, "right, let's get this over with." He didn't want to lay a finger on Hallie as he promised he would never hurt her. In his defence it was practise for tonight if not he would never do this.

Hallie swung first, then second, then third, all hits dodged by Seb. Her leg then swung around catching Seb off guard and smacking his bare skin on his abdomen. Seb returned with a low kick swinging under Hallie's legs taking them both out and her ending up on the floor. Quickly, Hallie rose back to her feet and continued with her punches, Seb however caught one and spun her close hold her in a tight grip.

Seb breathed in Hallie's ear, "ready to admit defeat darling." This however spurred Hallie, her left elbow went into his ribs causing him to release his grip slightly but just enough for Hallie to spin out of it making Seb lose balance, Hallie took this opportunity to then swipe his legs out and sit on top of him.

"I don't like to lose." Seb then sat up to meet Hallie's gaze, he grabbed hold of her and spun Hallie to her back while he then sat on top of her. Whispering in her ear, "neither do I." Hallie let out a breathless laugh and agreed to tap out. This fight could go on forever and Seb was right, they needed to reserve all energy for tonight.

However, Gibb soon ran in nearly as breathless as Hallie and Seb.

"You need to see this! What the... what you guys doing?" Gibb had the look of confusion on his face. Curiosity taking over however Seb and Hallie were still on the floor looking at each other.

"Look at what Gibb?"

"I think it is better to show you." From this both their eyes met Gibb's and could see that this was important. Seb stood up and bent down but ended up picking Hallie up rather than helping her up.

"I can walk you know." Hallie laughed.

"I know, I just like having you in my arms." The laughs and smiles soon faded when they walked into the office and saw what was on the screens, images, so many images. Seb slowly lowered Hallie down for her to stand as he walked over to the computer.

"How many have they got?"

Gibb looked up disheartened, "around 12 women, 5 men and 7 children. All are there to be sold to the highest bidder." This was more than what they expected, the images were for the people attending the auction to see what they like and what they would want to bid for. The terror in each person's eyes, you could see they have been through hell and back being trapped there. Gibb continued, "I am running ID checks on them all, around 7 have missing person reports on them, some are people who were just in the wrong place at the wrong time."

Hallie then walked up to the screen to get better look at these people, "Seb, we need to re-evaluate this plan, if we eliminate the people who are responsible for this, where do these people go? I mean before I would suggest Sergeant, but I don't trust that new detective." Gibb then stood up and looked to Hallie, "I am running checks on him, I recognise him but can't pinpoint where and because he seems so interested in Fowler I wonder if it has something to do with him." Hallie nodded then continued to look at these people's images, she had never seen anything like it. All she wanted to do was get them all out now.

Now, they needed to re-evaluate the plan and hope it would work out as there are too many lives at stake.

34

The evening was creeping in, and time was running out. After seeing all the victims that were being held ready to sell like cattle was sickening. The auction was due to begin at 9 pm, guests to arrive starting from 8 pm. The events theme was a black-tie masquerade ball. The masks to hide each person's identity. Dinner was chaos, everyone was away doing something whether that be research, weapon checks, surveillance checks you name it, not one person stayed in the same room. Ella had managed to find Seb as he was disappearing in and out.

Approaching his office door, Ella crept inside to see Wren and Gibb doing checks of the victims' names and where they are from to try figure out why they had been targeted. Wren looked up to Ella, "You okay Hun?"

Ella looked up and smiled, "Yes, I actually came here to ask Seb a question?"

This got Seb's attention, they hadn't really spoken much since patching things up. "Everything okay?"

Ella cleared her throat, "well, I know you guys are crazy busy and this case is just, well, fucked up. But I wanted to ask if you guys could use an extra set of hands?" Wren looked to Ella confused by the question.

Seb closed his laptop lid and leaned over his desk, "as in an extra pair of hands... doing?"

"Well anything, Toby is a very smart kid, and as much as I hate seeing him do this stuff, he is very good at it and enjoys it. So, I'm asking if Gibb could use Toby's help at all?" Both Wren and Seb's eyebrows raised. Surprised by what Ella was asking.

Before they could answer, Ella continued, "now before you call me a hypocrite and whatnot, he knows what is going on, as he has been sneaking around the manor for weeks hacking into shit he should not have touched!" Ella turned to the door to see Toby peering his head around the corner. Seb laughed from this.

"Gibb, you happy having Toby help ya?"

"Of course, always welcome." Gibb smiled and nodded to Toby to which he returned his nod. Ella noticed this and scowled at Toby, "don't think this makes you a hacker or whatever now, you are helping that is all, then you go back to doing normal kid shit after all this. Understand!"

"Yes mother." Toby walked up to Ella and gave her a hug. Toby was taller than Ella however, Ella still wore the trousers in that family.

From that, Wren followed Ella out to go and get ready for the evening events. Seb soon followed up, but when he walked into the bedroom, his eye line went directly to Hallie in a silk red tight dress which had a slit up the left leg. Hallie placed a garter on and slid her knife into this, a gun would show to much but better to be armed. Her hair was straight and fell elegantly down her back. Seb's eyes were taking in Hallie, noticing every inch of her. From her freshly painted toenails to the maroon red matt lipstick and finally admiring the red lace mask covering the top half of her face. Seb bit the inside of his cheek, he knew there wasn't much time before they had to leave but he could not resist himself. Hallie noticed Seb and slowly walked up to him. Seb was already in his suit all he needed was his mask.

On the dresser next to the bedroom door was Seb's black mask, Hallie picked this up and placed this on Seb's face. Looking directly in his eyes, Hallie's stomach filled with butterflies, there was something about him being masked which lit something inside her. Seb placed his thumb on her lips, gently pulling down on her bottom lip revealing her teeth, Hallie kept her gaze on Seb, not moving. Seb looked back into Hallie's eyes and smiled.

"You look good masked." Hallie whispered, a slight croak left her throat. Seb's hand then began to slide down to Hallie's neck holding a firm grip, enough for Hallie to tilt her head closer in Seb's direction.

"Do you enjoy the unknown darling." Hallie's response was a deep exhale which ignited something in Seb, a devious grin appeared, and he pulled Hallie in close and picked her up as her legs wrapped around his waist. Both were ready to leave, but this fuelled something inside of them both. Hallie was submissive, no words left her mouth, just remained staring into Seb's eyes. Gliding his hand slowly up Hallie's spine until he stopped reaching onto Hallie's neck and holding a firm grasp. Hallie smiled, "Think that makes my outfit." Looking down at his hand then back to reach his gaze. Seb looked puzzled, tilting his head waiting for an explanation from Hallie. Hallie took her hand to meet his around her throat and whispered, "My perfect necklace." Before Hallie could react, Seb instantly smiled and lifted Hallie pulling her close to his body but as he placed Hallie on the bed, there were knocks on the door.

Sighing, Seb's head hung low causing Hallie to laugh. "I meant what I said, soon as this is done, they are all being kicked out!" Hallie nodded in agreement, however Seb was still lying on top of Hallie.

"What you thinking?"

Smiling, Hallie admired Seb's perfect straight teeth, he had such a beautiful smile which Hallie was grateful she got to see often. "Just, you. Still to this day, you somehow manage to make me breathless. Somehow you make me feel, ease, calm." More knocks at the door however Seb still chose to ignore them, and Hallie was in no rush to move but before Hallie could answer Ashlyne was barging in with Wade and Wren.

"And that is the reason no one was answering the door. These dickheads thought you had been abducted or something!" Ashlyne laughed, Seb slowly got up and helped Hallie up from the bed.

"Well, in our defence it wouldn't be the first time!" Wren tried to defend himself.

"I mean, we can give you guys five minutes if you wanna continue with this." Ashlyne smirked winking at Hallie.

Seb stepped behind Hallie and helped her zip her dress back up then kissed the side of her neck, neither cared that they had a bedroom full of people. Hallie picked up her clutch bag from the dresser and walked to the door with Ashlyne.

"Right, let's get this over and done with then." Wren clapped his hands and rubbed them together with excitement, even if this was going to one of the hardest missions they were to ever endure, the adrenaline was kicking in with the blood that was ready to be spilled. Wren trusted Adam to stay at the manor with Gibb and his family just in case someone was to get scent of their base and attack while they were out.

Gibb had created a code word with just Seb and Hallie just in case they were under attack back at the manor by Tate's team.

"Hogwarts? Really Gibb? You want that to be the code word?"

"What? I think it is a great idea! No one will have a clue and unlike normal things like 'Olympus, White House, Palace, Manor, they are all so boring. Least this adds a bit of magic to the mix." Seb let out a small snigger rubbing his hand over his face to conceal his reaction. "Yeah, Hogwarts it is."

Gibb nodded then looked back at Hallie, "See, Seb doesn't think it is a stupid code word." Hallie looked to Seb noticing he was concealing his laughter.

"Okay, Hogwarts it is you great big nerd." Hallie pulled Gibb under her arm and hugged him. Neither one of them were fans of physical touch towards each other but Gibb and Hallie had developed such a sibling like bond that they acted like they were brother and sister constantly.

Gibb looked at Hallie, his face had lost all happiness he was once feeling and was now stern, "Hal, be careful. Okay?"

"You too!" Hallie tapped Gibb's arm and walked out to the hallway placing a long black coat on to complete her outfit. Seb however remained by Gibb's side. Lifting the side of his suit jacket, Seb revealed a jet-black handgun and held it in front of Gibb. Gibb did not take this straight away, he looked to Seb awaiting a reason he was holding a gun.

"Take this, and trust no one until we get back." Seb didn't meet Gibb's eye, his eyes remained on Hallie. Gibb took the gun and slid it in-between his belt and his jeans.

As Seb got confirmation that his teams were all in position around the perimeter of the target it was time for them to leave. Seb took Hallie in his black Jaguar, closely followed by Wren, Wade and Ashlyne. After waiting for what seemed like a lifetime, it was finally here. This was the time that they would take out this sick operation.

Pulling up at the remote location, Seb kept his hand on Hallie's leg the whole duration of the car ride, her hand held in his grip. As the car stopped before Hallie was about to get out, Seb pulled her arm back.

"What's wrong?" confusion on Hallie's face, was he having second thoughts?

"Here." Seb lifted the handle of the glove compartment and inside was a ring box. Taking the wedding band out carefully he gently lifted Hallie's left hand and glided the ring along her finger. Speechless, all Hallie was doing was admiring the ring and how it fitted perfectly alongside her engagement ring. Looking back to meet Seb's eyes he smiled, "I'm having no one touch what is mine."

Hallie laughed, "You think a ring will stop them."

"No, but gives them a second chance to leave you alone once you show them you're no one's but mine. We can go to the registry office after this, sign the papers and all if you like?"

Hallie leaned closer to Seb, "Sounds perfect! And if they still don't get the message after seeing the rings?"

Seb cupped his hand under Hallie's chin, "then I will have a collection of ring fingers of every man that touches you." Hallie sniggered; she knew he was being serious but answered with a kiss.

"Just be careful darling."

As Hallie put her mask on, she turned back to Seb, "the same for you."

As both left the car, a chauffeur took Seb's Jaguar and parked it around the corner. The location of Seb's car was pinged to Gibb's computer just in case a quick getaway was needed. The five of them slowly walked up the marble stairs to enter the large country manor, each one of them had studied the floor plan so they knew this place inside and out even though they had never visited. Seb made contact with his team ensuring all were in position ready. Seb gave a nod to Hallie and the others giving the go ahead to move in. As they stepped into the manor though, it was not what they expected to see.

35

The manor was filled with masked people whether that be guests, waiters, dancers, everyone wore a mask. Some more extravagant than others. The dancers wore small black masks which only covered around their eyes. The dancers were in boxes which surrounded the manors main hall, this was like a theatre. They had managed to convert the manor into their own private theatre, it included a stage, thick red velvet curtains with tables and chairs scattered across the marble floor. Seb pulled Hallie in close and squeezed her slightly before walking away with Wren to scope around to try catch Tate or Harold before this could all begin.

"Meet back here soon as the auction is about to start if we make no progress, agreed?" Seb said casually for all the team to respond through their earpieces.

"Agreed"

As Hallie was observing every part of the room, trying to get a lead of someone using a side door which looked heavily guarded by very large men all masked and suited. This was going to be one long evening, however Hallie had an idea.

"Ash, I need you to flirt with someone."

Ashlyne looked back to Hallie and smiled, "why can't you?"

"Because you flirt with them, keep them distracted while I check that door people keep slipping out of." Seb grunted through the earpiece, "Hal you are going nowhere alone."

Hallie looked to Ashlyne to which she nodded, "I'm not alone, have you all in my ear, the first sign of trouble I will already be out of there.

We only have 45 minutes till this auction is supposed to begin. Need to scope this place as much as we can before we can extract them."

A sigh from Seb, "fine, you have ten minutes down there then if you are not out we will be down there."

"Yes sir." Hallie sniggered, she knew Seb would be smiling from her calling him Sir. Gibb however interfered with the line. "Right, let's not do that as unfortunately I know what both your minds are like. Hallie, timer starts when you go in."

Ashlyne headed over to the large bodyguard who's lip instantly curled up at the sight of Ashlyne. She wore a tight sapphire silk dress and sliver stilettos. Pulling her hair to one side to expose her neck yet covering her other ear which held the earpiece, she couldn't be too careful.

"So, I am going to take a wild guess and say you are not a guest but working?"

Chuckling, the man nodded, "That I am. Least I have a view on everything though." His voice deep, husky yet recognisable to Ashlyne.

"Well, that is a shame, as I wondered if you cared to join me for a drink?" Ashlyne placed her hand on the man's shoulder to which he looked at her hand then looked Ashlyne up and down slowly.

"I can grab a drink with you, but then I will be back working."

Ashlyne smiled, "Good, I like a man who is career driven. Come." Ashlyne took the man's hand and guided him to the bar next to the door. Hallie found this the perfect time to slip through and was greeted by darkness with a downward stairwell. Hallie slipped her heels off and took the stairs barefoot to reduce her sound. To what she was greeted with made her speechless.

"Hal, talk to me." Seb tried to keep his emotions in check when he hadn't heard from Hallie.

"The- there are so many of them! What the fu- I can't believe this." Hallie was stuttering, whispering which made Seb's concern grow.

Calmly, Seb continued. "How many? Roughly so we get numbers right for extraction."

"Uhh" Hallie was muttering away trying to count. "There are around thirty, maybe forty people." Seb looked to Wren in shock, this was more than they expected. They needed to arrange for a way to get these people extracted safely.

Gibb intervened, "Hal, you have five minutes." Hallie nodded to herself, she continued through the long corridor. Each person looked drugged, none were awake, talking, nothing. Hallie slowly jogged to see the other end of the corridor. Every person was in a glass box, it looked like they had been their weeks considering the mess they were in. Hallie could hear some commotion at the other end of the corridor, so she slowly approached the sound.

Before getting too close she radioed back, "Gibb tell me when I got two minutes left, but right now, I can't talk as I am not alone." This made eyebrows raise but no one answered, the line stayed clear ready for Gibb's two-minute warning.

Hallie could hear muttering coming from one of the glass boxes, slowly she peered around to try and get an idea as to who was talking and it was Tate, but he was not alone. Joining him was a petite female, Hallie guessed it was Jessica.

"I told you, he would be here, and he will be so quit your moaning Tate!"

"It has been handy having him on the inside, but if this gets out, it will be his head I get first."

Jessica stopped Tate in his tracks and pulled him back to her, "my brother is not a traitor, he is in this just as much as you and I are. Harold has done enough for us, the least we could do is help in this little operation and surprisingly look how useful I have been."

Tate placed his hands around Jessica's head and tilted her head up, "you have been more than perfect. Especially since Katie made her disappearance. She never matched to you." A smile left Jessica as she kissed Tate however startling them a scream bellowed from one of the girls' boxes.

"Fuck you both, you sick fucking bastards!" Tate walked over to her box and smiled, "You will be the first one I look forward to being sold." The girl spat at Tate through the small hole where food and drink are transported, but he pulled out his set of keys and began to unlock her padlock causing the girl to back into a corner scared. Hallie was ready to step up and intervene when Gibb announced through the earpiece, "Two minutes Hal, need to get out now."

Hallie muttered under her breath and contemplated whether to stay and fight, get Tate off guard now, but Seb now demanded, "Hallie, get out. Now."

"Fuck." Hallie frowned and began to run as quietly as she could back along the long corridor, passing all the innocent, helpless humans who are being caged ready for auction. She felt helpless leaving them but as she ran, she whispered. "I will get you all out."

"Ashlyne, is it clear."

From this Wade answered, "Yes clear now." Hallie snuck through the door and walked to join Ashlyne rescuing her from the man's rescuing.

"Hey, sorry I'm late. Shall we find our seats?" Hallie looked to Ashlyne.

"Yes, we better. It was nice to meet you and thank you for the drink!" Ashlyne clinked her glass with the mans and began to walk away before he could respond. Wade was watching the man closely.

"I want him dead." Wren chuckled from Wade's comment. They all met back at their table and took their seats. Close to the back, an easy escape. Hallie was ready to quietly explain what she had seen however Harold Kingston took to the stage which made her speechless.

"Welcome everyone to Crescent Moon. I see some familiar faces and some new. So, an introduction is in order. We have held this once a year for the past five years and is always under the radar. To reassure you, we have people working from all backgrounds to ensure your privacy, your lives and your reputations are not affected by your attendance here. Now each one of you has something in common. You all want something money could not buy, that is taboo. Whether that be to work for you, to flatter you, to be used at full advantage, to allow you to fulfil your wildest fetishes. This. This is the place where your money can buy it. We have a wide range of humans available at your earliest convenience. So, grab a drink, sit back and the bidding will begin in fifteen minutes. Please be aware of my team working around you, and do not be alarmed by the armed team that surround these walls, we want everything to run smoothly as I am sure you do too. Enjoy."

36

Hallie informed the team in with what the contents of the basement was, and what Tate had said how they have people working elsewhere to ensure they are not caught. Seb placed his hand on Hallie's lap under the table which made her relax slightly. This was more intense than what she imagined. However, her eye line slowly moved away from Seb and locked onto two people close to the stage talking.

"Seb, that is Jessica, who Tate was talking to. And that, that can't be?"

Seb met Hallie's eye line discretely and his eyebrows raised, he looked back to Hallie to ensure that they did not look suspicious. "Is that Detective Roberts? He must be the one inside for Tate and his team." Seb nodded and looked back to Hallie and the others.

"We need to extract now before this gets out of hand. B team you in position on standby?" Another deep voiced man responded on the end of the earpiece, "yes sir, ready for your call."

Seb nodded and looked to his team, to which Wade and Ashlyne rose and began to walk out to the courtyard. Wren took the stairs to observe and eliminate anyone near and allow C team access to the building. However, before he could get to the balcony he was stopped by two men.

"This area is off limits, you can go join the party downstairs."

Wren smiled and continued walking.

"Hey, I said this area is off limits, don't make me remove you myself."

Wren stopped and slowly turned around, "like to see you try."

From this, the large man began to run towards Wren when he quickly took him out crouching and sliding his leg across the ground causing the man to fall with a loud thud. The other man went to pull out his gun when Wren was already charging at him and managed to catch him off guard to collect his gun. Releasing the barrel so all ammunition fell to the floor, gripping the stock of the gun Wren pulled back quickly and then jabbed the man in the throat causing him to bleed fast. Gurgles leaving his mouth, hands holding the gun in place as it was now lodged in his oesophagus. The other man had now stood up and grabbed Wren from behind. Crouching down, this caused the man to fall over Wren's shoulders, and with his knife he pressed into the man's throat slicing it quickly to allow both the men to bleed out. Wren quickly entered the bedroom with the balcony and unlocked the door greeting C team.

"Took you long enough bud." One of the masked men joked.

Wren sniggered, "Well I had company, which I need a hand dragging into this room to lock them in, I would but need to try keep as much blood off this suit as I can."

Another masked man spoke up, "so no one suspects you're killing them, right?"

Wren looked up and nodded, "sure that, and I rented this suit." This made the team laugh down the earpieces. Seb spoke up, "Really, you rented that suit, for this?"

"Yeah, what's so funny about that?" Seb continued to laugh with Wade.

"What's funny is you are not getting your money back on that!" Wren looked down then back up at C team.

"Oh piss off, haven't you two got things to do." Wren snapped back.

Instructing C team on how to get to where the victims were being held, Wren soon joined the table just as the auction was about to start. The auction began, as instructed there would be three sales then an interval, then another three, interval and so on to ensure that bidding would remain high and to allow each 'customer' a chance to re fill on drinks and get to know their acquaintances. As Wren took his seat, he nodded to Seb giving him the heads up that C team were in the building. Each one was armed however all suited to blend in with the surroundings. A gong went off which silenced the room and music began to play. Two men appeared with a woman in their arms. Placing her on the metal chair which was centre stage, this woman had been in darkness for some time as she squinted her eyes trying to adjust her vision to make focus of what was going on. Her mouth gagged to make sure she did not scream mid auction but judging by the beatings she had been through she looked like she had already been silenced.

The woman was just in her underwear, her skin had bruises scattered all over her body, her hair was in a messy ponytail which was now matted, but the thing that drew Hallie in the most was her eyes. Her eyes looked, tired, scared but most of all like she was ready to admit defeat, she did not care whether she died right now, she was done and that was noticeable even a mile away.

The bidding now begun, it took Hallie some time to focus back into the room to her surprise the bidding was already in the fifty thousand until the gavel slammed on the wooden board announcing the winner. A large, plump man stood and took a small bow along with what you would assume was his wife. She was over the moon with the new purchase and his smile did not disappear until he was told that he was not able to take his winnings until the end of the auction.

"Congratulations to number thirteen on the first purchase of the night. Right moving swiftly on." The man wanted this auction to move quickly as he did not feel comfortable with this situation, especially as he had two men either side of him ensuring he was not to move a step.

As the third woman was sold, it was now time for an interval, and this was the perfect time to begin shutting this auction down. Seb took Hallie to the bar and grabbed two drinks for them both. Ashlyne took this opportunity to go snooping around the manor, as for Wade and Wren, both were taking care of trying to grab as many of Tate's team as they could. Hallie leaned into Seb to ensure no one could hear their conversation.

"I think we should call Sarge?" Seb's eyebrows raised, he was unsure on this idea. Hallie continued when she didn't get an answer. "I will make a call in one of the rooms, I will just ask him where he thinks Detective Roberts is, for all we know he could be here undercover?"

Seb nodded, "I doubt it but okay, meet you back here in ten

minutes, okay."

Hallie nodded and walked out and noticed a room along the corridor. Walking slowly up to it she looked around before turning the doorknob. Luckily, it was unlocked, and the room itself was empty. Hallie pulled her phone out from her clutch bag and began to dial.

37

Waiting for what seemed like a lifetime, Sergeant finally answered his phone.

"Hello?" His voice groaned as if he had just woken up.

"Sarge, sorry if I woke you but I need to ask you something."

Clearing his throat he sounded surprised, "Hallie, didn't think I would hear from you for a while. Just so you know I had no idea that Fowler's ex would turn up. Well not sure if it is an ex or a…"

Hallie didn't have time for this, "Sarge, sorry. Hate to interrupt but kind of on the clock here. Where is Detective Roberts. Is he working on a case at the moment?"

"Roberts. No, he has taken a week of annual leave, last I heard he was on the plane to Barbados on Monday. Says he might extend his holiday then be back in two weeks to focus on the case. Why?"

Hallie sighed; she was unsure whether to trust Sergeant. To trust anyone for that matter.

"Hallie? Is he not away or is there something I need to know."

Hallie looked to the floor and closed her eyes for a brief moment. "Sarge, can I trust you?"

"Of course you can. You should know that!" Hallie sighed once more and trusted her gut.

"Okay, Roberts isn't who he says he is. He is working with the same person that targeted the station, that put me in a coma, that currently is part of a very large sex trafficking and human auction as we speak. Can you get an armed response team to surround a perimeter which my team is already on. We underestimated how many people would be up for auction, many have active missing person cases on them, others not yet. We have an estimate of 30-40 victims, some in unbelievably bad ways, others that will need treatments. We are going to begin extractions any moment now." Hallie paused, waiting for an answer, she knew Sergeant was on the other line as she could hear his heavy breathing. "Sarge, did you get that?"

"Yes, just shocked, I knew he was hiding something, but not that. I will get armed forces and teams out to you within the hour Hallie you have my word." Hallie looked relieved, after thanking Sergeant she ended the call and continued to stare out the window when she noticed a shadow behind her in the glass reflection. Quickly, she spun around to find she was not alone in the room.

"What are you doing here then?" The man tilted his head looking Hallie up and down. Instantly she knew who this person was.

"I could ask you the same question Roberts." However as soon as Hallie said this, Seb and Wren knew they needed to find her.

"I'm on a case, and the suspects are in this building. Now, your turn to talk."

Hallie needed to think quick, "Very similar to you, I had intel of a client who was going to be here that I needed to extract." Roberts didn't back down; he took a step closer to Hallie however he was getting too close now, so Hallie stood back.

"Now what are the chances, us being in the same place. Maybe even looking for the same person. Well, I know that is not the case. But gives me re assurance that the person I need is here." Roberts had a smile slowly starting to appear which made Hallie extremely uncomfortable.

"Who is your target then."

Roberts laughed and continued walking towards Hallie, "You." This instantly made Hallie's stomach sink, she froze and Roberts noticed this. He quickly reached forward to grab Hallie however she ducked and swiftly missed his grip. Instantly heading for the door, this was someone who was too heavily built to take on in a fight. As Hallie reached the door it was now locked. Hallie turned back around to Roberts to see him waving the old key, taunting Hallie.

"Don't think I won't kill you." Hallie spat. Seb was trying to get through to Hallie, try and get an idea of where she could be, but Hallie didn't answer.

Roberts laughed, "I will give you a good chance. But I need you alive to be worth more money." From this Roberts threw the key across the other side of the room, waiting for Hallie to run and grab it. Hallie did just that, Roberts was quick too, he grabbed Hallie from behind and picked her up. Hallie was kicking with all her power until she kicked him in the groin. Roberts released his grip causing Hallie to fall to the floor.

"Fuck this, I don't care if you are dead or alive now you bitch." Before he could start charging at Hallie she answered Seb's call through the earpiece.

"I'm on the first floor, fifth room along, prick has locked me in."

Roberts laughed and clapped his hands together, rubbing them slowly as he stood back up, "is that your little boyfriend. Tell him, I will leave my mark on you before he ever sees you again." Seb unfortunately heard this lighting a fire inside him, he was now running down the stairs to get to this room quickly.

Laughing at Roberts's comment, "You think you will have me, think again." This made something turn for Roberts, his smile had now faded. "Tell me Hallie, how did you do it?"

Hallie looks plainly back at him, "Do what?"

"Kill Fowler. You and I both know that he didn't kill those people. It had something to do with your new little boyfriend." Hallie remained quiet and allowed Roberts to continue. "You see, is don't add up. Your lead suspect is now the person you are so called working with. And after you somehow vanish, Fowler calls in explaining you have been taken. I do believe that. But I don't believe it was Fowler who took you, it was your new boss. What was it Hallie, did he fuck you, make you fall in love with him and lead you in with his web of lies. I mean I know Fowler, I know his wife very well and you are just the slag that got in the way of it all!"

Hallie's face was beginning to go red with anger, she shouted, "I had no idea about his baby mamma and you fucking know it."

Roberts laughed devilishly, he licked his bottom lip and began to look Hallie up and down, "I know, well, least he managed to keep getting his dick wet with you. I mean, I would do the same."

Hallie now charged towards Roberts kicking her right leg out she crouched to the floor turning on the ball of her other foot, this cause

Roberts to lose his balance. Hallie threw multiple punches, towards his face and abdomen and Roberts tried to fight back catching Hallie a couple of times. Hallie tasted blood which made her instantly think he had busted her lip. Remembering she had a knife strapped in her garter, she knew she would pull this out at the perfect moment, when she needed it most, so she wasn't disarmed too quickly. However, Roberts now had hold of Hallie, tightly, she could feel her lungs gasping for more air as Roberts squeezed. His arm slowly raised to her neck putting her in a headlock. The key was close to her, she was trying to reach for this, but Robert's grip was getting tighter. Hallie then tried to reach down to her leg to grab her knife. Roberts then whispered in her ear, "I am going to fuck you so hard while you lay there unconscious." Hallie could hear the door being kicked in. Her fingertips were just about touching her knife. Until she managed to build enough strength to whip her head back and headbutt Roberts, this made his grip loosen once more giving her room to grab her knife and stab him in the neck. His grip was now completely released, Hallie leaned forward and grabbed the key, running to the door out of breath she quickly fought with the lock and the door was open. Seb greeted her first as she fell into his arms. Wren and Wade instantly went for Roberts.

"Where are you hurt." Concern over Seb's face he was looking at Hallie all over until his eyes focused on her lip, he gently placed his thumb over the cut to stop some of the bleeding.

"I'm fine, we need to do the extraction now. Armed responses are going to be joining us shortly." From this Seb looked up and nodded to Wade and Wren which made them leave the room quickly to find Ashlyne. The plan was about to take action.

Hallie walked up to Roberts as he was slowly bleeding out. Roberts smiled as blood was filling up his mouth, his once white teeth were now stained red. Attempting to get the words out, he stuttered, "you...are" coughing in-between words, "no...hope." Hallie crouched down to Roberts smiling back, "Maybe, but least I won't be dead for it." Hallie then pulled the knife from his throat but instead of pulling it out slowly she ripped it across his neck slicing it wide open. Seb stood back and just smiled as he watched this.

"Fuck you." Hallie spat down as she watched the life fade from Roberts's face. As she stood back up, she looked to Seb confused.

"What's with the smile?"

Seb raised his eyebrow and half-smiled, "would it be too much to say you killing someone is a very big turn on." Hallie giggled from this, after cleaning her knife with Roberts's suit she slowly walked up to Seb.

"Well, this is going to be one big turn on tonight then as I don't think he will be the only body we have on our hands."

Seb pulled Hallie close by her waist and smiled, "I hope fucking not darling." Just as they shared a kiss with one another Wade was shouting through the earpiece.

"Boss, got a situation here."

38

As Seb and Hallie joined Wade and Wren both were curious as to what had happened. Hallie was looking around the hall, "Where is Ash?" Wade then looked towards the stairs. However, before anyone could talk Ashlyne spoke up through the earpiece.

"Think we need to hurry up with this plan." She sounded breathless, curious as to where she was Hallie still continued to look for her.

"Where are you."

Breathless, Ashlyne responded, "taking care of a little mongrel feral dog." However, in the background you could hear a woman shouting back at her. "I am not a dog, you fucking psycho." Ashlyne giggled, "yes you fucking are. When are we going ahead with the plan, give me time to silence this thing." Hallie smiled to Seb, she enjoyed how crazy Ashlyne could be, she would make anyone smile on such a shit day. But before Seb could answer an announcement interrupted.

'The auction will resume in five minutes. Please could guests find their seats."

Seb looked to his team and smirked, "I reckon five minutes and its lights out. Everybody copy?" Throughout all earpieces you heard a variety of people responding, 'yes sir.' Seb continued, "Gibb you and T ready?"

"Yes sir. Five-minute countdown has started until lights out. I will channel into armed response and give them the heads up, the telephone mast will also be out of action so will be radio silence for the meantime with our line being the only one live and encrypted just for us." Seb nodded to Wren and Wade to get in position, B team were in the surrounding forest and driveway with snipers and C team remained close to the victims hiding in plain sight. As for Seb and Hallie, their target was Tate, and he was nowhere to be seen. Seb looked down to Hallie, his eyes darkened, "ready to play a game darling."

Hallie smiled and kissed him, their lips touched gently before Seb pulled Hallie in closer, his taste was intoxicating. "Thought you'd never ask." Seb then passed Hallie a handgun he had spare and they parted ways.

4-minute warning.

Ashlyne knew she couldn't let Jessica's death be shown as a murder, so instead she went into her clutch bag and pulled out a ready drawn needle filled with some sort of medication to make her death look natural. Jessica's eyes widened, she began to struggle however her restrains were too tight.

"Ashlyne, please, you don't have to do this. I can help you."

Ashlyne laughed flicking the readymade needle to get the last air bubble out from it. "You cannot help me, I am beyond help. Now need you to open your mouth for me. You will feel a sharp scratch."

Jessica spat at her feet nearly catching Ashlyne. Her eyes went to where her saliva landed on the carpet. Ashlyne frowned, "Did I stutter, open your mouth or I will get someone to open it for you!"

Jessica shook her head and kept her lips tight close together, "You have no one!"

However, Ashlyne's frown now turned into a smile, "Fancy getting your hands dirty?" Jessica thought Ashlyne was talking to herself which is something that wouldn't surprise her. The door slowly opened and Jessica's eyes widened, "help, help me, she is crazy, please!" she began to plead which made Ashlyne laugh even harder. Walking over, she put the needle on the bed ahead and put her arms around Wade. As she kissed him, she opened one eye slightly to see Jessica's reaction which was priceless. Her mouth had fallen open, she had no words.

"Oh, yeah he won't help you." Ashlyne taunted. From this Wade walked behind Jessica and pulled her mouth open. Screams bellowing causing Ashlyne to work fast. Taking the cap from the needle she injected the solution underneath Jessica's tongue which silenced her almost immediately. Instantly, she went limp, her head hung low and her once stiffened body now relaxed. Wade felt her neck for a pulse, nothing.

2-minute warning.

As Seb and Hallie returned to their seats, they waited for the others to join them. Wren followed, trying to adjust his suit from which Hallie leaned towards him and helped adjust his tie. Ashlyne and Wade then took to their seats and all looked slightly breathless.

"You all ready for this." Seb looked around the circular table, it was too late to back out now, but he wanted to make sure.

"Yes boss. How long we got." Wren was eyeing up the bar ahead.

Gibb responded, "40 seconds." Wren contemplated running to grab a drink when Hallie slid hers to him. Thanking her he swallowed the contents in one without guessing what the drink contained.

20 second warning.

Hallie slid off her heels, this was better barefoot. Ashlyne also noticed Hallie's actions and followed suit. Seb placed his hand around Hallie pulling her close.

"Stay safe." He whispered, Hallie leaned close placing her lips to his gently.

"See you at the end."

Gibb now spoke. "Three. Two. One. Lights out."

All power was now gone from the manor, screams and uncertainty filled the rooms. People were trying to escape, chaos was unravelling.

Seb then announces to his team, "Time to play!" From this they all stood and ran to their points. The main aim was to extract all of the victims safely and capture Tate and Harold. Running to the door that led them to the victims in their boxes, they needed to get everyone out.

B team were explaining through the radio that armed response had just arrived and they were stopping everyone who tried to escape the manor. They believed everyone was a suspect. Hallie and the team needed to work fast before they got caught.

39

Each person was in their own box. Some roamed free, some were restrained down with thick rope. Hallie started on the left while Ashlyne was on the right. Wren had managed to swipe the master keys from a guard so he was unlocking every box. Instructing everyone who could run to the stairs and to run and run fast.

"Gibb, I need you to patch into the armed response and tell them victims are coming out, they will stand out as all are wearing the bare minimum each has a number on their left arm, advise not to shoot or attack they need help."

"Copy." Toby was already typing away and had Sergeant on the other line ready for Gibb.

"WHO IS THIS?" Sergeant was in the mood for no jokes.

"Sarge, it is Gibb. Victims are now being freed, tell your team not to attack and they need help before they get taken by these sick bastards. Understand."

Sergeant was silent, he never heard Gibb speak to anyone like this.

"Sarge, do you copy?"

"Yea-Yes Gibb. Copy. But who is behind this Gi-." Before Sergeant could get an answer, the line went dead. Gibb couldn't explain anything now as it looked like Tate was trying to get back into the system. Gibb was putting every coding, every hack he could to keep him from getting back into the system.

Meanwhile, gunshots were now being fired across the manor. Seb looked to C team and instructed them to continue getting victims out safely. Meanwhile Wade, Wren and Seb would go to track down

Harold and Tate. Seb wanted to get his hands on them both before the police did. He never worked well with the police as he liked things in his control, so this was very unfamiliar territory for him. Seb managed to get eyes on Harold and Jake Henderson. Seb pulled his gun out and took a shot which hit Jason in the shoulder causing blood to splatter along the wall surrounding him, Harold however did not wait up for Jason he continued to run up the stairs. Wade ran for Jason. As he stood on top of him Jason attempted to pull his gun at Wade and shoot but Wade managed to knock his arm and the shot fired across the room hitting an old painting which now came crashing down to the floor. Wade wasted no time, with a couple of punches to the head, he then placed his gun in the centre of his forehead and shot. Blood pooled from this singular hole and the pressure from the shot caused Jason's eyes to bulge out from his sockets. Wade wiped his face and continued up the stairs in a hunt for Harold. Seb's thoughts would be that he was running for Tate, so he ventured up the staircase in search.

Wade and Wren waited outside on of the doors of the long hallway, nodding to Seb he shot at the door handle and Wren barged through the door gun in hand. Harold spun around quickly with his hands in the air.

"Ahh, gentleman, this is a misunderstanding. Do you not know who I am." With the power still out all you could see was Harold's silhouette from the moonlight. No answer to Harold, until he took a step closer and squinted, instantly his eyes widened.

"Now I am surprised you are on me and not my partner."

"Speaking of, where is Tate." Seb responded bluntly.

Harold laughed as he lowered his hands. "Sebastian Chandler, I have been informed about you and your team. Well played. But as to Tate's where abouts that all depends on one person." Harold chuckled deeply which began to annoy Seb instantly, he had no patience so instead, Seb lowered his gun to aim for Harold's shin and pulled the trigger. Harold fell to the floor almost instantly, swearing at Seb for shooting him.

"I won't ask you again. Where is Tate."

Harold was rolling around the floor squirming in pain. Seb looked to Wren who walked to Harold and hoisted him upright pulling his arms behind his back.

Harold now had plead in his eyes, "I told you, it depends on where she is!" shouting back, saliva was forming around the creases of his lips.

Seb crouched to meet his level, "where who is?"

Harold looked up slowly, a smile forming, his eyes squinted as he spat the words, "Hallie. Precious little one isn't she. Well, she was when I looked after her. I say I done a surprisingly decent job sending her off to the army. Even now, look how she turned out, she would be worth a pretty penny I think for that bod-." Before Harold could finish his sentence Seb shot the other leg. They needed to keep Harold alive so he could rot in prison if he got the sentence he deserved, if not Seb would end his life the hard way.

Seb pressed his earpiece and radioed to the others, "We have Harold, Jason has been eliminated and there are still no eyes on Tate. Are all the victims out."

A member from C team answered, "all victims are out of the manor."

Seb smiled to Wren and Wade, "and Hal, Ash what's your location?"

But when he had no answer, their smiles began to fade.

"Ashlyne, Hallie. Need an answer. Where are you?"

Nothing.

Seb pressed his earpiece once more, "Gibb, can you get through to Hallie or Ashlyne, get their location."

Seb heard typing but no answer. His patience was wearing thin.

"I have no location."

"Right, I need two members of C team to take this piece of shit to Sergeant to get him arrested, as much as I would like to kill you myself, I haven't got time for that right now, but it will come." Seb was pressing his gun firmly into Harold's mouth making him squirm even more with fear.

"Copy."

Before Seb had left the room, he heard a rustle through the earpiece. Wondering what it was, he looked back to Wren frowning.

"Seb, he has her." It was Ashlyne, she sounded hurt.

"Ash?"

"He-," coughing in-between words, "Hallie has run, he is going after Hallie." Wade stood up quickly, hearing Ashlyne like that made his heart sink.

He responded, "Ash, where are you?"

Before she could answer they heard her scream, more rustles went through the earpieces as all the boys looked to one another. C team had finally arrived upstairs to take Harold.

"She's mine now, she's a fast runner Seb, but I will catch her first." Tate had taken an earpiece from one of the team, the line went dead.

Seb ran as fast as he could down the stairs, Wade and Wren closely following. As they approached the basement where the victims were being held, they found Ashlyne on the floor holding her abdomen tightly. Blood began to trickle down her mouth, she had internal bleeding. Wade went straight to her and knelt by her side.

"Ash, where did she go." Seb was pleading that Ashlyne would not lose consciousness before he could get an answer.

"The forest, she has no weapon, she gave me her gun." Seb sighed and looked to the floor. "Wade get her to a car and to a hospital now!" No argument from Wade, he picked Ashlyne up holding her close to his body and ran for the door. Meanwhile Seb and Wren began to run to the forest which surrounded the country manor.

A member of B team had eyes on Tate, "he is east of the manor running towards the sea, I have lost contact." Seb made no time to respond but he began to run. Run faster than he ever had.

40

A breeze began to pick up throughout the night, leaves rustling together as the gentle wind whistles throughout. The once open country manor now seemed non-existent as Hallie tackled the terrain of the forest floor. However, this forest was bigger than Hallie first expected. Each tree looked the same, with only the moonlight as Hallie's source of light, it was a struggle to know whether she was making any progress or running in one big circle.

Animals of the night began to stir the further she got into the forest, with a fox barking in the distance and random scuttering across the forest floor. Hallie had no time to think, she needed to act and act fast.

As the trees creaked upon one another, the unknown sound lurked in the distance. Hallie paused to try and steady her breathing, try and notice any distinguished noises, something out of the ordinary however, this all felt out of the ordinary for Hallie. Looking around, she was surrounded by trees, brambles and uneven pathways. Hallie contemplated hiding, climbing up one tree or peering from around one of the bushes, but if she was found, then she would be trapped. Attempting to press on her ear to get a feel of her earpiece, her heart fell to her stomach when she realised it must have fallen out escaping from Tate. She did not want to leave Ashlyne behind, she could be dead for all she knew, Ashlyne screamed for Hallie to run. So Hallie did, but into the unknown. The opposite end of the area that was supposed to be being watched. Hoping someone would know she had run, she was not about to be some damsel in distress, it was time to fight. Pulling her hair up, she had no hair tie so instead, lifting her leg up she glided her garter down her leg and used this to tie her hair back. Darkness had formed as clouds floated past the moon, one moment she had sight, the next was complete darkness. Standing as still as she could, she waited and waited.

A snap of a twig caused Hallie to spin around and try to see what was close to her. With only the moonlight giving her sight, this was futile. Another snap from a twig, Hallie began to run again. Her feet were becoming sore from wearing no shoes, but adrenaline had kept her from causing any extreme pain, it was her time to escape. A gunshot bellowed in the distance. Whoever this was, they were getting closer. Hallie began to panic, looking around, she contemplated trying to run back to the manor, only she had no idea what direction she needed to go in to get back. Now she was beginning to regret running away.

"Hallie... come on, I won't bite." These words sent a chill down Hallie's spine. Instantly she knew Tate was close. Picking up the largest branch she could, she crouched behind a bush, seeing a silhouette coming closer to her she attempted to steady her breathing.

"Hallie... come out, come out. I haven't got time to find you. I know you're close. I can smell you from here!" Remaining still, Hallie wondered if Tate would carry on walking so she could run back. Instead, he stood still, tilting his head up to the stars and staring to the moonlight. Engrossed as to what he was doing, Hallie didn't realise that her arm began to relax causing the large branch to move, which made a slight snap against the bush she had hidden behind. Tate's head spun around, "found you." Pointing the gun, he fired but missed. Before he could aim at Hallie again, she pounced towards him knocking him off guard causing him to drop the gun to the floor. Tate's large build was proving a struggle for Hallie to tackle however, Hallie was determined to not give up. Tate quickly bent over causing Hallie to fall over his head. Landing on her back with debris from the trees causing her to squirm on meeting the floor. Before Hallie could move, Tate managed to pin her down but unlike anyone else Hallie had been caught in a fight with, she sensed how dark Tate was. Wriggling around to try and get out of his tight grip, Tate managed to slam her back to the ground. His eyes darked with his lips beginning to tug at the sides. Hallie looked around the forest floor to attempt to find something to hit Tate with. To her surprise, the gun was lying close to her. Reaching her arm out she attempted to grab this while keeping eye contact with Tate.

Unfortunately, Tate managed to pick up on what Hallie was trying to do and he pulled her arm back in. Leaning to the gun, he threw it across the forest floor.

"You're not getting away that easy. It feels so good watching you squirm. No wonder Seb has you."

Hallie scowled back to Tate, "Fuck you."

Tate rolled his head back then focused back on Hallie. "Oh, I plan on doing much worse." Hallie's eyes widened, no response came from her, she was speechless. Tate took this as an opportunity to lean down to Hallie and whisper in her ear. "And I intend on making sure you feel every piece of me." Tate began to kiss Hallie's neck but because she was squirming so much this caused Tate to become agitated. "You better keep fucking still." And he bit down on Hallie causing a scream to bellow from her throat.

Hallie could hear Seb call for her, she tried to respond but Tate had placed his hand over her mouth. "Let's hope he finds you when I am inside you." Tate began to attempt to restrain Hallie, flipping her over so she was now laying on her front. Hallie was trying to think of a way to get out of Tate's grip. Until she thought the unthinkable, play him at his own game.

"You are fucking sick Tate, you know that right?" Hallie groaned, she was in pain from how much he was pulling at her every muscle. Tate released one of Hallie's hands and quickly reached for his belt, pulling it out from its clasp he pulled the belt from his waist and attempted to use this as a restraint for Hallie. Hallie however spun from his grip and swiftly swung her arm around the side of Tate's head. Quickly escaping his grasp, Hallie aimed and ran for the gun. But before she could grab it, Tate picked Hallie up and swung her back to the floor. Beating Hallie to the gun he reached down and picked it up and pointed the gun directly at Hallie's head. Stopping from making any other movements, Hallie's only sight was down the barrel of the gun.

"Now, I don't want to ruin that beautiful face of yours, but I will. I think you will be worth more if you look like that. Regardless, I might not even sell you but keep you for my own."

Hallie frowned and began to talk, her throat was dry, she had no idea what was going to come from this. Seb screamed Hallie's name once more causing her head to turn and look in the direction of the voice, tears began to fill her eyes. But Tate pushed the gun closer to her and made Hallie remain still.

"You make one sound Hallie, and I will shoot you."

"Do it, I would much rather be dead then go anywhere with you."

Tate sniggered.

Placing the gun closer to Hallie's head it was now pressing in between her eyebrows. Hallie was not going to stand down but she had no where she could go.

41

Seb hears Hallie yelp in pain, he instantly shouts for her losing Wren in the forest. Battling the brambles, branches and the uneven terrain, he leaps over any fallen debris Seb was still unaware that his mask lay tightly on his face. Looking around, every tree looks the same, he clicks the earpiece to channel into his team.

"I need some sort of imaging or… just anything of where the fuck I need to go." Seb was looking around trying to get his eyes to adjust to the darkened forest. Clouds now began to clear away from the moonlit sky causing his surroundings to lighten up slightly, just enough to be able to see where he was going.

"Sir we have a drone from B team going over the forest, thermal imaging will possibly give us coordinates." Gibb seemed breathless even though he had not moved a muscle all evening, the suspense on this evening's events had taken its toll on everyone.

As Seb continued throughout the forest he heard another scream from Hallie. This made his stomach churn, she had not screamed like that in a very long time. Seb felt like his whole body was on fire, he needed to find Hallie.

"Gibb." He shouted, very rarely did he shout but time was running out.

No answer as of yet. Seb inhaled ready to shout again but Gibb spoke up, "We found them, they are east from you." Seb didn't answer back but began to run again. Gibb tried to keep track on Seb to ensure he was on the right track, he had the footage of the drone above in the office. Until Toby spoke up,

"You're not alone in there. You have company." Toby surprises Seb and Wren, curious to who would be in the forest Gibb begun the hunt to see whether it was members of Seb's team or whether it was unwanted guests.

"Gibb, am I going in the right direction?" Sidetracked from confirming the additional people in the forest, Gibb looked up to the TV screen which had the thermal imaging footage from the drone.

"Yes, keep going, you are close. Looks like they are still together." Gibb then attempted to hack into another radio frequency to see if the other unwanted guests were using earpieces. They could be working with Tate and he could have something up his sleeve. They needed to get ahead. Harold was extracted from the manor but now it was time for Tate to get captured.

Seb continued on through the forest, clouds were beginning to cover over the moon which now made the forest completely in darkness. Seb was being attacked by branches which he could not see in the distance. His suit was snagged along the side of a bramble bush causing it to rip slowly. He ripped off his suit jacket and left it attached to the bramble bush. Determined, he continued through the rough path of the forest, the manor was now completely out of sight.

All Seb could think about was Hallie, he had promised her he would never lose her, that she would never be in harm's way ever again. He couldn't break that promise to her. Seb needed to focus, however his mind was thinking the worst. What Tate could be doing to her, how he should have never left her alone. Yes, she had intense training, she had her wits about her, but deep-down Seb always knew she would be the prime target. As he was running through the forest, it was like he wasn't even there, his mind had wondered into the unknown. Flashbacks were flying through Seb's mind, all his happiest memories which all included Hallie. His life with her, what he looked forward to with her, the future he wanted with her. Then darkness, the time he nearly lost her, her in the coma, what pain he inflicted on Hallie all those years ago when he believed she was the target and worked close with Fowler in the army. Seb's blood began to boil once again, he tried to erase these bad memories from his mind, but the voices began to take over, they were screaming at him, then on repeat was Hallie's scream in his mind. It was getting too much, too loud, everything was spiralling out of control.

That was until he heard the worse. The one sound which made all the noise stop, the birds to fly from the trees, to disturb the forest surroundings. This made Seb freeze. A gunshot echoed throughout the forest, it sounded close. He was close. But was he too late to save Hallie?

42

Wade was running to the closest ambulance he could find from the outside of the manor. Holding Ashlyne tightly in his arms, she was stirring in pain, blood was trickling from her abdomen. Tate had managed to stab Ashlyne thinking he had left her for dead, but Wade was determined to save her. Wade shouted for help when he saw an ambulance ahead. They seemed to be treating one of the victims when Wade began to run towards them. Instantly, one of the paramedics saw Wade holding Ashlyne and began to clear the way for him to carry Ashlyne into the ambulance. Placing her on the stretcher, the paramedics began to hook her up to the machines to check her vitals. Giving her dressings to hold onto her abdomen as they attempted to place a cannula in her arm. The ambulance driver turned on the blue lights which illuminated the surroundings and the sirens went on. The race to the hospital had begun.

Wade stayed close, putting pressure on the wounds Ashlyne had sustained while the paramedic injected drugs into Ashlyne's body. Her body was starting to react to the pain she had sustained causing her to shiver. A large silver blanket was placed around Ashlyne to try and keep her warm, she was drifting in and out of consciousness. This caused the paramedic to call ahead to the hospital, get a hold of the blood bank to order a transfusion and ensure the top doctors were to hand. Just as she had finished the call to the hospital, Ashlyne had lost consciousness and was not responding. Her vitals began to drop significantly and was now going into cardiac arrest in the ambulance.

Pulling up to the ambulance entrance of the hospital, there were doctors already at the door ready to whisk Ashlyne away. Wade remained close and he kept the pressure on her wounds. There were too many people surrounding Ashlyne, Wade knew he needed to step back and let them work. Until he heard the words.

"We need to take her to theatre now." Wade realised he would now be separated from Ashlyne, he couldn't leave her. Following them to theatre until he felt an arm on his shoulder. A nurse looked him with kindness in her eyes, "sir, I am so sorry but you can't go any further. They will do everything they can and more I can assure you of that. Here, let me take you to the waiting area." Wade was tempted to ignore her and just walk straight through. The nurse was small, he could easily push straight through her, but what use would that be. Wade didn't answer and just nodded following the nurse to the waiting room. His clothes were covered in not only Ashlyne's blood but others from the events of the night. As he sat down, he placed his head in his hands. He couldn't deal with this. The uncertainty of Ashlyne surviving, of his teammates surviving, what is happening back at the manor. Just was all getting to him. Without him realising his hands were beginning to shake, emotions were getting high.

Hearing footsteps getting closer to him, Wade looked up and surprisingly was greeted by a young girl. This girl could not be over six years of age. Her hair was tied back and into a braid. Hugging a white cat soft toy which was wrapped in a blue blanket she sat next to Wade. Wade looked down at himself then back to the child, he didn't like the idea he was covered in blood especially that a child might have questions. The mother just gave a reassuring smile to Wade.

"Who are you waiting for?" The young girl asked, her tone was soothing and pleasant.

Wade sniffled and lifted his hands from his head to turn to the young girl. "My girlfriend. How about you?"

"My daddy. Is that from your girlfriend?" pointing at the blood from his clothes, Wade sniffled again and fought back his tears.

"Sure is, she was hurt, but here, the best people are to fix her." Looking to the mother she nodded. The mother stood and walked over to a cupboard which was on the wall, she pulled out a hospital blanket and walked back to Wade. Draping the blanket over Wade's shoulders, she noticed he was shaking. It could be from adrenaline or that he was cold, but mothers' instinct was to care and that she did.

"Thank you." He recognised the mother, but could not pinpoint as to where, that was the least of Wade's worry at the moment.

"So, you say you're waiting for your dad huh?" He looked to the mother then back to the child.

"Yes, he has an issue with his heart and is currently having a transplant. We have been waiting for this day for three years." The mother smiled, but her smile had uncertainty behind it, there must be high complications to this surgery. What if the heart rejects the new host, what if the patient crashes on the table, his old heart can't take it. So much risk yet both seemed so hopeful which gave Wade some assurance for Ashlyne.

"Well, I hope all goes okay for you all."

"And same for your girlfriend." Wade smiled to the girl, he was about to reply when the waiting room doors opened. A doctor emersed in theatre scrubs and a nurse behind him.

"Mrs Stanton, your husband is out of surgery. It went very well, he is now in recovery. Nurse Stone will take you to him of you like." A breath of relief came from the mother and a big smile. Her hand laid on her chest whilst receiving this news. Pulling the young girl close she praised the lord for allowing her husband's surgery to go well. Wade smiled to the mother to which she responded, "I hope all goes well for your girlfriend, you will be in our prayers." Wade nodded and smiled back to the mother.

"Thank you, hope the recovery is smooth for your husband." The mother followed the doctor and just as the young girl was leaving, she turned back and ran to Wade. She wrapped her small arms around him, he was shocked and unsure what to do.

"My mummy tells me a hug helps sooth the mind, stops you feeling trapped in a bad place." The young girl took her arms back and looked to Wade with a smile then ran out the room to catch up with her mother. Wade remained shocked yet heartfelt a young child could feel such emotion. He had hope that Ashlyne would be okay, until a doctor came in to give an update on the surgery.

43

From the gunshot that rippled through the forest, Seb knew he was getting closer to Hallie. Ignoring every person that tried to interfere through his earpiece, his mind thought the worse. Instantly he began to run as fast as he could, ducking and hitting branches from his path, he was shouting after Hallie. Until he saw the worst.

Seb arrived at an open path of the forest, the moonlight had begun to illuminate the night sky and beaming down ahead of Seb, the sight in front of him made his heart break, shatter. Tate stood over Hallie, gun still pointing at Hallie on the forest floor. Without thinking, Seb sprinted towards Tate, however Tate heard him coming and began to spin round but shot too soon missing Seb, Seb continued towards Tate and another shot fired, grazing Seb's arm. Seb ignored this and tackled him to the floor. Tate tried to shoot again however was now out of bullets, the handgun was just clicking. This caused Seb to smirk, Tate had nothing.

"You are a dead man, you hear me." With that a punch to his head with such force that you could hear his jaw crack out of socket. Grabbing Tate by his thick hair, Seb pulled his head up and smacked it down again, and again, and again until he heard her shout "STOP!"

Instantly, Seb's head looked behind him and saw her standing there behind him. Standing up to meet Hallie, he was hoping she wasn't a figment of his imagination. "Hallie?" He began to walk over to her before she ran to him and jumped in his arms. A heavy breath left his chest and a tear had formed in his eyes. Hallie's legs slowly dropped for her to meet the floor. Seb however didn't release his grip. His head stayed burrowed in Hallie's neck. Hallie placed her hands on either side of Seb's face guiding his head to look at her. Placing her forehead to meet his, they both gazed into each other's eyes.

"We need him alive. As much as I want him dead, so badly want him dead right now. He needs to stay alive." Seb nodded with Hallie and smile, but that smile soon faded when he heard Tate's voice.

"I know you enjoyed the chase, Hallie. You want to be mine." Both Seb and Hallie's smile faded, Seb released his grip from Hallie and went to straight to Tate and kicked him on the side of the head knocking him unconscious. Relief flooded through Seb's body, he took Hallie in his arms and picked her up close again letting out a breath of relief, with a single tear rolling down his cheek.

Hallie found her feet again and looked to Seb with tears forming, noticing his tear she grazed her hand across his cheek wiping the tear away. "Thank you. Again."

Seb frowned, confused on Hallie's comment, "For what?"

"For always finding me."

Seb let out a small laugh, placing his hand on her face cupping her chin to tilt her head up, "I will always find you darling."

A few moments later and B team had arrived. Seb had instructed Gibb to get some of the team to collect Tate whilst they head back to the manor. Luckily for Hallie, B team had arrived with rope and tape to be able to keep Tate quiet. To Hallie's surprise, one person had brought a taser with him. Taking advantage of this, she pointed the taser straight to Tate then pointed slightly lower than usual. As she fired the taser, her aim was impeccable and hit straight to Tate's dick. Voltage had implanted himself throughout Tate's body causing his muscles to spasm.

44

Arriving back at the manor to see what chaos had been left in. Blue lights illuminated the path ahead reflecting the manors exterior. As they approached the manor, both had noticed Sergeant in the distance, but before continuing Seb stood in front of Hallie.

"You sure you wanna go there. Tonight has been... well tough." Seb looked defeated.

Hallie smiled and leaned up to Seb and kissed him. The kiss was passionate and lasted longer than it should. As Hallie pulled away she still had a smile on the face, that was until she noticed Seb's shirt was now turning red.

"You're bleeding."

Seb didn't look, he kept his gaze on Hallie's face. "Knew you cared."

Hallie looked up to Seb with a stern look, "of course I care you big idiot." Laughing mid-sentence, looking around she had nothing to put pressure on the wound. "We need to get you to the hospital." However just as Seb began to speak, Hallie interrupted once more, "and not your private doctor." Seb's mouth remained open and closed quickly with no response.

Hallie shook her head and took Seb's one good hand. Walking back to the manor she caught the eye of Sergeant who discharged himself from the current people he was speaking with.

"Hallie, Seb. I have a ton of questions for you." Sergeant showed no emotion from his comment. He looked like a disappointed father just about to tell his children off. Hallie looked up and began to talk.

"And I will be happy to answer them, but right now he needs a doctor." Seb looked down to Hallie and smiled, he loved how much she cared for him. Hallie kept her eyes on Sergeant awaiting his answer.

"Looks like you need to see one too." Puzzled by this she ignored the comment, she had been hit a few times but continued. Sergeant joined them both to the ambulance so Seb could have his shoulder looked at following the shot he received from Tate. As they approached the ambulance, the paramedic knew instantly what to get, Seb however being as stubborn as he was refusing to be taken to hospital. Seb needed to ensure that everything was taken care of here and that his team would not have too many questions asked to them.

Seb clenched his fist from the pain of the needle being injected into his shoulder, making Hallie smile. He noticed this and scowled back at her, "you can wipe that smirk of your face." Hallie let out a breath of laughter from this comment. Seb had endured so much pain in his life, yet needles would still make him squirm like a child.

Trying to distract himself from this, he looked to Sergeant and grunted, "So, what do you need to know."

Sergeant looked to him and shrugged his shoulders, "where do I bloody begin. For starters how the hell did you figure out this place? Why is one of my officers dead when he is supposed to be in fucking Spain? How many of your so called team do I need to eliminate from questioning? And how the hell did you know Harold Kingston was behind this?" Hallie let out a sign, she had no idea where to begin so fortunately for her Seb took over.

"We had a way to access this auction a couple months ago to allow enough prep time for extractions. We had no idea on the location until the day before the auction. Your detective never was planning on going to Spain. He was close with an ex-officer that used to work for you and is close with the mother of his child. No guess for you as to who that would be."

Sergeant frowned, "Fowler?"

Seb continued, "Bingo. They trained together for the detectives' exams which you know about as you trained them. Unknown to you is that they stayed in contact up till he died. He never had any interest in working for you, but to be someone on the inside for this operation. Unfortunately for you he kept a grudge on Hallie thinking she was the reason for his death, never believed Fowler would kill anyone and he was the one who arranged the unexpected meeting with Hallie and the mother of his child. As for his death, him and his sister worked with Harold on this sick operation. The aim was to keep him alive, but he was the one who did that to Hallie." Looking up to Hallie noticing the split lip and the redness on her face which would slowly become bruises. "As for our team, none should be in questioning and all I believe disappeared before armed response arrived to take over the manor. Two are currently in the hospital so they will not have anyone bother them, I hope." Raising his eyebrows, Hallie noticed his darkness appearing slowly in his eyes, Seb had lost all respect and was dealing with a great deal of pain. Sergeant didn't answer but nodded. Seb took this as his word he wouldn't touch them. "As for Harold, he has been running this operation for a few years, we have, well extracted shall we say, all ties to this as Harold is the cause for all these innocent people's lives."

Sergeant placed his hand to his head, rubbing his forehead, he had no idea that it was this serious and the level of depth of the operation. Sergeant nodded, clearing his throat, "And for this, Tate. Location on him?"

Hallie looked to Seb as her eyes widened, she knew Seb wanted to keep him, taken him himself but Hallie knew how the law worked, and they would need him in questioning.

"We have him."

Sergeant looked to Hallie hoping she would understand the severity on keeping a wanted man. "You know we need him for questioning and sentencing right."

Seb let out a small laugh, "Harold was behind it all, Tate was just the sick fuck who ensured it would carry on. You choose, either you take Harold, sentence him make him rot in prison or take Tate and we take Harold. Your choice." Seb was not messing around, as the paramedic even raised her eyebrows from the situation, fortunately Hallie noticed this and spoke to her, "You repeat none of this, understand me." The paramedics eyebrows went even higher, panic flooded through her body as her cheeks had a rose blush flush through from this comment.

"No— no of course not. Believe me I have heard nothing." Hallie smiled from this response and continued to look at sergeant awaiting his response.

Sergeant looked around and then back to Seb, "I don't think I have much of a choice, it depends what you intend on doing with one of them?"

No response from Seb, he just raised his eyebrows slightly and stayed quiet.

"Keep Tate, we can say he died here. I want to watch the media blow this up about Harold. However, your little operation stays under wraps you understand me. If this gets out to, well anyone…"

Seb introjected before Sergeant could continue, "believe me, you won't hear from us ever again."

45

A few hours later, the police and armed response were now cleaning up the mess at the manor where the auction was once being held. Hallie thought it would be wise to get Seb checked at the hospital even to have just an x-ray on his shoulder to check there are no remains from the bullet in his shoulder or if it went through bone. Seb agreed with this just to shut Hallie up. After being x-rayed showing the bullet went clear through, no fragments left, just went straight through flesh this was a relief for both Seb and Hallie. After some proper stitches and a sling Seb was allowed to go, no questions asked also thanks to him knowing one of the doctors in the emergency department.

Hallie and Seb joined Wren as they headed to the waiting area to check in with Wade and get an update on Ashlyne. As they walked past the waiting room, the large window showed Wade was the only one in the room, with a blanket around his shoulders. He hadn't moved a muscle since arriving. One of the healthcare assistances saw them looking through the window and asked if they knew him. All nodding the assistant continued, "I have tried offering him a drink or something to eat, even to clean his wound on his face but has declined it all."

Hallie looked to the healthcare assistant and smiled, "thank you, can I take a bottle of water in for him, might help if we check in with him. How is Ashlyne?"

The assistants face dropped, trying not to reveal a lot but it was inevitable the outcome, "they are doing all they can." Nodding from this comment they walked into the lounge and sat next to Wade.

Seb places his hand on Wade's shoulder, Wade manages to snap out of his daydream and join them in the room. A small smile appeared but showed no emotion, he was hurt and it showed. Hallie knelt down in front of Wade and smiled, "You really like her, don't you?"

Wade nodded, no noise left his mouth as he closed his eyes. Placing a hand on his knee his eyes opened once again meeting Hallie's gaze. Before Hallie could continue a doctor walked into the room. All eyes lead to him, and Wade stands up first walking over to him. As he places his hand out to shake, the doctor met his shake and exhaled deeply. Wade knew this look instantly, but he waited for the words to leave his mouth.

"Are you all together?" The doctor didn't want to disclose anything about Ashlyne unless he was convinced they were all together.

"Yes, we are all the only family she has." Wade looked to the others and smiled, then return his gaze to the doctor.

"Very well, please." Gesturing his hand to the chairs, he joined them sitting down and begun. "Ashlyne had suffered a significant amount of damage on her abdomen, we had to reconstruct her intestines and place a colostomy bag in place due to the damage the injuries had sustained. Altogether, she lost a high amount of blood and she has a rare blood type proving it difficult to give her the amount she needed. I am unsure on the outcome of Ashlyne at this moment. She crashed three times on the surgical table, however we now have her monitored and is currently on the intensive care ward. I will say that the sight of her on all those machines helping her breathe and just keeping her stable is not something we advise however, judging by the looks of you all, you seem like you have seen your fair share of trauma." Instantly looking to Seb and nodding, a nod in agreement however Hallie was confused how he knew Seb so well. From that they followed the doctor to the Intensive Care unit.

Arriving to Ashlyne's room, the doctor was right, this was a sight. One machine was pushing oxygen into Ashlyne's lungs which extended her chest out then back in, another machine to monitor her vitals, another pushing medications into her system. Wade ignored all machines near Ashlyne and walked straight in and grabbed Ashlyne's hand sitting next to her. Seb placed his arm around Hallie as she cradled into him, this was an upsetting sight for her. Wren stepped outside to answer a phone call from his wife to give an update on what has happened.

Many hours had past and Wade hadn't moved a muscle since sitting with Ashlyne, the only time he took his hand away was when nurses were checking her cannula ensuring there was no leaking from the number of medications she was having administered. Another doctor who supervised the intensive care unit entered the room. Seb took a seat in the large patient chair which was in the corner of the room with Hallie on his lap asleep, she hadn't even stirred when the doctor entered and Seb wanted to keep it that way.

"Hello, I am Doctor Abdul. I will be taking over the care on Ashlyne and wanted to introduce myself to you. I can get a bed made up for you if you wish to stay with Ashlyne." The doctor gave a sympathetic smile to Wade to which he returned, "Thank you, that would be nice." The doctor nodded to the nurse which joined him to get a bed brought around and made up for Wade.

"Is there any update medically for Ashlyne?" Seb spoke up asking the question that Wade was contemplating to ask. The vibrations from his chest as he spoke woke Hallie slowly and she noticed she had been asleep this whole time, attempting to get up Seb pulled her back tightly and ensured she was okay on his lap.

"It's just time unfortunately. So far, she has proven everyone wrong and has fought the hardest battle, the fact she has not crashed since is a good thing. But tomorrow we will try some neuro stimulant tests, see if her brain will respond."

"And worst case?" Wade finally spoke, his voice cracked when saying this, however he did not look at the doctor but straight to Ashlyne rubbing her hand.

"Worst case is she is brain dead, or she doesn't make it through the next twenty-four hours. It is just a matter of time right now."

After the doctor explained everything to them, Wade assured he would be okay staying here with Ashlyne and that they should all go home. Agreeing they said their goodbyes and would come back in a few hours. The thought of leaving Wade alone and with Ashlyne being in a very vulnerable state was risky, but Wade assured he would call if any changes. Ashlyne had become a member of their dysfunctional family, they cared. But the next twenty-four hours were literally a matter of life of death.

46

6 months later

"This just in, breaking news.

Former chairman and aristocrat Harold Kingston has now been sentenced to serve life in prison following the extent of crimes he had committed following the kidnapping, slavery and sex trafficking of innocent people. Targeting mainly younger people, Kingston had accomplices to help capture and hold an auction at a remote country estate he bought three years prior. These victims have now been under the best of care by the relevant services and their identities will remain anonymous until the trial has been completed.

We will be holding interviews with two of the victims who were a couple at the time of their taking and what life was like before being sold to be a human slave.

Associates working with Harold all died on the scene of the invasion by armed response teams and all identified.

Harold Kingston will be held in a maximum-security prison with life without parole."

All had returned back to the manor. Wren held his family close, Hallie and Seb joined hand in hand, Wade and Gibb walking slowly to the bar. The day was not one anyone looked forward to. As they took their seats in the large lounge area, not a spec of colour on anyone's clothing. Seb stood and raised his whiskey glass to the sky, "To Ashlyne, always expecting the unexpected." All followed raising their glasses and cheering to Ashlyne. The ceremony was small, only Seb and his team attended. Sergeant had called Hallie hearing the news of Ashlyne's passing and sent his condolences, the hunt for Ashlyne for recall back to prison was now non-existent despite Seb's earlier efforts to have this removed. Wade however was distraught with the news of Ashlyne. The day she had passed he was back at the manor showering and getting fresh things for Ashlyne when Seb arrived to give him the news.

Seb noticed Wade looking more down from the funeral, he went over to him, Hallie followed giving Wade a hug. Wade was unsure on this but returned the hug, placing his hands around Hallie's waist. He exhaled slowly and struggled to hold back the tears. As Hallie pulled away from this hug, Wade placed his sunglasses back on his face and walked out the room to the garden to try get some fresh air. Hallie looked to Seb, the look on her face suggested she is trying to give Seb a message with her eyes. Seb rolled his eyes and nodded to agree causing Hallie to smile instantly.

A couple hours had passed and before Hallie could go give her news, Wren emerged from the stairs with Ella close behind. All had packed and ready for their long holiday to the other side of the world. Toby walked up to Gibb and exchanged a look to which Gibb handed him something, however under Ella's eagle eye she noticed this and snatched this from his hand to quickly.

"Really Gibb, a hard drive?" Ella looked disapproving from this. He laughed and looked back to Toby.

"I tried mate, you'll have to get one out there." Gibb sniggered however his face soon changed when he met Ella's eye.

"He is not getting a hard drive when we are in Australia. It is a holiday." Ella looked to Wren for back up and he nodded.

"Yeah, a holiday." Ella returned her gaze back to Hallie whilst Wren looked to Toby and smiled, he returned his with a smirk.

As Seb helped them with their bags to the car and returned the hugs, they were thankful for Seb for allowing them to stay with them all this time especially after this was not an easy time for any of the family. As they all entered the car, Wren took a little more time in saying his goodbye to Seb.

"I really am thankful for what you have done for us, despite everything that has happened. Thanks." Wren lifts his arm and gives Seb a brief hug, with pats on each other's backs they released each other from their grips and Wren stepped into the car driving off along the gravel driveway.

Gibb followed suit shortly after with a packed bag and his walking stick. His ideal break away was in Madrid, Spain. He believed Spanish women would like his nerdy side and his accent. When in reality that is where his mum lived, but not to hurt his ego, Seb and Hallie went along with his call for being a stud on the prowl for women. Packing as many electrical items as possible, Gibb was finally ready to say his goodbye. Thanking Seb for the opportunity to work alongside him, to watching Katie die in front of his eyes from her lies he was ready for a well-deserved break. The biggest question was, how long of a break was he to take.

"You call me when you land alright!" Hallie demanded helping him lift the last of his luggage into the car.

"I will." Answering like he was being told off, making Seb snigger behind them. Gibb was a valued member of this dysfunctional family, and it was sad to see him go spread his wings. Hallie knew he would come back if she ever needed him, but it was needed for everyone to take some time apart from working.

Walking back into the manor hand in hand, Hallie noticed Wade was now sat in the armchair with a whiskey to hand. Seb stepped ahead taking the seat next to Wade.

"We have something we need to show you." As his eyes slowly met Seb's gaze he nodded and followed behind. Walking towards Wren's old truck he wondered where he was going. Hallie smiled to Wade to give some reassurance as to what he might be in for. But Wade was numb, he had endured a high amount of emotion these last few weeks.

Seb didn't take to the driveway but headed straight through to the forest. Wade knew there was a cabin hidden among these tall trees however was unsure what was necessary for him to see.

As they pulled up outside the cabin Seb walked over to the solid oak door and begun to unlock it. Looking back to Wade he smiled. "Think you'll enjoy this." As he opened the door, there was a single chair with someone tied up on it in the centre of the cabin. Wade squinted and took a step inside the cabin to get a better look as to who was tied up in there. However, to his surprise, it was Tate.

As the door closed behind them, Wade looked to Hallie and Seb with confusion. "How did you manage to not get him taken in by police?"

"With my excellent ways around things and the people we know, we made a compromise. They kept Harold, made out Tate was dead when in fact we kept him alive long enough for today to come." Hallie sniggered.

The confused look still on Wade's face, "Why today?"

Hallie looked to Seb for him to answer this question, they were unsure on how Wade would respond to this. "Now don't be annoyed we didn't tell you sooner, it wasn't our idea this okay?"

But before Wade could answer this the door swung open abruptly.

"Sorry I'm late." Wade's face changed instantly, shock, uncertainty, confusion. Wade had so many questions, yet he was speechless.

"W-what the actual…" Unsure whether it was anger or the element of surprise lurking however Ashlyne instantly walked over to Wade, pulled him in close and placed her lips onto his. Wade's face moulded into Ashlyne's, he was still shocked by this.

"I thought you were dead. The doctors told me you were dead!"

Ashlyne looked back to him, down to the floor then back at him. "Technically, I am dead. Well, I had a death certificate made and everything. I came around when you were back at the manor, it was my idea to be made into another identity, convincing the doctors to go ahead with this to protect my identity they agreed. I thought wise to tell no one including Hallie and Seb. If it wasn't for mister fucking noisy then this surprise would have been for you all not just you Wade. I am sorry for keeping it a secret, but I had to have lots of physio and get back to somewhat normality before being able to execute this plan the way I wanted to." Once again, Wade frowned with confusion, Ashlyne could count his small indents of frown lines which spread across Wade's forehead. Wade then looked to Seb, his eyes had softened slightly from Ashlyne's touch. However, their moment was shortly extravagant by Tate banging his feet on the wooden flooring. From this sound, Ashlyne rolled her eyes and slowly walked over to Hallie, with a limp and slight crouch because of the pain she had spreading across her abdomen, determination was what was keeping Ashlyne moving. Nodding to Hallie, she pulls out a small handgun and passes it to Ashlyne. Instantly, from taking this gun, Ashlyne lines it up to meet Tate's head. Slowly limping towards him she kept the gun aiming for his head. Until she reached him and the barrel of the gun was now touching his forehead.

"You know, I have replayed this moment in my head for so fucking long. How to kill you. And to think, I nearly didn't get the chance to. But now look where we are. I wanted to inflict pain on you, to take you, ensure you had no moral or will to live any longer, make you beg for your life. But now, I just can't be fucked to know you are still breathing and wasting valuable oxygen on your pathetic lungs." Before you knew it, the gun had fired. Blood spat across the floor, walls and across Ashlyne. Luckily for the others they were stood far enough away from the mess. Shocked looks were on each of their faces as they expected something more in depth, but this was a relief for them all. Not even a chance for him to say his last words. Which would have been a struggle anyway as Seb had cut out his tongue that morning and cauterised it to stop him bleeding to death. This was the end to one hell of a nightmare.

1 year later

47

Summer was Hallie's favourite time of year. The soothing sun on her bare skin was like a warm hug every day. From the trees adding a colourful pallet to the scenery, to the wild animals scattering the fields in the distance. Everything seemed perfect.

Wren and his family decided to stay in Australia for a while longer than expected. Much to Wren's dislike as his fear for snakes grew every day the longer he stayed out there. Toby however had young love down under and was determined to stay there for this, not wanting to risk his heart being broken for the very first time.

Gibb travelled back from Spain every three months, just to prove he still had a job with Seb despite not being in the line of work he once was. Seb had contacts in Madrid and Barcelona who needed someone with Gibb's talents to help them with inside operations. Gibb was promoted to Senior Analytical Operator. Which his mother loved to praise about to her work colleagues. Much to Gibb's disgust, he never explained the real things he done in his job just that it was bit to technical to explain.

Wade ended up forgiving Ashlyne for not telling him that she was going to fake her own death. Even though he hated showing he had a soft side, him and Ashlyne remained in Seb's cabin which was tucked away in the forest. They preferred keeping out of the way and what they got up to, Seb didn't want to know. As long as it didn't bring trouble on his doorstep he couldn't care less. Which in Ashlyne's case was perfect, her most recent target Wade had managed to capture, she had him tied up and injected expanding foam down his throat. This person deserved it none the less for attempting to murder his girlfriend and for domestically abusing her for five years. Luckily for the woman, she had bumped into Ashlyne in the supermarket, got talking about her black eye and Ashlyne took care of the rest. This pair were never going to fully retire just do volunteer work to keep the numbers low.

As for Hallie and Seb. The manor was finally empty. A time that they had awaited on for what seemed like forever. Being able to roam freely and do anything they desire was incredible. Seb made sure he took time away from work, as he promised Hallie he would take her away and that he did. To many different countries in such short amount of time Hallie never quite believed how much of the world she could see in under a year. But this was all made possible by him.

Seb was already outside tending to the garden, since being back home he had taken time to plant an assortment of the most colourful plants he could find. His only task was to keep them alive for the summer which he took very seriously. However, from his usual day to day antics, he was disturbed by knocks on his front door. Knowing Hallie would take a while to get downstairs he walked around the manor to meet whoever was at the front door.

"Hello Sebastian. Long time no see." Seb was not expecting this person to arrive at his doorstep.

"I could say the same about you Sergeant. What can I do for you?" Seb kept his secateurs in his hand with a firm grasp. He hadn't seen Sergeant since the auction, hoping this was just a flying visit. The front door however opened and it was Hallie on the receiving end.

"Oh, sorry, didn't hear you answer the door. Sergeant?" Hallie's face was similar to Seb's which answered his question of did Hallie invite him over.

"Hallie, oh wow. I'm sorry I didn't know, well, you know. I guess a congratulations are in order?" Hallie returned this with a smile as she cradled her bump. That was another reason the travelling was cut short as Hallie had no idea she was pregnant for the first twenty-two weeks of her pregnancy.

"Thank you sir. Yeah, not long now really." Looking to Seb, her eyes widened with her smile, she was beyond happy with how her life was at the moment. Nothing could damage this, well she hoped.

"Well, this makes this ask even more harder." Sergeant looked down to the floor then back up to Hallie and Seb. As they both exchanged looks to one another, Hallie invited Sergeant into the lounge and offered him a drink. As he took a seat in the armchair, Hallie brought over a whiskey on ice and another for Seb. Taking a seat, Seb remained standing next to Hallie. Placing his hand on her shoulder, he didn't know what Sergeant wanted let alone what his ask would be. Remaining quiet, they both waited until Sergeant was ready to talk.

"I have a bit of bother and unfortunately this is something I don't want to involve my superiors about. However, we have recently issued another interview with Harold Kingston regarding some of the victims who he had attempted to sell. Anyway, we now have reason to believe that a specific person who he dealt with in the sense that he was always one of his highest bidder. It turns out he had quite the turn around of people who he…" Sergeant paused, he was sickened by the thought of what he was about to say. "Let's say he used and abused every one of them. Luckily, one escaped from his hold hence why he was bidding again at the auction. However, the man responsible is someone I least expected to be involved in something like this." Hallie frowned and tried to lean forward however her large bump proved difficult. As she shifted to another side, she was waiting for Sergeant to explain more.

"Do we know this person?"

Sergeant nodded, however he did not want to say the name. Seb continued. "High profile I am guessing? Surely if that is the case then the police and the media would be having a field day with this type of news. Getting them exposed quicker."

"It would, if I wasn't asked directly by one of the members of family to keep it under wraps unless I didn't value my life or my family's lives." Sergeant snapped back at Seb. Hallie raised her eyebrows, she was getting uncomfortable, she thought this line of work was behind her. However Sergeant's face showed desperation, he needed help otherwise this would just get worse.

"We need a name."

"The Duke of Kent." Instantly, Hallie leaned as far forward as she could. Both remained speechless from the name. They thought Harold was a shock when they found out what he was up to, but a member of the royal family involved in such a scandal was unexpected.

"You're certain?" Seb raised an eyebrow and took a swig from his drink. Sergeant nodded then continued to drink the rest of his whiskey in one mouthful.

Clearing his throat, Sergeant moved to the edge of the seat placing his elbows on his knees. "Certain. I have been informed by the palace to keep my mouth shut. Hence why I have come here. If I go further with the force, they will find out. Whereas I do not know the extent of your line of work, yet I am optimistic you could help me." Seb looked down to Hallie, meeting her gaze she nodded and placed her hand on Seb's lap. Seb met Sergeant's eyes and nodded in return. "We will help. I need all information you have, then you need to pretend you know nothing. That you are doing nothing like they think you are. No questions asked to us, any additional information you receive we must get immediately. Understand." Sergeant was not used to taking orders, however he was happy to compile with Seb's demands.

"Yes, then you better start with this." Sergeant pulls out a plastic wallet with images and paperwork, Hallie took this from Sergeant and laid all the pages out on the coffee table. This had surveillance images, in depth layouts of his house. However, worst of all were the images of the deceased victims he had kept tally of. Hallie was sickened by this, Seb pulled out his phone and placed it up to his ear. Hallie met his gaze with confusion.

"Looks like our little dysfunctional family is having a reunion. Wren, need you help with something. When are you back..." As Seb walked away on the phone attempting to get his team on board with this task Sergeant looked to Hallie with a smile.

"What?"

Shrugging his shoulders, Sergeant smiled, "You look, just so happy. I am over the moon for you Hallie. But I feel horrible dropping this kind of news on you. Especially when you have your own shit to deal with."

Hallie chuckled, rubbing her belly and then trying to stand up as gracefully as she could. "Believe me, we can handle it. But thank you, I am very happy. Let's just hope this is the end of it when he is dealt with. My word of advice, I know must be odd to take orders from someone else but do as he says if you want this to go smoothly."

Before Sergeant could answer Seb walked back into the room tucking his phone back in his pocket. "Would you like another drink?"

Sergeant stood shaking his head. "Thank you, but I have taken enough of your time. I am grateful for you both, any way to keep my family safe, I will. Somehow Harold let slip that I would investigate further and that put me in firing line. Believe me, any other way around this I tried to get there but all ends led to you."

As Sergeant left, Seb placed his arm around Hallie's waist and his other hand on her bump. Seb did not want this to affect Hallie, he was worried, and Hallie could sense that.

"When are they all coming."

"Two weeks darling."

Hallie sighed, "well, least we have two weeks of a quiet house until then. Well, somewhat quiet."

Seb's face puzzled, his hand remained on Hallie's bump feeling it contract. Raising his eyebrows he looked to Hallie and she met his eyes with a smile.

"My waters broke on the sofa." Seb's mouth fell open, this was the first time Hallie had seen him flustered. Unsure whether to help Hallie to the car, get the hospital bag, get the keys he just froze. Hallie however was calm, "Any chance you can grab the bag from upstairs and we can go to the hospital." Without thinking, Seb ran up the stairs taking them two at a time to find the hospital bag. Nearly tripping over himself, he picked up his keys and went straight to the car. Meeting Hallie there he pulled her in close and kissed her. The kiss slowly became more intense. Parting their lips, he rested his head on her forehead looking closely into her eyes and smiled. Hallie then began to feel the sudden pain of another contraction causing her to frown slightly. Seb took this as an instruction to get in the car and drive.

The thoughts of Sergeants news were now out of their minds. The most important thing was that they were about to become parents. One thing neither one of them had ever thought they wanted. Never would have married one another. Never would have fought for each other. Kill for each other. Lie for each other. From how they first met to now, this love was pure and one that was worth fighting for. For once in her life, Hallie had found her person, her home and her life she never thought she deserved.

ACKNOWLEDGMENTS

Where do I even begin! I am beyond grateful for so many people in regard to this book!

Firstly, my wonderful fiancé. The amount of patience, asking questions on whether parts make sense and hearing me go on about this book. The support and the motivation you have given me is indescribable.

My incredible family. Without you being there for me with this writing process I would never have believed I could achieve what I have. The support and guidance you show, not to mention the family group chat attempting to describe best ways to inflict pain on someone! You are just the best!

To Kate and Chantelle. Now, you two have paid such a significant part in writing this second book. Helping me and being the best editors, I could ask for. Even though you both live your own day to day lives, I could not wish for better people to trust this book with. Thank you for your honesty, your opinions on what works and what does not throughout the book. Forever in your debt.

To my wonderful ARC readers. Well, you are just too incredible. From sharing this journey on social media, I never would have believed that you guys would be interested let alone want to be a part of this journey with me. You are all too amazing and so happy I could share the book with you before any eyes would see it!

My closest friends, (of course you know who you are) for being there on dark days when I didn't believe I was good enough, you showed me what was possible and for that I am so proud to have you as my friends.

And to you! You especially! You are the reason I do this. You are incredible and I am thankful for you for reading this book. Even if you loved it or didn't, that's okay. You gave me a chance and for that, I could not ask for anymore.

Asked myself if I was crazy for doing so much... we said yes!